THE KINFOLK

THE FIVE STONES TRILOGY — BOOK 3

# THE KINFOLK

## G. A. MORGAN

ISLANDPORT PRESS

ISLANDPORT PRESS

Islandport Press

PO Box 10

247 Portland Street

Yarmouth, ME 04096

Islandportpress.com

books@islandportpress.com

ISBN: 978-1-934031-82-7

Library of Congress Control Number: 2016931240

Printed in the USA by Versa Press

Cover and back cover artwork by Ernie D'Elia

*For John, one of the bravest people I know;*
*and for my grandmother, with gratitude.*

# THE KINFOLK

# THE ISLE OF AYDA

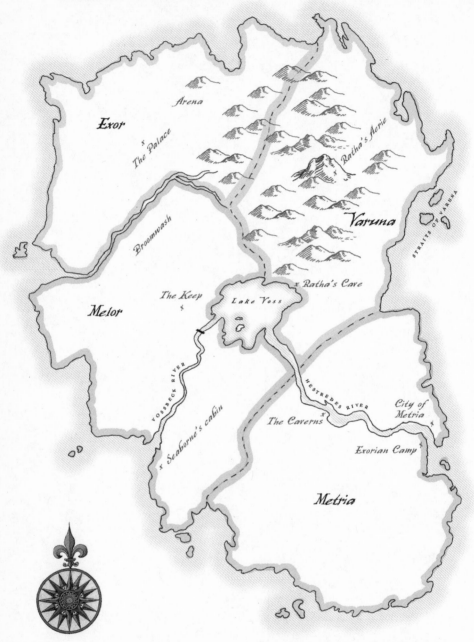

Exor

Arena

The Palace

Varuna

Ratha's Aerie

STRAITS OF VARUNA

Broomwash

Melor

The Keep

Lake Voss

Ratha's Cave

VOSSBECK RIVER

HESTREDES RIVER

City of Metria

The Caverns

Seaborne's cabin

Exorian Camp

Metria

NORTH ATLANTIC

# Contents

*Bay kou bliye, pote mak sonje.*
"The giver of the blow forgets, the
bearer of the scar remembers."

—Haitian proverb

# AYDA, DURING THE GREAT BATTLE

Remiel crosses the snowfield slowly so his wife, Rachel, will not fall behind. She follows him, her robes wrapped tightly against the wind that bears down on them from the summit. They have climbed through the night, leaving the clamor and bloodshed of battle behind them. A pale, just-risen sun sheds light, but no heat, and the ice glitters blue beneath their feet as they push forward. Below, to the west, a column of black smoke pollutes the low-lying clouds that ring the mountainside. A singed odor penetrates the air.

Remiel's eyes are drawn forward and up. Spindrift spits and swirls off the snow-laden peak, veiling their destination. He stops and waits for her, mother of his children and, once, a long, long time ago, catalyst of the evil now befallen them. But this is not her fault. It was never her fault. The blame is his. His weakness for her. He turns to watch as she makes her way toward him in the thigh-deep snow. The weight in his chest threatens to fold him in half, leave him moored in the snow on his knees. He knows it is the weight of regret. A wholly human pain, once foreign to him—but no longer. His time among the human race has made him accustomed to pain—to cruelty and to death. Inevitable, since this pain had spread to every corner of the Earth.

He looks past Rachel, across the blue ice, toward the thick black smoke unspooling into the lightening sky. And now cruelty and death have come here, to his home. If he wavers, all of Ayda will burn.

When his wife reaches his side, he smiles at her, still moved by the feeling she creates in him—as if his own heart has leapt from his chest and taken on human form. Her form. He has known such joy with her and their children. He had been told it could not be so, and would not be so, but for a while he was happy.

They climb the last hundred paces side by side. Gusts of snow lash their chapped faces. The sun is higher, all hint of war extinguished. The only sound is the screech of wind song across rock and ice, the only sight, a sky so blue that it shades to indigo. Here, he allows himself one moment to collect his wife to him.

She lifts her face to his, smiles through frozen lips, unaware it is to be the last time.

"What is faith?" he asks her, leaning to speak directly in her ear, to be heard above the wind. She smiles a little at the familiar question.

"Belief in what you cannot see, touch, taste, or hear, but know in your heart to be true."

"Do you have faith in me?"

This question surprises her.

"Yes," she says after a moment. "Of course." She squeezes his arm gently to make her point. He looks away.

"Would you have it if you could not see me?"

She studies his face, wary of all these new questions, then nods.

"Good." He removes a stone from the folds of his robes. It is gray and smooth and rounded, the size of a human palm, and very heavy—but not for him, as he is simultaneously something greater and something less than human. He is the last remaining Watcher, sent at the dawn of humanity to guide and protect the children of the Earth. Friend, these children had once called him. Teacher. Brother. Father. Husband. But no longer. His love for Rachel has led them all to the edge of ruin.

The wind subsides as the sun rises. Rachel gives to him the four smaller stones she has chosen for this task. They are of equal heft and shape, smaller than his stone: one black, one amber, one blue-gray, one white. He squats to dig a shallow recess in the snow and places his stone at the center, arranging the other stones around it, equidistant and aligned along the direction of the four winds. He stands over them. His dark silhouette blocks the glare of the sun.

"You must take cover below now. I will meet you when it is done."

She is suddenly, inexplicably, afraid. His voice is removed, as cold and distant from her as the stars that lay hidden by the sun's light.

He senses this and turns to her, himself again.

"Do as I ask, love; your daylights will not survive this. You must go down."

She steps back, eyes on his. "You will find me when it's done?"

He bends his right arm and raises his hand chest-high, fingers lightly splayed. She mirrors him with her left hand. Their fingertips touch.

"*Go*," he urges.

She turns and follows their broken trail down the mountain a good distance. She looks back only once when she thinks she hears him call her name. The wind comes screaming back over the summit with a blast of snow. He has all but disappeared into its vapor, yet she can just make out his tall form, backlit by the sun. He is looking down at the stones.

Already a glow is forming at his feet, as if the stones have been lit from within by a white flame—a cold heat getting hotter, brighter, casting orange and red hues against the blue and white of the sky. He raises his hands above the stones. His lips move. The wind and snow begin to funnel, circling him and the stones like a cyclone, obscuring her view of him.

Blood surges to her temples in a riot of emotion and pain, squeezing out breath. Her heart thumps wildly; the edges of her vision blur. She must hurry down before her daylights fragment.

Still, she lingers.

The ground surges like a wave beneath her feet, and a great seam in the mountainside tears apart. A wall of light and ice explodes from it, as bright and potent as the sun's own rays shining down. The snow is blinding, golden. Around her, the mountain throws off its mantle, ripping its solid husk apart in great heaves and rumbles and cracking booms that burst forth like groans of relief. Another explosion spits an avalanche of snow and rock that flows toward her, a river of rubble. She runs. The avalanche tumbles over itself, gaining speed and momentum.

Shelter appears as a deep fissure carved into the mountainside. She throws herself into it. Rock and ice and snow rain over her head and bury her. The sound is deafening, but in time, it passes, leaving behind a deadly quiet. She waits for him to find her.

Hours.

Days.

She is patient. Faithful. But he does not come.

When fear for her children finally overcomes her, she struggles back to the summit, now black and gouged as if clawed by a giant hand. Weight drops into her bones, a heaviness she has not felt since her girlhood, since the day she first encountered Remiel. So many years have passed since that day, and only now does she feel her age. More than anything, this new ache in her bones tells her he is gone.

She crawls the last few feet, digging at the blasted ground with frozen hands until she finds the place where Remiel laid the five stones, now buried under a layer of purple filament. What she sees fills her with a feeling close to fear: The center stone is pierced by four veins of color: black, amber, purple, and white—the colors of the stones that encircle it. She touches each in turn and names them out loud, as she has been instructed.

The black one becomes Exor, stone of fury and strength. The amber is Melor, stone of resilience and growth. The purple is Metria, stone of memory and healing. And the white is Varuna, stone of vision and invention. Her hand hovers over the center stone. The Fifth, the heart stone, is the most important of all, the great balancer of the four. She does not speak its name, for it is beyond her knowledge.

She looks up as if to congratulate her husband—as if he were still there—but her eyes meet only air. He has given himself to the stones, and, in them, left her with hope for the future. She grieves for him, silent and unmoving, until a soft wind sings up the south side of the mountain.

Go, it says.

She gathers the stones gently, as if they were eggs, precious and fragile beyond imagining. They are heavier than normal stones of this size—weighted as they are, she thinks, with fate. She uses her robe to heft the lesser stones over her shoulder. The Fifth Stone she wraps in a scarf from her head and ties close to her body, next to her skin. Something in her has shifted in this exchange. Her daylights are stronger despite being so close to the stones. She, too, is now something greater than human—and, with the loss of him, something less.

The sky above her is clear and almost purple once again. She pauses for a moment, in the still of the morning, her eyes raking the blackened pit. Then she turns to face the smoking lands below.

Ayda.

She straightens her back under the load and retraces her steps toward the Voss. She will take these stones down the mountain and give them to her children. And then, she will teach them to fight.

*Chapter One*

# THE HUNT

Knox leapt easily over a smoking pile of fallen tree trunks and bracken, sprinting full tilt around a blackened grove. The scream of a *tehuantl* behind him made the hair on the back of his neck stand up. An Exorian raiding party was gaining on him. He ran faster, the ground under his feet a blur. The inside of his poncho was damp with sweat. The basket of dried fish he had spent the last few days catching and preparing thumped against his back. His new machete was drawn, and he was running for his life.

Dankar had been pressing without mercy into Melor. The once-great forest was now completely overrun, and the Exorians were burning everything they could find. The only unconquered expanse was at the heart of the Wold, beyond the springtime glen and the swamps of the deathfield. If Knox could make it there without getting caught or killed, his strength would double and he would shake the Exorians.

He'd also have backup. Most of the remaining Melorians—those who had not fled or been driven out of Melor—were holed up in the Keep, doing their best to fend off the enemy. Thus far, they'd succeeded. No

Exorian had passed alive through the deathfield; their own black deeds kept their minds paralyzed and their bodies wandering in the swamp—easy prey for a Melorian with a bow, or the hounds of Melor—two giant, brawny beasts named Axl and Tar. The *tehuantl* did not even try to go into the deathfield. They knew better.

Nonetheless, the siege was taking its toll. Food was so scarce that each day the strongest Melorians in the Keep were forced to venture farther and farther from its safety to find anything to eat; even snakes were precious meat now. And Knox needed to find food. His mother and Teddy were in Melor, led there, as he and Evelyn had been, by the strange creature Chantarelle, who lived beneath the surface of the earth and traversed a vast system of tunnels between worlds.

The thought of his mother and Teddy and what it might mean for them to be here made all the air in his lungs evaporate. He did not dare let his mind wander to his father, all alone now beyond the fog, except for Frankie and Mrs. Dellemere. And who knew if Frankie was even still alive? And what about the others: Evelyn and Chase and Captain Nate. Knox was sure that Chase was well-protected in Varuna. The Exorians were not bold enough yet to cross that far north, but he was worried about Evelyn. Melor was no longer a real buffer. It was only a matter of time before the enemy swept into Metria. He consoled himself with the thought that a river lay between the Exorians and their objective: the great Hestredes. The Exorians had a love-hate thing about water, so it might take them a while to figure out how to cross it.

The *tehuantl* screamed again—too close for comfort. Knox scanned the forest in front of him and saw a large cavity gouged into a charred tree trunk. He threw himself into it. Once he was inside, he climbed a few feet off the ground by jamming his knees to his chin and crab-crawling up with his feet and hands against the inside of the trunk. He was completely hidden and could take a minute to catch his breath and weigh his options.

Hiding in the tree was as good a tactic as any. With the brush cover and much of the tree canopy gone, it was harder to move in the forest undetected, even under his hood. If he could stay still and not call attention to himself, the Exorians might run right past him.

The only problem was that when Knox stayed still, he couldn't stop worrying. He shoved the fur collar of his poncho into his mouth and chewed on it, an old habit. If he was going to get out of this jam, he needed to focus. His time in Melor had taught him that thoughts weaken as easily as wounds, and he had to stay strong. He had to feed his family. It was the most basic custom in Melor: A hunter must provide for their own, or starve trying. Seaborne and Calla helped Knox by sharing what they hunted, but they had their own worries. Mara was dying. The passing of Calla's father, Tinator, had loosened her daylights, and her vessel was not strong enough to survive the siege. Rothermel tended to her, but even his powers could not reverse what now seemed to be inevitable.

Knox grimaced at the thought of Tinator's death, and now, Mara's. They felt as much like family to him as Seaborne and Calla—all of the Melorians did. They had taken him in and treated him like one of their own, and now they were doing the same for his mother and Teddy. They had taught them all how to survive.

A shout from somewhere outside made his heart rocket inside his chest. He fingered the hilt of one of his throwing knives. He was happy that he'd had the foresight to sharpen the blades on a rock at the beach, and was confident of his aim if he could just crawl to the top of this trunk and gain the higher ground. He wondered how many Exorians were out there. He was fairly sure there was only one *tehuantl*. He would not kill it if he could help it. He would not kill any of them if he could help it. Only if they tried to kill him. This was another lesson the Melorians had taught him: Blood is paid with blood; better to avoid the debt whenever possible.

He calmed himself by breathing in and counting to four, holding it for four counts, and breathing out for the same count. It was a method Seaborne had shown him on the journey back to Melor, after the battle with the Exorians at the Voss. Once his pulse returned to normal, he closed his eyes and listened intently, trying to get a bead on his enemy's location. The forest outside was deathly quiet—unnervingly so. Dankar had destroyed Melor on so many levels—even sound. It was only when Knox entered the heart of the Wold and traveled through the springtime glen that he once again heard the natural chittering, peeping, and rustling of the forest—the sound of life.

But a distance lay between him and the Wold yet, he reminded himself. He and the hounds of Melor had traveled far in search of food: to the shore, all the way to Seaborne's cabin, where he and his brothers and Evelyn and Frankie had spent their first night on Ayda so long ago.

Knox hadn't been sure at first if he would be able to find the cabin, but as he retraced the steps they all had taken so many moonrises ago, it was as if his muscles knew the way. After three days, he had found himself on the little footbridge that crossed the stream, staring at the blackened foundation, crumbling chimney, and charred hull of the waterwheel where Seaborne's cabin once stood. Exorians had burned everything in the clearing but the footbridge—more proof that their fear of water was strong.

He had squatted there, surveying the damage and resting for a moment, remembering the cabin as he had first seen it, and how confident he'd been that day: how carelessly he'd thrown the stone from the beach—like a solid ostrich egg—over the cliff, and how stern Seaborne's reaction had been. His eyes had traced the patch of ground where he and Tinator had had their duel.

"I'm sorry," he remembered saying to the blackened trees and gray sky. "I was an idiot."

Then, he had heard Chase's voice in his head reply, *Yup, you got that right.*

If he tried, he could almost conjure up Chase's voice now, but he didn't want to.

Being at the clearing by the cabin had made him miss his brother so much that he couldn't stay there. Instead, he had turned back toward the path through the forest, taking it with long strides, until he heard the gentle thunder of waves crashing on the beach. At the cliff's edge he had stopped again, thinking back to the moment their boat had come ashore on the beach below. How were any of them to know what they would set into motion that day at Summerledge? It had all started out so innocently—he had just wanted to wring some fun out of a bad day. How could he have known about the fog of forgetting, about the five stones, about Dankar?

Memories jabbed at him with their sharp edges, bringing a stabbing pain in his ribs. Since when did thinking about things hurt so much? Because he had a lot to think about. His father left alone beyond the fog. The Fifth Stone and Captain Nate. Keeping his mother and Teddy safe. He wondered what Ratha might be doing to Chase, and how long she would make him stay in Varuna. Forever? The pain in his ribs amplified.

After explaining Ayda itself, Chase's absence was the second-hardest thing Knox had had to explain to his mother. When he and Seaborne and Calla returned to the Keep from the battle at the Voss, he and Seaborne had made a beeline for the place where Knox remembered emerging from Chantarelle's tunnels. Chase had seen his mother and Teddy in one of his visions, in the tunnels, headed for Melor. It only made sense to begin the search where Knox was sure there was an opening. But when they got there, they found no one.

They had then spread out in different directions, using the rock ledge that ran parallel aboveground to the river that Knox knew ran beneath the forest. But after searching through the night and following day, they had not found them. Darkness fell again, bringing with it doubt. Maybe Chase's vision was wrong? Or—worse—Grace and Teddy were lost in the maze of Chantarelle's tunnels. Maybe they had emerged in the Broomwash, or Exor? Seaborne had said nothing, but Knox had known at the time that he was thinking the same thing.

And that's when they had heard it. A little *hoot*. A pause, and then another. It came low and soft through the darkness. They waited. And then they heard another. Seaborne took a chance and hooted back. It was immediately followed with a response. Teddy's signal! It had to be.

They followed it all the way to the source: a deep-rutted V in a granite ledge. And there the two of them were, dirty and starving, and armed only with Bob the turtle and a penlight that had run out of juice. Chase's vision had been true.

"I knew you'd come," Teddy said, climbing up out of the rut to leap on Seaborne.

"Knew I'd come?" Seaborne's face was hidden in darkness but smiling by the sound of his voice. "How did you know such a thing, you rascal? If you only knew what we've been through to get here, you'd know we're both lucky to be anywhere and not roasted."

"Knox?" His mom's tight voice had come from right behind Teddy's in the dark.

"Hi, Mom," he'd said.

She cried a little, and then she asked about Chase.

How long ago all that seemed! But it didn't matter anymore. He was not the same person. None of them were. The past was like Seaborne's cabin—already gone. It did not serve a Melorian to linger there.

✛     ✛     ✛

He had camped by the sea unmolested for six moonrises, catching fish.

It was on his return that the trouble had begun. He and the hounds had followed one of Chantarelle's tunnels to the Vossbeck, then surfaced, and run smack into the Exorian raiding party. He was faster than the Exorians, and had thought he could slip by them, but the *tehuantl* had caught his scent and then—well, the race was on. The hounds had run off, trying to divert the cats, but the *tehuantl* were getting too used to Melorian tactics. And now, here he was, stuffed inside a burnt-out tree trunk like a terrified squirrel.

Knox lowered his hood, straining his ears to hear any movement or breathing. Nothing. Maybe he had lost them? He went over the terrain with his mind's eye. It wasn't too far to the northern bridge, which he would have to use now that the sky crossings were toast. If he ran full sprint he figured it wouldn't take him long to get there. He was as agile as a deer now, swift and strong, and could leap a hurdle of five feet as if it were one. The fish in his basket would go far in the Keep, and his mother and Teddy were on the lookout for him. He couldn't stay in the tree forever. He needed to get back.

He let go of the tension in his feet, and let himself slip down the smooth bark of the inner tree, landing without a sound on the forest floor. It helped that he had traded in his old Converse sneakers for the soft moccasins of a Melorian. He could feel the terrain much better with the moccasins, almost like running barefoot. He poked his nose out of the cavity, then exploded into a sprint. He only made it a few yards before the telltale roar of a *tehuantl* overhead made it clear that he had not tricked the Exorians with his hiding place. He glanced up through the haze that always lingered in the burnt forest—a mist of ash and smoke—and saw a *tehuantl* perched on yet another pile of charred stumps.

As burnt and black as the trees were, the *tehuantl* was an altogether different kind of black: shining and sleek, with impassive yellow eyes. Eyes that locked on to Knox's. Knox had looked into those eyes before, back at the Broomwash, as one of the animals was dying. The experience had affected him deeply. Even now, Knox was more impressed by the majestic jaguar than scared. He remembered how soft the fur was between its eyes when he'd stroked it. He remembered how frightened it had been. Maybe that cat was this one's brother or sister. Long ago, the *tehuantl*, like the Exorian people, had been the most noble and brave of creatures on Ayda. Only after Dankar had abused their daylights did the cats turn on humans.

"Good kitty," he said, as if the animal might understand.

The *tehuantl* roared again, but did not move from its perch. It was acting more like a sentinel than a killer, but you never could tell what a *tehuantl* was thinking. Better to be safe than sorry. Knox glanced over his shoulder without breaking his sprint. He tried not to think about how far one of them could leap.

*Just run*, he told himself. *Run fast.*

He heard a shout, an answering call, and then a flaming spear whizzed by his head, landing on the grass ahead of him and fizzling out. The Exorians were now on the chase. Normally he would stop to pick up the spear, but there was no time. He had to get to the bridge.

It occurred to him to try to lead his pursuers into a *tehuantl* trap, but he was not far from the Wold, and from there the glen was very close. He could lose them there. No matter how hard the Exorians had been trying to raze the glen, it defied them, growing thicker and lusher despite every attack.

Knox ran full tilt until he hit the wooden planks of the bridge. A volley of cold spears landed behind him, their metal points sinking into the wood. The Exorians did not dare to burn this bridge; they needed it to cross the river more than the Melorians. Knox resisted the impulse to use the open air of the bridge to look back and scan the raiding party.

Now that he knew Louis was his lost uncle Edward, it was hard not to stop and see if he was there among the Exorians. He wanted so much to bring Louis to his mother. To show her that her brother was not dead, and had been living on Ayda all these years since he'd gotten lost at sea. But Knox knew it was a bad idea, even if he could find him. Louis had been transformed into something almost unrecognizable in a ceremony at the arena. His own sister would not know him now: an Exorian covered in a warrior's hide, drunk with a raging thirst to do Dankar's bidding. The only thing that made Louis stand out from the other Exorian warriors was his blue eyes and his human-looking right hand. And the fact that he could swim.

Knox raced over the bridge and sped into the forest, which still held an aura of its old self. Fern groves grew between the trees and the scent of pine could be made out beneath the ever-present smell of smoke. Out of the corner of his eye Knox caught a flash of green and yellow bracken that delineated where the glen began, and made a beeline for it. He was almost there. The Exorians could feel it, too.

Another flaming spear whizzed past his head, then another, both landing unsatisfied on the ground ahead of him. This time, Knox took the time to swoop by and pick them up.

*Two more for me, two less for them.*

His bounty of dried fish slapped against his back, and the machete thwacked against the side of his leg, but he was so close now. He should be tired after how much he had run, but his daylights were only gaining in strength as he approached the glen. With a single leap, he jumped a ten-foot ravine that acted like a dirt moat to protect the glen. A few more running strides took him across the meadow where he somersaulted, headfirst, through a wall of flowering yellow shrubs and into the full protection of the glen.

He peered back through the bushes to see the Exorians massed at the ravine, shaking their raised spears in anger. In the time it took them to climb down and back up again, Knox would be long gone. He shuddered as he took in the full sight of the warriors—reptilian-looking, with thick, cracked skin the color of dried mud and blood. He quickly examined their hands, looking for one that looked even remotely human.

Knox shuddered again, remembering the terrible transformation of his uncle at the arena. Of all the horrors that Dankar had visited on Ayda, ruining the people of Exor was the worst, his uncle among them. Dankar had turned an entire generation of Exorians into slaves—and the unlucky ones who became warriors, into monsters. The thought of his uncle jabbed at him again. He knew Louis was out there, somewhere, and that he should tell his mother. But how? How do you tell someone that their brother has been turned into a monster?

He slowed his pace, breathing the good, green scent of the glen deep into his lungs. It was as refreshing to him as a full night's sleep. Ahead lay the moss-covered trees and swamp of the deathfield, and beyond that, the Keep, his mother, and his little brother. Seaborne and Calla. Rothermel. Knox felt the weight of the full basket on his back. Tonight, they would all eat well; and for the briefest of moments, Knox was truly happy.

*Chapter Two*

# WILDEST DREAMS

Chase was dreaming . . . the same dream he'd been having every night since his arrival in Varuna—heck, since even before then.

It was *that* dream: the one where he was standing on the porch at Summerledge, his bare feet brushing the softness of the weathered cedar planks. He looked out over the ledges of granite that slumped into the sea. The waterline that colored their flanks was green and mossy, while years of bird droppings stained the tops white. The sky directly above him was clear blue, and beneath it lay the darker blue—almost black—expanse of the Atlantic Ocean, undisturbed except for the occasional whitecap and a festive scattering of candy-colored buoys bobbing on the surface like leftover party favors.

In the dream, Chase sees the low, pine-laden islands far off to the east, their leeward side shaded, and beyond them, the sky folding in on itself in a gauzy layer of fog. His eyes sweep the sea to the west, then back again. He is searching for something. When he sees it—the flash of orange—the dream launches him up and off the porch, swooping him high into the air above the house and out over the ocean. He heads straight for it, knowing, in the way one knows in dreams that recur, what he will meet. He does not want to go, but yet he flies on, propelled by someone else's vision. He is not in control; the dream is—or Ratha is. He doesn't know which, as the line between his dreams and Ratha's visions have blurred since coming to Varuna.

From somewhere else in his brain—as if there's another Chase in there watching, conscious and awake—he recalls Seaborne's warning about Ratha: "She doesn't need weapons; she can drive you to madness with visions." This other Chase wills himself out of the dream—the ocean, the sky begin to fade—but not for long. Something stronger pulls him back in. The dream takes hold.

He is hovering above the source of the orange flash, a life jacket on a body that is floating facedown. He has seen this image countless times before in this dream: the halo of hair undulating like kelp; the dark, rolling sea pressing toward a far-off shore. The rise of a wave, the body turning, turning, turning to face him. He is expecting the face beneath the hair to be Knox's or Evelyn's or Teddy's or Frankie's, as it has been every time since he began having this dream. But this time, Ratha has a surprise for him. This time, she does not show him his brothers or his friends, but the blue-white features of his mother, lifeless, her eyes fogged over and staring.

"MOM!" he yells, and plunges into the water beside her. He pulls at the life jacket, but the swell pushes his mother's body away from him. She floats on the surface of a wave and then disappears on the other side. He sputters and swallows water and uses a name he hasn't called her since he was a toddler.

"*Mommy*," he cries.

Seagulls begin to circle above him.

"Somebody, HELP ME!" he screams, in the dream, or out loud.

✛     ✛     ✛

Like a train passing through a tunnel, Chase was thrown out of the dream in a violent lurch into darkness. He was aware of being awake again, but his body would not move. He opened his eyes and saw only blackness. He yelled again, but no sound came out. He was stuck between being asleep and being awake, and he didn't know which was more terrifying: being alone in the dream, in the water, with his mother's body, or being in the sudden darkness without her.

"Stay with her, Chase," said a low, whispering voice he recognized as Ratha's. "Stay with them all."

Chase fought her, trying to keep his mind blank. He did not want to go back into the dream, but she wouldn't let him stay out, either. She had warned him on his first night in Varuna that she would continue to send him the dream until he grew strong enough to make her stop. Night after night he had been helpless to do anything but watch. Tonight was no different. The force of Ratha's mind pushed his own back down through the tunnel, back into the brightness of the dream.

✛     ✛     ✛

He is in the ocean again, beside his mother, yanking at her life vest, trying to pull her from her cold grave. Something bumps into him from behind. He lifts his eyes from his mother's face. Another body has floated against him, then another. All around him are bodies floating on the surface of the sea, lifeless, rolling closer and farther apart with each swell. He sees the faces of Seaborne, Mara, Calla, Adhoran, Urza, Captain Nate, Bodi, Emon, and countless more: Melorians, Metrians, Exorians, Varunans, whose names he will never know. And then his own family: his brothers, his father. Evelyn and Frankie. All dead. He is alone, at the mercy of the sea, without a single hope and with no one to save, for they are all gone. Every single one.

Panic floods him, blind and thrashing. He begins to swallow seawater in great gulps. Soon it will be his turn to let go, and allow the sea to claim him as it has the others. He feels something akin to relief; at least he will not have to be alone anymore.

And then, just like that, Ratha sucked him out of the dream. The ocean receded into blankness and Chase lay fully awake on a daybed set under a window open to the stars, backlit by the ghostly light of a distant borealis. He was drenched in sweat and his head ached. A flash of his mother's eyes as they appeared in the dream made him retch. He turned his head over the side of the bed and puked up the contents of his stomach.

✛    ✛    ✛

Chase dared not close his eyes again. He lay in bed until the first gray light of dawn began to illuminate the bare flagstone floor of his room. He rose and wiped up the vomit as best he could with an old rag, throwing it in the fire that burned perpetually along the opposite wall.

The room was perfectly square, like a cell, and built of stone blocks mortared so closely and evenly that the walls appeared as smooth as marble. Some attempts had been made to make it cozy: A woven rug covered the stone floor, and a circle of candles lit the room, held aloft by a rope that stretched to the ceiling. His Metrian sword lay against a chair by a long table in the center of the room that served as a desk and a dining area. Assorted tools of navigation lay on the desk, as well as a gold statue of nine spheres. His bed was placed under the only window and piled high with blankets and furs. These articles were his only furnishings. The large fireplace took up the distant wall by the door, while ancient books lined the opposite side from floor to ceiling. Chase had begun to try and read them, but many were written in a strange language, and others were just hieroglyphs. He could make no sense of them. Still, it was enjoyable to look at the pictures. Time was moving slowly in Varuna, and aside from Ratha and the few Varunans that attended him, he had had no company.

Chase bent down to pick up one of the fur coverings on the bed. It was a robe given to him by the Varunans when he first came. He swung it over his shoulders, happy for the warmth it provided. Somewhere, south of here, he knew it was still summer in Ayda, but here in Varuna, it was cold. He missed his brothers, and Seaborne and Calla. And Captain Nate. And Evelyn. A lump rose in his throat. He closed his eyes and tried to conjure a vision of them. He wanted so much to see the ones he loved alive, as they were back in Exor at the wadi. It seemed only fair that after all this time in Varuna, he should be able to get a real glimpse of them, not just in his imagination or a dream or a memory—wasn't that what he was here for? To learn how to see things the way a real Varunan does—in real time?

"How do you know that what you see is not real?" said Ratha, who had appeared silently at the door. She looked as she always did: severe and pale, her translucent eyes probing his, her shimmering robes wrapped closely around her. As far as Chase could make out, Ratha did not sleep.

Chase did not reply. He had learned quickly that Ratha did not require a lot of conversation. She couldn't care less about external expressions or manners or gestures; rather, she probed what was happening on the inside. Every thought—however humiliating—was on display.

Instead, he thought about Rothermel, Ratha's only remaining brother, and the Keeper of the stone of Melor. As far as he knew, Knox, his mother, Teddy, and the rest of the Melorians were safely under his guard deep in the forest—and far from the sea. Evelyn and Captain Nate were a different matter. Chase had last seen them boarding Metrian ships alongside the Exorian warriors they had taken prisoner.

Ratha crossed from the door to the table, her robes undulating in an unnerving fashion, as if she were floating and not walking.

"Your fear will do little to help them," she said to him out loud, referring back to the dream. "They will need strength, not fear, when the time comes—and it is coming."

"I know," Chase said, exasperated. "I'm not trying to be afraid. It just happens. It's a messed-up dream!"

"Dreams are expressions of what we most desire—and also what we fear. They are a way to rehearse all forms of possibility. If you examine them, they reveal your relationship to yourself, and where your weaknesses lie."

Chase looked at the fire. He couldn't deny it. Despite everything that had happened on Ayda, he knew he *was* weak. He'd always been weak: the nerdy, asthmatic kid whose little brother had fought off the bullies.

"You do not give yourself enough credit, Chase," said Ratha, with more warmth.

"What do you mean?" he asked, turning toward her with some surprise. This was the first time Ratha had said anything even vaguely complimentary to him.

"Exactly what I said."

Chase ignored the spasm of irritation that had become almost reflex. Ratha was infuriating to converse with. He took a deep breath.

"Let me rephrase: Why do I not give myself enough credit?"

She stopped speaking out loud, and instead replayed in his mind the instant in the dream where he had felt the presence of the other Chase, the awake Chase, repeating Seaborne's warning. Then she spoke to him in his head.

"There, you were aware of the presence within you that is constant, that is more than and less than the sum of all your fears and emotions. It is that presence of mind that we need moving forward. I was wondering when it would break through."

Chase shook his head. Ratha spoke in riddles.

"I still don't understand. Are you saying there's another Chase inside me?"

"I'm saying there is something more powerful than the one you call 'Chase' inside you." She pointed out the window, and then said aloud, "Look outside."

He did as she requested, kneeling on the bed and putting his elbows on the windowsill. The snow-covered peaks of Varuna were turning rosy with the rising sun. Pale starlight faded into the greater day. A ring of mist lay along the flanks of the mountains. It was stunning.

"Do not admire it," Ratha admonished, coming to stand next to him. "*See* it."

"I see it," he said.

"Tell me what you see."

He described the view outside his window as best he could.

"Everything you describe is true, but it is not all. It is like the paint on the exterior of a jug. If you take the paint away, the body of the jug is still there. If you take away the sunrise, and the snow, and the mist and the clouds, the sky and the mountain still exist. Whether it is night or day, fair or foul, winter or summer, they simply are. It is the same with you: your fears, your worry, your emotions, your ideas about who you are—they are like the colors in the sky right now. In an hour they will all be different, but the sky itself remains what it is: eternal. Just as the core of you is eternal."

Chase looked again out the window. The sun glinted off the snow, so bright it made his headache flare. He squinted. The sun had already risen several hundred feet over the mountain range in the time they had been standing there. He felt its warmth on his face. Soon it would be higher, less intense, but still the same sun. Even when it set tonight, falling beyond his vision, it was still there. A thought clicked.

"You're talking about the daylights," he said.

"Yes," said Ratha. "Good." She took a few of her gliding steps backward and reached a hand out to touch the statue of the spheres. Reflections of the flames from the fireplace burnished the gold on the statue beneath her hand. It was a strange contrast to the tomblike chill of the room.

Chase followed her with his gaze. She stared deeply into the statue, her mouth downturned, her brow contracted.

"What's wrong?" he ventured. He had never seen her look distressed, but he imagined it might look something like this.

She spoke out loud, almost wistfully.

"It is as if there is another kind of fog—in my mind—that obscures from my sight the nature of the battle before us. I do not know what lies ahead, and I don't like not knowing because then I cannot plan."

Chase got off his bed, crossed to the table, and faced her. It seemed incredible that she might be confiding in him. He studied her for a minute, then said, "Captain Nate is coming soon. He'll be here. He told me he would—when we left Lake Voss. He'll tell you everything you need to know, and then you will be able to see what we should do."

Ratha flashed her pale eyes at him. "You have great trust in this man. I wonder if he is worthy of it. I have known him to be otherwise."

"He'll be here if he can, I know it. He will keep his word."

"Ah, yes, but you hit on something most important. While he may wish to keep his word, he may not have the ability. Whatever is coming to pass, it will happen in Metria. Of that, I am convinced. Your Captain may find his allegiances trying."

"I *know* he'll come," said Chase, raising his voice. He didn't want to think what might happen if Captain Nate didn't come soon. He couldn't stay here much longer without going crazy.

"You might not feel the same way once he gets here," snapped Ratha, having read his thoughts.

She glided to the chair and removed Chase's sword from its scabbard. She weighed it in her hand, holding it so it caught the firelight. Then she moved around the table toward him and pointed the tip at his heart.

He froze.

"You humans rely too heavily on weapons of steel, Chase, which may win battles but never win the war. Your strength must rise from what lies *inside*. From the daylights. You think I give you no peace of mind, that I roam your thoughts like a crow picking crumbs from the grass. But I do so for a reason. I must know you, so that I may trust you. Do you trust me?"

Chase almost laughed at the question. Instead, he glanced at the sword pointed at his chest, and shrugged.

Ratha lowered the sword. "Ah, I see. Well, I suppose it is only fair to doubt me, as you have not been allowed to read my thoughts. Here, I shall return the exchange for a moment."

With a force that practically threw him back against the bed behind him, Chase's mind was bombarded with a cascading onslaught of images. He saw Melor ablaze and the bright orange eye of a giant hound. He saw Dankar holding aloft the belt that Rothermel wore, connecting him to the stone of Melor. He saw Metria, abandoned, its byways and waterways prowled by roaming *tehuantl*, its people underground or dead. He saw Hesam's ship, shattered on the rocks along the straits of Varuna. He saw the rubble heap of the arena in Exor and scribes no older than Knox being forced to drink firewater, regardless of whether or not their daylights could survive it. Like a nightmarish slideshow, he saw Ayda in ruins—her beauty and her peoples destroyed.

"Has this happened?" he choked.

Ratha was silent for a moment, then sighed. "Not yet. But we are but a hairsbreadth away. Dankar advances on Melor. He is intent on gaining Rothermel's stone. I fear he will succeed, and then he will take his troops all the way into Metria, to the city, and its stone. If that should come to pass, little will stand between him and your world. He will lift the fog and use the ships in Metria's harbor to sail his army to your lands. This has been his goal since he slaughtered my brother Ranu half a century ago and stole his stone."

"But what about the stone of Varuna? Can't you use it to stop him?"

"The stone of Varuna is powerful, and it can allay him, but it cannot withstand the assault of the other three for long. It will ultimately fail—unless—"

"Unless what?"

"Unless the Captain is able to do what I asked him to do in the first place, and bring the Fifth Stone to Ayda. It is our last and best chance. Melor has all but fallen; Metria will be next. We are out of time."

"What do you mean, Melor *has* fallen? My brothers are there! My mother is there!" Chase sprang to the window as if he could see through the mist to the lands below. "I need to get down there and help them."

"Chase, calm your emotions and heed your daylights. Remember what we spoke of earlier. You are Varunan. You are tasked with seeing the larger implications, not just reacting to the whims of the heart. We must focus on the return of the Fifth Stone."

"No!" Chase turned on her, lunging to rip his sword out of her hand. "I'm not your captive! If you won't let me go, I'll fight my way out!"

Ratha reared back to her full height, her robes flashing like a strobe light. She raised the sword as if to strike him. "Do not forget that my kin also resides in Melor!" she roared. "If I can trust him to fight his own battles, surely you can do the same?"

Chase glared at her, his mind reaching for the right words, but there was nothing to say. She was right. They were going to have to do the best they could under the circumstances. Knox and Teddy were miles away with Seaborne and Rothermel and Calla, and their mother. Evelyn was far away in Metria with Captain Nate.

And he was stuck on the highest peak in Ayda—with *her*. He took a step back and raised his palms in surrender.

Ratha lowered the sword.

*Chapter Three*

# DANKAR IN ASCENDANCE

The water in the fountain in the courtyard burbled along, as if nothing had happened at the Palace. As if a battle had not taken place, the arena had not collapsed, the scribes had not revolted, and the Melorians had not escaped.

At least one victory could be claimed from the rubble of the arena: the water-hoarder, Rysta, Keeper of the stone of Metria, had not made it out of Exor alive. Of this Dankar was sure; he could feel it, in the shift in his own daylights and in the air around him. If ever there was a time to strike and make all of Ayda his own, it was now. Without Rysta's influence to dampen the fires of Exor, his army was unstoppable. The last remaining Keepers, his cousins, Rothermel and Ratha, would be dealt with in due course. He would see to it that they did as he wished, or suffer the fate of their siblings.

But he must not hesitate. He must not waste the imbalance that the death of Rysta had created in the daylights. Soon enough, nothing would be able to stop him. Not even the fog.

He paced the hallway, circling the courtyard in long strides and looking down at the lush garden he had raised from sand that surrounded
a burbling fountain. He admired the garden less for its beauty than the
sheer will it had taken to create it. *His* will. With enough of it, even
the Earth would bend to his vision—it was just a matter of what one
was willing to sacrifice. Look at what he had already built: a palace and
an army, out of rubble and dust. He would not falter now, despite his
recent setbacks.

Outside the walls of the Palace, continuous windstorms raged across
the plains. The air was yellow and heavy and filled with sand. Ratha was
up to her old tricks, trying to hem him in like a child in a playpen. But
Dankar had found that the tunnels that had allowed the Melorians to
enter into Exor unseen could be used two ways. At first, his warriors had
balked at the idea of traveling underground, but he knew how to handle
insurrection. He had only to point to the bodies of the scribes who had
helped his old enemy, Caspar, hanging on the rock spires outside the
Palace, so much flesh and bone for the vultures' pickings. There had
been no more grumbling after that.

*Yes,* he thought to himself. *I have subdued the rebellion in my own
house. Now it is time to grind into dust all of my enemies. I will fill the air
with the soot of their remains.* Ratha. Rothermel. Caspar. And whoever
now protected the stone of Metria.

At the thought of Metria, the sound of the fountain began to grate
on his ears. He would have it stoppered, just as he would raze Metria
to the ground and take possession of its stone. The garden would die
without the water from the fountain, just as Rysta had died, cut off from
her lands and her stone. Just as the Metrians would die as the flame of
his army advanced across their lands. Their Keeper would not be there
to save them this time.

He made a fist with his hand, feeling the weight of his dagger as he pictured holding it above Caspar's unnaturally long-lived heart, ready to drive it through the man's ribs. Rysta had used the last of her strength during the battle at the arena to save him: the man she loved.

Dankar almost spat in disgust, but he would not waste his body water on the word.

*Love.*

It was always the same. Love—specifically for humans—had been his family's undoing, but it would not be his. Pleasure he could abide, and the making of children as a necessary act. There was no counting the number of children in the pit-houses that he had sired, and done so intentionally—hoping to fill their Exorian veins with enough Watcher blood so they might survive the transformation necessary to become warriors. His Ayda would require soldiers, not scribes, to bring down the fog and venture into the lands beyond it. For it was the world beyond the fog that preoccupied him now.

Once he was restored to his rightful place on Ayda, he would rise, and claim dominion over all of humanity, as was his birthright. First son of a Watcher, sent to Earth by the great Weaver to rule over all. This was his destiny, and he would not succumb to the call of his human blood or fall into the trap that had doomed his predecessors.

Death was contagious for humans, he knew this. He had seen it here on Ayda, in the pit-houses, and so many times in the lands beyond the fog. The greater the love between the humans, the more catching the idea of death was for those who survived. Kill one, and their loved ones would soon follow, loosening their own daylights in despair or surrender or bloodlust for revenge.

It gave him great satisfaction to know that the passing of Rysta would come as a fate worse than fragmentation for Caspar and many of the

Metrians—and perhaps even her surviving brother and sister. They would be weakened, their daylights stirred with grief and imbalanced by loss, and vulnerable to the rot of emotion.

*So bound to one another*, he thought to himself. *So easy to control.*

His ears pricked up. The *fwop-fwop* sound of bare footsteps marching on the steps up to the Palace brought him back to the present. He could hear his warriors' spears thud against the sandstone with every other step.

*Finally*, he thought, and went out to greet them.

A party of newly minted warriors was amassed in the antechamber that served as an entrance to the Palace, hastily made replacements for those lost at the arena. Dankar assessed them from the landing of the main stairway. The raw-looking cracks between the scales on their skin were bloodied still, but would scab over in time. They were younger than their predecessors, and he had lost more than a few in the making, but he would master it soon enough, and have an ample supply.

First things first: He must conquer Ayda before he set his sights beyond the fog.

Dankar raised his hand in greeting, putting his palm face-out. The warriors responded by thudding the hilts of their spears to the ground in salute. As soon as the hilts met the finely packed dirt, their tips ignited into flame. One warrior pushed his way to the front of the group. He was encrusted in yellow sand and grit, having spent days coming through the sandstorm. He did not carry a spear, and his right hand was strapped close to his chest, as if it were broken. The effect made him appear more like a statue with a broken-off arm than a man. He stood at the bottom of the stairs, and blinked. His eyes flashed a disconcerting blue against the yellow of his skin.

"You may approach," said Dankar.

The warrior made his way up the stairs, stopping on the step just below where Dankar stood. He bowed his head and groped at the belt at his waist, removing a small, golden flask. He unscrewed the cap and took a sip from it.

Dankar's gaze raked over the warrior, taking in his defective right hand.

Admittedly, the daylights were a tricky business, and this had been a hasty job. But also special. The warrior had once been an outlier, washed onto the shores of Exor as a boy. He had been raised on Ayda, and the resilience of his daylights had grown stronger, but he was still only human. The first outlier to undergo the transformation. The fact that he had survived at all gave Dankar renewed hope in his strategy. Perhaps those who lived beyond the fog would not die when confronted with the same fate.

"What say you?" he commanded the warrior.

Louis raised his gaze and spoke in a tired voice.

"We lost them at the Voss. They had ships, and many Metrian soldiers. They took a number of us captive. I only just got away. The camels are gone."

"So they *are* in Metria, then?"

Louis shook his head, dispersing a cloud of yellow dust. "I don't know. Melorians were there, and those hounds. They might be in Melor. The ships must be bound for Metria . . . I don't know where the others went."

"Never mind," grumbled Dankar. "I don't care about the others, except the grown outlier, the man. Where is he?"

"I don't know. He was on one of our camels when last I saw him."

Dankar turned away in frustration.

Caspar was a threat. He would need to be dealt with swiftly, but how? The outlier did not have the strength of a Keeper, but his mere existence after all these years meant he had *some* kind of power aiding him. Only Watcher-blood or the stones of power could grant longevity to a vessel like that. Perhaps his lover Rysta had given him a trinket or charm that protected him with the power of her stone, and that was what was keeping him alive.

The idea of the Fifth Stone gnawed at the back of his mind, but he swept that worry away. Surely his cousins would not be so stupid as to waste an opportunity to use the Fifth Stone if Caspar had brought it with him. The upset at the arena was a nuisance compared to what the Fifth Stone might do. If Caspar had it in his possession, all of Exor would be at the bottom of the sea right now, he was sure of that.

No, Dankar argued with himself; it had to be some charm of Rysta's that could be undone when he had the stone of Metria in his possession. Dankar smiled at the symmetry of it all: The stone would be Caspar's undoing, not his own. He turned back and addressed the troops in the hall.

"For too long the water-hoarders have kept their bounty from us! Why should the Metrians grow fat and rich off food and water, when it is the sun that gives us *all* life? They live in great houses with plump beds and fine clothing, while we grub in the dirt to grow enough food! Let me ask you—when is the last time you had a bath?"

Dankar smirked at their confusion. Most of his warriors did not even know this word.

"The Metrians loll about in great vats of water and then"—he paused for emphasis—"they let it drain, only to refill the same amount the next day."

The warriors grew silent at the thought of so much water going to waste.

"I ask you," continued Dankar, "is it not fair that we should ask them to share? After all, have we not shared the sun as it shines on their land? Is it not time that we demand what is rightfully ours? Should we not now go forth and take what has been kept from us these many years?"

A wave of excitement passed through the warriors; they thudded their spears on the ground in unison. Dankar's voice was electrifying.

"You have all sacrificed. Your mothers have sacrificed. Your sisters have sacrificed. Is it not just that you see some reward? The city of Metria lies unprotected, its Keeper spent, its people lost and frightened. Yet they will not give up their riches easily! It is not their time, however; it is OUR time. Exor's time. We have already won! It is time for us to find the stone of Metria and collect our due!"

*Ex-or! Ex-or!* the warriors chanted in time with each thud of their spears.

The firewater in Louis's veins pulsated to the rhythm of the sound of the spears hitting the ground. He felt a flame of injustice ignite in his heart, and a hatred for the Metrians—for anyone who was not Exorian—swept through him. Had they not suffered long enough in the desert? Friendless, isolated, scraping an existence out of nothing? Ayda belonged to *them*, and them alone. They had earned it. Let the Melorians and the Metrians find out what it was like to live under a burning sky, as Exorians had been doing for all this time. The new world would be born of flame, and it would only have room for those who could survive hardship and thirst.

"We will take back what is ours!" cried Dankar, lifting both of his arms in the air. "We will not stop until we are victorious! To Metria—and beyond!"

The warriors took up the cry, chanting *To Metria—and beyond!*

Dankar allowed the wave of fervor to crest before raising his palm again; this time, in benediction.

"Go now! Rest, fill your flasks, refresh your firewater supply. Ready yourselves, for our day is close at hand."

Louis's right hand throbbed against his chest, but he pushed the pain away with his mind. He would see Exor take what it deserved. He turned to go.

Dankar stopped him.

"Not you," he said. "You will leave at the next moonrise and take a small battalion into Melor. Waste no time. Burn whatever you have to in order to find the Keeper, Rothermel. Smoke the Melorians out of their warrens, and kill anyone who does not surrender."

"And those who do surrender?" asked Louis.

"Drive them east, into Metria, where I will meet you at the banks of the Hestredes. We will enter the city together. Prisoners will be useful to show the Metrians how easily we took their neighbors."

"The Keeper will not go easy."

"I want him alive," Dankar snapped. "For the time being."

Louis nodded his assent.

"And I want his stone."

Louis's facial expression remained blank, but his blue eyes were troubled.

"How? Even our best men are no match for a Keeper in his own land."

"The outliers—they are in Melor?"

"Yes, or Metria. I'm not sure. Maybe both?"

Dankar raised his hand and laid it on Louis's shoulder. A small puff of yellow dust rose around it.

"Love for humans curses the blood of Remiel's line. It has ever been so. His children were born of it, and they will all die of it." He pinched Louis's shoulder hard enough to make Louis visibly wince, despite the new, tough hide he'd grown.

Dankar leaned in and whispered in his ear. "I have a plan."

*Chapter Four*

# HOSPITAL

Far away, across a fog-enshrouded sea, the monitor by Frankie's hospital bed beat out a regular rhythm. *Bleep-bleep. Bleep-bleep. Bleep-bleep.* As if to say: *No change. No change. No change.*

*Annoying and reassuring at the same time*, thought Jim Thompson, who had been watching the jagged spikes on the monitor like it was a video game for the last hour. Outside, rain beat hard against the window, as it had for weeks in Fells Harbor and the surrounding area.

"We'll need an ark if this keeps up," announced one of the day nurses, there to record Frankie's vitals yet again.

Jim did not respond. He didn't care about the rain. He didn't care for conversation. He was living at the hospital these days, rarely venturing outside. He ate in the cafeteria or out of the vending machines, and wore doctor's scrubs. He showered in Frankie's bathroom. He hadn't been home in days.

*Home.*

*Where was that exactly?* he wondered, fixing his stare on the rain-streaked window. He used to think he knew what home was: the pitched roof and widow's walk of Summerledge. The granite ledge that slumped off into the sea. The patchy green lawn between the house and the beach where his sons liked to kick a soccer ball back and forth. He saw in his mind's eye the white-painted kitchen with its ancient table and woodstove. He heard the sound of leaking pipes and a slamming screen door. That was home, once upon a time. But he knew better now. Home was not a place—home was the people who *inhabited* a place. It was where the people you love are, and that could be anywhere, really. As long as they were there.

"She's a sweet little thing, isn't she," said the nurse, glancing down at Frankie before stepping out of the room. "You are very lucky."

Jim followed her gaze to the small girl tucked tightly into the hospital bed. She seemed dwarfed by the expanse of the bed, just a gentle ridge that broke the otherwise flat plane of blankets. It seemed to Jim that if it weren't for the dark hair fanning out in ringlets across the striped pillow, she would barely be noticeable at all. One could walk into the room and not realize she was there. She lay so quiet and still, her rounded face revealing how young she really was. Not much older than Teddy.

He hadn't noticed her age before. In fact, he hadn't really noticed *her* at all, or her sister, Evelyn. He had some vague notion of them from before. Passing in and out of the kitchen at Summerledge. A voice on the telephone. Teddy singing a song they had taught him. But the girls had had no real shape or form. Not until the night they had been pulled out of the ocean with his own kids, Frankie burning with fever, after that stupid prank the boys had pulled. Jim was glad now that the Whaler had sunk in the accident. He would never again allow any member of his family out on the open sea.

*Stupid, stupid*, he swore to himself, thinking back to that day. The phone call from the lab that had called him back to the office; his wife,

Grace, driving him to the airport. If he and Grace had just stayed at Summerledge that day, none of this would have happened.

But the boys had used the opportunity to break the rules and take the girls out on the boat, despite what their mother had told them year after year about the fog. How quickly it moved in, how fast you could be stranded and shipwrecked. And that is exactly what had happened. The boat had floundered and capsized and dumped all five children into the sea. If it had not been for Captain Nate, and his superior navigation skills, they all would have drowned. As it was, only Frankie had suffered any long-lasting damage.

The other four kids had come out of the water just fine—a touch of hypothermia and some odd behavior, but otherwise in perfect health. Frankie, on the other hand, had grown steadily worse in the days after the rescue, her cells succumbing to some unknown illness. Jim was an immunologist and specialized in viruses, and for a few weeks, he feared the worst for Frankie: some kind of rapidly moving cancer or infectious agent. Though he had been hesitant to say it out loud, he had never truly believed her condition to be related to the accident; it had to be a coincidence. An example of bad timing.

But as the weeks went by, he grew increasingly stumped. He had never seen anything like what Frankie was experiencing, and neither he nor Frankie's other doctors could predict whether she would survive. Antibiotics had no impact, and there was not much else they could do. Her doctors had decided, with the consent of Fanny Dellemere (Jim's neighbor, and Frankie's adoptive grandmother and guardian), to put her in an induced coma, to help her body heal. It had worked; her condition had stabilized. She was no longer deteriorating.

Then Grace, the boys, and Evelyn had all disappeared with no trace but a mystifying note. Jim and Fanny Dellemere spent their days now rotating between searching for their missing loved ones and watching over the one who was still with them.

Jim smoothed his hand over the bedsheet and pulled up Frankie's blanket. The hospital overused the air-conditioning in the summer, and it was even more unnecessary now, in late August, when the season was turning. In other years, the boys would be feeling the dread of the school year approaching.

With a pang, Jim realized that he had never understood why his children felt this way. As a boy, he had always enjoyed school—its rigors and examinations—and his own summers had felt too long and open-ended. To this day, he still preferred routine and schedules. It was one reason he liked lab work: orderly stacks of test tubes and calibration regimens and result tabulations. Data could be quantified and reasoned with; aberrations were simply that, and easily disqualified. When he met Grace and married her, she had appreciated his steadiness and his caution. She liked that she always knew where he was and what he was doing. It made her feel safe.

But then the children were born, and their lives changed. Their routines were upended. He would never have admitted, out loud, how surprised—and, if he were perfectly honest—how distressed he'd been to discover how messy and disruptive and loud family life was, and even more so at Summerledge, where nothing could be relied on, not even the weather. He saw clearly now how he used the excuse of the office to escape the chaos: the petty griping between the boys; the endless activities and chores and maintenance; Grace's exhaustion and the gloomy memories of her brother that still haunted the house.

He jumped to his feet and paced the confines of the room.

Oh, how gladly he would take it all back now! Trade the dark, relentless peace of the empty house and the sterile routine of the lab for the sloppy uproar of his old life. He would quit his job forever and stay home and play whatever games his boys wanted him to play, for as long as they wanted, if only they would come *back*. He would never say an angry word to Grace again.

*Please, please come back*, he pleaded silently, stopping at the window. Night was descending, and the sky was thick with rain clouds. He pressed his forehead to the window, his spectacles clinking against the glass.

*Don't leave me.*

Frankie moaned lightly behind him. Jim crossed the few paces to her bed, removing the stethoscope he now wore around his neck like a scarf. He listened to her heart and checked the monitor again. Her pulse was normal. She was doing better. She was fighting. If it continued, they would be able to bring her out of the coma soon.

But then what? What would he and Fanny tell her? He hardly knew what to tell himself. All he knew for sure was that Evelyn, the boys, and Grace were gone.

For the thousandth time, Jim mentally went over the note that had been left on the kitchen table. Evelyn had written that she and Knox were going to the hospital, but the police had found no evidence that that was the case—it was more likely that she'd lied, especially considering what she wrote as a postscript to Teddy:

*Knox and I found the thing that lives in the cave. It explains everything. If you have any questions, go to the cave.*

Jim had read that and immediately organized a search party of townspeople and neighbors, with the notable exception of Captain Nate, who hadn't been sighted since the night of the kids' rescue. Everyone else showed up with flashlights and rain gear—even Fanny Dellemere, who had left Frankie's bedside to join in. Together, they formed a line and scoured the forest between the house and Secret Beach. Their search revealed a small cave, set above the ground amid a jumble of granite, but the entry was filled in, and any animal that had lived there was long gone.

The plain truth was, Jim Thompson had no clue where his family was. Evelyn and Knox were together. And it seemed likely that Teddy was with his mother. But where was Chase? And why hadn't any of them been in touch?

The door behind him swung open and Fanny Dellemere came through it. She had a singular way of filling up a room. She was tall, granted, made taller by the swoops of whitish-gray hair she wore piled on her head, but it was something else that demanded space. A way of being. Even bowed by age and grief, she was someone who commanded attention.

"How is my girl doing?" she asked, clearly trying to sound chipper.

"Fine," replied Jim. "Good, actually. No dip."

"I'm glad to hear it."

She moved to Frankie's bedside, opposite Jim, and bent down to kiss the girl's forehead. When she stood up, she caught Jim's eye.

"And how are *you* doing?" she asked.

He shrugged.

"I've learned that no news is usually good news."

"What makes you think that?" Jim snapped. He didn't mean to sound so angry, but he couldn't help it. Why had they left him behind?

Mrs. Dellemere reached across the bed and put her hand over his. She patted it.

"I don't know. I guess I'm just feeling optimistic."

Jim shrugged again. Mrs. Dellemere squeezed his hand with surprising strength.

"Do you have faith in your wife, Jim?"

"Of course."

"So do I. I've known her since she was a girl, and she suffered a great deal when her Edward was lost at sea. She was too young to have endured so much grief, her own and her parents'. It might have taken another person all the way down—but not her. She is a survivor, and she worships those kids. Wherever they are, I *know* she will protect them. I also know that she will be in touch with us, if and when she can."

Jim struggled to swallow, his worst fear rising up out of some sick, sad place in his belly and swamping the flash of anger.

"But that's what I'm worried about. I know she would certainly try to reach me—I mean, if she was still able to—and she hasn't, which means she physically can't, or someone is stopping her—" He choked on the words. "If they are still alive, I think they must be in terrible danger."

Mrs. Dellemere suddenly stopped patting his hand.

"I agree," she said.

"You do?" He swallowed hard. However bad his fear was, it felt worse to have it confirmed. He pressed his fingers into his closed eyelids under his spectacles.

"What do we do?" he whispered.

"The only thing we can: We wait, and we watch, and we help whomever needs it."

Jim removed his fingers and stared at Mrs. Dellemere.

"As if that's going to make a difference?"

She returned his stare.

"You'd be surprised, Jim. You'd be surprised."

*Chapter Five*

# RESEARCH

"What use is it, then?" Evelyn grumbled.

She and Hesam were poring over scrolls in the whitewashed public library of Metria, part of a larger complex of low, blue-domed buildings that served as the city's civil headquarters. The complex was built around a large square, at the center of which stood a fountain from which water poured across three levels, first as a stream, then as a sheet, and then as droplets that filled the air with the sound of rain. It was the defining characteristic of Metria: Wherever one went, there was the sound of water, splashing against the foundations of the buildings, rushing under the footbridges that spanned the waterways, slapping against the stone-and-wooden piers along the harbor. To Evelyn's ears, the sound was like a reproach for what had happened to Rysta in Exor.

*Bring her back*, it seemed to say.

But Rysta would never come back. Her imprisonment and torture at the hands of Dankar had made her too weak. Captain Nate—Caspar— had come all the way back through the fog to rescue her. He had sworn to Rysta's sister, Ratha, to give up the location of the Fifth Stone, all in the hopes of returning Rysta to Metria. But it hadn't worked. Despite everything Captain Nate had done—along with Evelyn and Chase and Knox and the Melorians—they had been too late. Rysta had given her only chance of survival—the necklace that connected her to the stone of Metria—to Louis before he was transformed. Without it, her daylights were loosened, and she fragmented at the wadi outside Dankar's palace.

No, Rysta was never coming back, no matter how much the water pleaded.

"We can't give up, Evelyn," said Hesam. "There must be something in here that will cure them."

They were looking through every possible source in the library. They had been at it for days, trying to find any possible clue as to how to undo the transformation that Dankar had performed on his warriors with the firewater. In the north, at the caverns, Hesam had thirty miserable Exorian warriors being guarded under lock and key. She had ordered the removal of the flasks at their waists, the contents dumped on the ground, and then a daily bath in the waters of the Hestredes, but it had not been enough. The warriors were somewhat improved by the treatment, but not cured.

"We are making progress, you know. It's slow, but they are changing." Hesam pulled down another scroll from a shelf and blew the dust off of it. "At first the bath was a torment to them, and now they don't even notice it. Maybe time is all it will take."

Evelyn shook her head.

"We don't have time—we have to find a cure now. If we can find an antidote to Dankar's poison before he attacks Metria, we can use it to change all his warriors back. Dankar won't have anyone to fight his stupid war." She opened the scroll on the long, wooden table.

"You act like they want to be changed back. I haven't found that to be true."

"They don't know what they want. Dankar is a *bokor*—a sorcerer. We have people like him in the country where I was born. They use a dark magic to take over the will of other people and enslave them. They don't even know what they're doing . . ." She paused, thinking about Louis. "It's a curse, and a curse can be lifted. We just have to figure out how."

She stooped over the open scroll and groaned in frustration. This one, like so many of them, was written in an ancient script that was completely unrecognizable.

"What language *is* this?"

Hesam shook her head, bewildered. "I think it is the tongue of the ancients, but I do not know. These all predate my birth."

"I wish Chantarelle would come back. He might know." Evelyn sighed.

"He has been gone a long time."

Evelyn was silent. Neither she nor Hesam wanted to voice what both of them, and Urza, were most worried about. Maybe Chantarelle would *never* come back. Maybe the Keeper of the Fifth Stone would not respond to their pleas. Maybe they were truly alone.

After all, it had been several days since the little man had descended into his tunnels to take a message back to the world beyond the fog: a message from Captain Nate for the Keeper of the Fifth Stone. Captain Nate would say nothing about the specifics of it, just that it had been sent. As soon as he and Evelyn had entered the city, she had parted ways with the Captain, and saw him only on occasion. She knew that he had secreted himself with Chantarelle, and that Chantarelle had left soon thereafter, but nothing more.

Since then, Captain Nate had kept to himself mostly, waiting and watching the water down by the harbor. He was probably there now.

She stood up and let the scroll rewind itself on the table.

"I need to check on something," she said. "Keep looking. There's got to be something in here that we can read. I'll be right back."

✝     ✝     ✝

Captain Nate leaned into a wooden post at the end of a pier. The pillars that demarcated the entrance to the city's great harbor rose above the mist, but his eyes were not drawn to them. Instead, they were glued to the small circlets and half-moons that pebbled the surface of the sea. Every now and then a smooth patch would appear, and the Captain would lean over, watching it intently. But despite his vigilance, he had not seen it stretch or widen into a ribbon as he'd wanted it to do. Ever since Rysta's death, the watchwater had disappointed him. Perhaps the map that she had given him so long ago was lost. Maybe the secret she had told him—how to come and go from Ayda as he pleased—had died with her. He was now like every other Aydan, or outlier: stuck on one side of the fog or the other.

He put his hand to his chin, surprised once more to feel rough skin and not beard. Ever since his return to Ayda, his daylights had resumed their former potency, and he appeared to be a much younger man than he was. Good Lord, he was old, he thought to himself. Over five hundred years old. He had lived the majority of those years on the other side of the fog. And, he had seen that world remade over and over again, at great cost. Would he live to see it remade again—or destroyed utterly?

Captain Nate closed his eyes, trying to imagine what might unfold if Dankar were to pierce the fog and return to his birthland. Descendants of the Others still existed there; one did not have to go far to find their petty fiefdoms and tyrannies. There was small mercy in the fact that not all of the lines were evil, and many were now so diluted as to be practically powerless. Since the loss of the Fifth Stone, the daylights of all who lived beyond the fog had dimmed as a whole, including—thankfully—those that belonged to the heirs of the Watchers, which begged the question that most nagged at him: If he actually succeeded in bringing the Fifth Stone back to Ayda, what would happen next? Would the daylights of the Others beyond the fog resume their strength? And if so, who would they pay allegiance to? If history was any lesson, it was a thought worth troubling oneself over.

A sudden break in the fog allowed a beam of light to shine through the overcast sky. It hit the water and the surface turned to molten silver. At the same time a school of purple-and-silver fish breached the water's surface and leapt into the air, shattering the stillness. They hovered, then dropped and swam below, and the sea grew still.

He studied the harbor again, and the fog obscuring the horizon, longing for the watchwater to tell him that his message had been received.

✠    ✠    ✠

Evelyn, too, had seen the school of fish jump into the air and then dive back under the surface. She was standing behind the Captain, wondering how best to interrupt his reverie without startling him. As it turned out, she didn't have to.

"Have you found anything?" he asked, not turning around.

"No; have you?"

The Captain shook his head.

"What about the fish. Is that a sign?"

"Not one we are looking for. But maybe."

"How do you mean?" She came abreast of him.

He pointed at the glassy surface of the sea. "Perhaps it means that no matter how disruptive or violent an action, eventually peace will reign."

She looked at him sideways. "And you really believe that?"

"No." He gave her a rueful grin.

"You are thinking you'll have to leave soon, aren't you?"

"Not exactly, but yes, I made a promise to Ratha; I won't break it."

A flutter of fear took ahold of her. As long as Captain Nate was in Metria, it felt possible that the Fifth Stone could arrive at any time. It made her feel confident that a power existed that was stronger and better than any one of them, and she knew she wasn't the only one who felt that way. Urza, Hesam—everyone in the city shared the feeling. Even the soldiers. Captain Nate was the closest thing they had now to Rysta.

She felt the strongest impulse to fall to her knees and beg him to stay. Instead, she kept her voice calm and tried to reason with him.

"But you've already sent the message to the Keeper of the Fifth Stone. You said it was out of your hands after that! It's up to Chantarelle to find the Keeper and ask for the stone. What more can Ratha want from you?"

"She wants what all Varunans want: thoughts, memories, dreams. They are a source of information and, perhaps, inspiration. Or it is possible she just wants to punish me. I don't really know. "

"Will she let Chase go, if you fulfill your promise?"

Captain Nate shrugged by way of an answer.

"That's ridiculous. We need some kind of guarantee, no?" she objected. "You can't just go up there and let her keep you both on some mountaintop! We need you here. We're at war! The Exorians could break our defenses any day!"

"Do you think I don't know that, Evelyn?" The Captain groaned. "But who knows what Ratha has in mind—for any of us, for that matter. All

I know is, she will do exactly what she wants to do. And I must stay true to the only thing I have left that matters to me: my word."

Evelyn digested this.

"I feel bad for Chase," she murmured, thinking of his face when she'd last seen him, on the shores of the Voss, exhausted but resigned. Leaving Knox, especially when he knew his mother and Teddy were in Ayda, and that Louis was free and out of control, was the last thing he had wanted to do. "I forced him to beg Ratha for her help, and she used it to trick him into going with her. Now he's her prisoner."

"It's all right, Evelyn," said Captain Nate. "It was the right thing to do under the circumstances. We would never have made it across the desert if you hadn't. Ratha is a manipulative piece of work, to be sure, but I trust she will not hurt the boy"—he grimaced—"at least, I don't *think* she will."

"That doesn't exactly fill me with confidence."

"Me neither, but it is the truth." He laid a light hand on her shoulder. "Either way, I will find out soon enough. I leave for Varuna before the next moonrise."

*Chapter Six*

# MARA

Knox did not break stride as he entered the deathfield and quickly crossed toward the edges of the swamp. He headed straight for the great mossy ledge of rock at the far end: the hidden doorway to the Keep. No one could get in or out without Rothermel's knowledge. Armed sentries hidden along the ledge would kill anyone trying to enter without permission.

Knox toed his way around the edge and onto the narrow footpath by the ledge. The swamp stank of rotting vegetation; the moss on the ledge dripped muddy, rank water. Knox paid it no heed, cupping his hand over his mouth and hooting once, like an owl. To anyone who was not a Melorian, the signal would blend in with the rest of the normal chitterings of the forest—or at least, what used to be normal.

Knox cocked his head, lowered his hood, listening.

*Hoot-hoot* came the reply.

An invisible seam in the ledge cracked open and a blinding light poured through the space. The two sides of the ledge shifted to make room for

Knox to pass. As he went through, a small, hooded figure dropped to the ground in front of him.

"Hiya, Tedders." Knox smiled at his little brother. "Hungry?"

Teddy looked up at him from under his hood. "What took you so long? Mom was getting worried."

Knox nodded at the spears he was carrying.

"I ran into a few Exorians on the way back, and had to improvise. You'd better tell Duelle and rest of the guard to expect them."

"Okay, but you need to find Mom. It's not good."

"Whaddya mean?"

Teddy paused for a second, then said, "Mara."

Knox grimaced.

Ever since Seaborne and Knox had found Teddy and Grace and brought them back to the Keep, Mara had taken Grace under her wing—as much as she could, before she got too weak. It was as if the two mothers had an immediate understanding, and Mara knew it was her job to pass on whatever information she could to Grace about her children's time on Ayda. They spent hours huddled together in conversation, often inside one of the long row houses in the Keep.

After a consultation with Rothermel about Chase, Grace had taken almost everything Mara had told her in stride, but more often than not, Knox caught his mother staring at him like he was a stranger. She seemed worried about him, but distant. It made him wonder how she'd feel when she found out about Louis. She had only heard about Exorian warriors, never seen one in the flesh. Knox hoped he could keep it that way.

He passed through the towering grove of trees on his way toward the hillside that marked the beginning of the village of the Keep. He couldn't help but pause a minute and look up. Massive branches intermingled overhead, filtering the light into a mellow golden glow. Here in the heart of Melor, it always felt like midsummer, even as the forest beyond the wall fell into ash and frost. It never failed to make his heart soar.

Once he was in the village, he headed straight for one of the row houses. Narrow spirals of smoke wafted from the open holes in the roofs. Beyond the houses, a few scattered Melorians were harvesting what they could from the struggling gardens. He waved to Adhoran, who waved back.

Knox pointed with his thumb to the basket on his back and grinned. "I caught a lot of fish!" he shouted.

Adhoran put his palms together under his chin and bowed his head. He had not spoken since the battle at the arena. Rothermel had found him in the Broomwash, his body badly broken and close to death. He was brought back to the Keep and was healed enough now to be put in charge of the gardens. If his injuries or the change in occupation bothered him, no one would ever know. Melorians did not complain.

Knox paused to look at the carefully tended garden, feeling once again grateful for the weight of the dried fish on his back. At least they would all eat well tonight. As if on cue, his stomach growled. He paid it no mind; he was used to it. He was always hungry now. They all were.

Rothermel had used the stone of Melor to speed the growth of what had been planted in the gardens, but even his power could not grow what had not been seeded. And, without the ability to hunt and gather regularly in the forest, and the milk goats and cows sacrificed for their meat long ago, the remaining Melorians had very little now to fall back on. It surprised Knox to find that even the daylights couldn't fend off the pit of desperation that hunger gnawed into his stomach. He was no different from anyone in the Keep: He was willing to do anything, go anywhere, challenge anyone, to get food.

Fights had begun to break out, and there were whispers of hidden stores of food being stolen from one family to feed another. But mostly, everyone in the Keep just grew thinner and weaker. Mara was not the only one to fall seriously ill, and an atmosphere of fear lay over the village. It wasn't enough that they were being hunted from the outside; things were also falling apart on the inside. Nobody said it, but they all were thinking it: The power of the stone of Melor was fading as Exor's grew in strength.

Knox made his way to the threshold of the northernmost building and stepped inside. The houses were lit only by firelight and the blocks of sunlight that passed through the open doors and windows, and it took some time for his eyes to adjust to the dimness. Once they did, he saw that at the far end, a fire burned with great intensity, giving off a sage-like odor. His mother and Calla squatted beside a prone form.

Mara.

Knox crossed the room and set his basket down by the fire. He knelt beside his mother. Her face was shaded by the hooded poncho she wore. One of Mara's. Calla kneeled across from them.

"How's she doing?"

"She is fading," said Calla, matter-of-factly. She stroked Mara's forehead.

Mara lay utterly still. Her eyes were open and only blinked sporadically.

"I brought food. Will it help?"

"She is beyond that now, Knox," said a rich, rumbling voice from the doorway.

Rothermel emerged into the firelight, his mouth drawn down, his head un-helmeted and haloed by the shadow of his mass of hair. The creases and folds of his face were more deeply etched by the dim light, and Knox was overcome suddenly with an awareness of how long Rothermel had been on the planet. How many deaths had he witnessed?

"Mom?" Knox whispered.

"I'm here, honey," she answered, but her eyes flashed between Calla and Mara. It was hard not to recognize that soon, Calla would no longer have her mom to answer her.

Mara stirred.

Calla wiped her mother's lips with a wet cloth and squeezed a few drops into her mother's mouth. Mara's eyes focused on Knox.

"Did you succeed?" she whispered.

Knox nodded, too choked up to say anything.

"Good," said Mara, patting his arm weakly.

He glanced over at Calla, wondering how she was doing. Not good, by the looks of it. Her eyes were hollowed out and her lips were a thin, compressed line. He couldn't remember the last time he had seen Calla sleep, let alone smile. He couldn't blame her. Since when had she had anything to smile about? So many Melorians had left the Wold to flee into Metria, or had been killed. And now her mother was dying.

He glanced at his own mother again out of the corner of his eye. How would he feel if she was dying? She looked smaller, and more fragile. He could see the bones of her skull beneath her face. For the first time since they had found her, he had the real sense that his mom could die here. They could all die here.

A memory of his dad flashed across his mind. Knox remembered how he'd looked from the backseat as they drove up to Summerledge, that crazy day when they had lost the bikes. He saw his dad's profile looking down at his cell phone, the bare spot on the back of his head where he was losing his hair. The indents on his nose from his glasses. For all Knox knew, his dad believed his whole family was already dead.

Knox swallowed hard.

Mara patted his hand with a touch as insubstantial as a bird's feather. Surprised, he brought his gaze back down to her. The gold flecks in her eyes had multiplied, and it was as if Knox was looking into the aura of a candle flame. Her eyes were more gold than brown now.

"Tinator was right," she whispered. "He knew from the first time he saw you that you had the makings of a fine Melorian. He would have welcomed you at our fire, as I do." She raised her head slightly to scan all of their faces. When she got back to Knox, she asked, "Where is the little one? Teddy?"

"He is at the wall, standing guard. Duelle is looking after him."

Mara nodded and then gestured for Knox to come closer. He leaned in, and she reached for him, pulling the collar of his poncho until his ear was close to her mouth.

"You have become strong in your time in Melor."

Knox nodded.

"You must use this strength in ways you have not imagined. It will be difficult, but you must let him be taken," she said, her voice like a creaking door.

Knox froze for a second, not understanding. He frowned.

"Who? Teddy?"

Mara clamped her hand down on his neck, keeping him close. She raised up a little and said more clearly into his ear, "When the time comes, you must let him be taken," she repeated. "The others will not want to allow it, but you must prevail. Then, go from here. Find Evelyn."

"I don't understand," said Knox, raising his eyes to Calla's for explanation, then back down at Mara.

Mara had shut her eyes. Her breath grew raspy.

He wondered if she had lost her mind. Why would Knox let anybody take his little brother? He'd die first.

Rothermel pulled Knox back to create room for him to stoop beside the dying woman. He put a hand on her forehead. Her breath grew less labored, but more shallow.

Calla moistened her mother's lips again. Grace smoothed Mara's blanket and took one of her hands. Behind them, the room began to fill with people.

Rothermel started to chant in a low voice. Knox could not understand a word of it, but somehow it seemed familiar. Then he remembered. It was the same chant he had heard Tinator and Mara use at Seaborne's cabin when they had saved Tar's life after Frankie was taken.

Heat began to emanate from Rothermel's hands, spreading down across Mara's body. His chants grew more insistent, as if he were calling to her. But then, suddenly, he stopped.

He raised his head to look at Calla, and shook it slightly.

"Your mother's daylights go to mingle with their source. Bless her now, child, for her vessel is passing." He reached for Calla's hand and put it on her mother's chest, then lifted the back of his left hand and used it to gently trace the outlines of Mara's face, lingering along the rough outlines of her scar. Mara's skin started to glow as if lit from within, mimicking the embers of the fire that burned beside them. The scars she had worn for years grew smooth and indiscernible.

Rothermel covered Calla's hand with his own.

"Mama," Calla whispered, bowing her head. "You are the spear of new grass, the budding leaf, the unfurled flower, the tree sapling. You are the soft earth that is dug each spring, the fruit that grows close to the ground, and the frost that blankets them each winter. You are the needle and the bough. We honor your daylights with ours . . ." She took a deep breath and put her other hand on top of Rothermel's. "In me, you go on."

The glow beneath Mara's skin grew stronger.

Knox's mom instinctively put her hand on top of Calla's.

The glow radiated over their hands.

"In me, you go on," Grace repeated, like a prayer.

Knox placed his hand on top of his mother's.

"In me, you go on," he said.

"In me, you go on," echoed another voice, and then another, and another.

Knox looked over his shoulder. The house was full. Every single Melorian in the Wold had assembled to witness the passing of Mara's daylights. One by one each person intoned the prayer, intertwining arms with their neighbor. Duelle, and other members of the guard joined in. Seaborne was here now, and so was Teddy.

Adhoran stood closest to Knox. He reached out a hand and put it on Knox's shoulder, linking him in the chain.

"In me, you go on," he rasped—the first words he had uttered since the battle.

Then, the room fell silent but for the sound of the fire.

The light emanating from Mara rose and filled the spaces between the Melorians with the golden light of a late summer afternoon. It hovered there, encompassing them all, as if waiting for something.

"Go now," said Rothermel, finally, raising his open palm chest height, fingers splayed. "Be free."

The light dropped, and the room fell into shadow.

Mara's body lay by the fire, no longer weary, finally at peace.

# Chapter Seven

# THE ANTIDOTE

E velyn was taking a break outside the library. A feeling of foreboding had passed through her only moments before. She ran out of the dank room to find some warmth.

Something bad had happened, she was sure of it. Her thoughts went immediately to Frankie, but it could be anyone. How would she know? She chewed on her lip and fretted, watching the fountain at the center of the square. A weak sun fell across the paving stones, filtered by the ever-present mist that wrapped itself around the foundations of the buildings. The air was filled with the sound of water falling, but the city itself was quiet. Captain Nate had left for Varuna early that morning and Urza was secreted away with the captain of the city guard, going over tactics for what now seemed to be an inevitable invasion.

A wagon trundled through the square pulled by two donkeys and a driver. It was filled with provisions. The Melorian refugees and Metrians who were not at the front were busy with preparations: stockpiling food, making and storing weapons, and establishing an evacuation plan. If worst came to worst, the inhabitants of the city could swim to safety in the underground caverns. How long they would last down there was another question entirely. Evelyn did not like to think about it. If they were forced down there, it would be the last resort.

Evelyn looked up at the sun riding almost overhead. It was midday. Normally, Urza would check in on their progress, but today Evelyn knew she was distracted with plans for those Metrians who could not fight: the very young and the wounded. The Melorians, however, were a conundrum for the Metrians. They had a strange malaise upon them—one that made them more of a burden than Urza would admit to Evelyn. The refugees would not eat, and spent much of their time crouched and huddled beneath their hoods, their eyes turned to the west where a billowing smoke rose constantly. Urza believed it to be a kind of homesickness for Melor, and had said as much to Evelyn and Hesam on her last visit to the library.

"Their daylights long for the forest and the dappled light through the tree cover. It is not good for them to linger here in Metria," she had explained.

Urza, too, was not herself. The death of her Keeper had rendered her gaunt and downcast. She did her duty, but it was very clear that her heart was no longer in it.

The sense of foreboding amplified and Evelyn began to pace. She could not help feeling that everyone was acting as if they had already lost. She crossed the square to stand at the base of the fountain, letting the spray from the water fall on her. It felt good. Real. An antidote to all the phantom worry in her head.

The fountain was at least twenty feet tall, with four streams of water that poured from the top out of trumpet-shaped shells. The streams hit a shelf above Evelyn's head, where they intermingled and fell again as a clear wall. At her navel, there was another shelf where the water was sent through small holes, forming droplets that fell onto the basin at her feet and got sucked back up to the top where the process would begin again.

Evelyn stared at the fountain for a long time. She walked around it, watching as the shape of the water changed. As she circled the fountain again, and again, a feeling grew that tempered her anxiety. There was something important about this fountain. Something it needed her to understand. She stared down at the basin where the raindrops collected into a shallow pool, wishing Captain Nate were there to ask.

The sun went behind a cloud, and with the change in light she was able to see it: an image, just like the one Chantarelle had shown her in the puddle by the underground lake. Frankie, lying in a hospital bed, with glowing machines flickering beside her.

Evelyn hovered over the image, wondering if this was the communication she had desired only moments before. Was the pool trying to tell her that her sister was gone? She moved closer, standing over it, looking down, directly over her sister.

"*Frankie,*" she said out loud.

At the sound of her voice, Frankie's eyes opened and latched onto Evelyn's. They were the same deep brown as they had always been, only now flecks of orange danced in them like flames.

Evelyn recoiled in understanding. Frankie wasn't dead, but she was *changing.* The balance of her daylights had been corrupted by Dankar, and she was becoming an Exorian. Just like Louis.

Had Dankar given Frankie firewater when she was a prisoner in Exor? Evelyn had never even thought to ask. She tried to remember how Frankie had looked when she was in Exor. Her little sister had been strangely connected to Dankar, watching him all the time, but even more so to Louis. Evelyn had not seen her drink firewater, but that didn't mean anything. Who knew what other kinds of spells or poisons Dankar had cooked up? Plus, as far as Evelyn knew, Dankar had not tried the warrior transformation on a female. He used the women in his tribe for free labor in the Dwellings, but not to fight.

Evelyn stared down at the image.

Frankie stared back at her.

Something tugged at the edge her memory. She frowned, trying to bring it to mind. Then she remembered the bracelet that had encircled Frankie's bicep. Louis had snatched it off before he'd helped them all escape. It had left a nasty, scarlet-colored mark, like a brand. Maybe that's what Dankar had used to poison her. Could it be possible? Could Dankar change the balance of someone's daylights from the outside?

Evelyn felt the strange lens of her own daylights click into place and saw the fountain now with a telltale clarity that confirmed they were speaking to her. The image of Frankie receded as a web of light rose to the surface. It stretched across the pool at the base of the fountain, all the way to the top, and shone through the levels of water in an endless, perpetual chain. No matter whether the water was a plume, a droplet, or a mist, the web stayed unaltered. She extended her hands. Water beat down on her palms, heavy and solid. Her hands and arms began to glow, and she saw the same web of light beneath her skin.

"*Thank you*!" she whispered, thunderstruck.

She dried her hands on one of her scarves and ran back into the library.

Hesam was bent over yet another scroll.

"We've got it all wrong!" she cried. "We can't change them from the outside. We have to change them from the *inside*!"

"What are you talking about?"

"That's what Dankar does. We were right!"

She quickly described the image of Frankie in the fountain and everything that she'd seen. "It's all the same thing. The warriors. Frankie.

The *tehuantl*. He's figuring out ways to feed their Exorian daylights—so we have to figure out a way to put them out, from the inside."

"How can we do that?"

Evelyn told her what she was thinking.

"Go find Urza, now," Hesam said.

⁜   ⁜   ⁜

Evelyn sprinted through the long hall that felt like a dormitory, with all the Melorians who were now living there. Hammocks hung in rows from the pillars that lined the room, and clusters of baskets and weapons and clothing were piled against the walls. Light spilled into the room from the open aperture at the top of the walls, catching the smoke as it spiraled toward the vaulted ceiling from the small fires that some of the Melorians had begun to build on the floor. It was a depressing sign. The Melorians had come to Metria thinking they would only need a temporary refuge, but now they were transforming the hall into more-permanent quarters, as if they had given up any idea of ever going back.

Normally Evelyn would stop and try to cheer them up, but she was on a mission. She had to convince Urza to let her use the stone of Metria. And she had to do it fast. It was like the old game she and Frankie used to play when their father had a chore for them to do: Rock, Paper, Scissors. Paper covered Rock, Rock smashed Scissors, and Scissors cut Paper. Whomever had the stronger sign, won. Wasn't this kind of the same? Evelyn reasoned. If the daylights all came from the source, the *atar*, but were more or less influenced by the stone they were aligned with, then shifting alliances might change the effects of the daylights, but—and this was the piece she had missed—*not* their essence.

Dankar used the stone of Exor to create firewater, which the warriors *drank.* The solution was to use a different stone of power to create a healing draught to counteract this process. And what quenched fire better than water? If Urza would let her use the stone of Metria to make an antidote, they could heal the warriors and Frankie and Louis and all the rest of the Exorians. The Metrians could dip their swords and arrows in the potion. They could feed it to any prisoners they took. The healing waters would make their way inside the warriors and soften their Exorian daylights. Dankar's hold would weaken.

Dankar could not win a battle if his warriors would not fight.

She hit the stairway to the main tower in a dead run. She willed Urza to be at the top, and took the stone stairs two at a time. There was no time to lose.

✛　　✛　　✛

Urza was in the tower, seated at a desk covered in maps. Three armored Metrian soldiers attended her, their curved swords poking out from the folds of their purple tunics.

"We must use the southeastern boundary lands of the Hestredes for our last defense. There are no bridges. Without boats, the thrust of the advance will come from the north, just by virtue of the fact that the Exorians must walk," said one of the soldiers. He was pointing to the map.

Urza followed his finger with her gaze, saying "I believe what you say to be wise, Letham, but I worry yet for the river defenses. Are we sure they have no boats? The destroyer came to our lands long ago by boat."

"I know of no vessel that could be sea- or river-worthy after five hundred years," said Letham.

"Still, do not abandon the river defenses. Set a watch."

"Our line runs thin, Urza. We do not have the troops to guard the whole river. We must be strategic . . ."

Evelyn made her presence known by moving forward into the center of the room. The soldiers' hands fell immediately to their swords, then relaxed when they saw who it was.

"Evelyn," said Urza, with a welcoming tone, turning halfway in her seat to face her.

"I have something I need to talk to you about," said Evelyn, panting a little. "But first, I overheard what was just said. If we are having trouble guarding the river, why don't you ask the Melorians? Every Melorian is trained to be invisible in the forest as soon as they can walk; maybe you could ask them to patrol? There is no one better"—she stopped herself and said, diplomatically—"I mean, after the Metrians, of course."

Urza cracked a small smile. "You are very polite, Evelyn."

"I think it would make the Melorians happier. They are just wasting away sitting around all day. They need to be outdoors, doing something useful." A quick flash of Knox crossed her mind. "And preferably dangerous. It's their nature."

Letham nodded.

"It's not a bad idea. We could use their help, and they are savvy in the wild."

"So be it, then," said Urza, dismissing the soldiers. "Assemble the Melorians and I will propose it to them, but first I will speak privately with Evelyn."

The soldiers exited the tower, and Urza stood. She beckoned for Evelyn to join her at one of the open windows. Together, they gazed across the blue-and-gold rooftops of the city of Metria, out toward the great harbor, and beyond where the bank of fog lay like a wall to the south.

"All my life, I have seen no other view," murmured Urza. "I am far older than you, Evelyn, but my knowledge of things is sparse compared to yours. I do not know my neighbors—their strengths and character—as I should. The Melorians' customs are strange, and their nature even stranger to me, and so I have not thought much about them. It would not have occurred to me to enlist their help. I am grateful for the insights you bring me, outlier."

"You are welcome, Urza. Don't take it to heart. Everyone feels the same way about people and places they've only heard about. Besides, you didn't have a choice. You've never been allowed to leave Metria. It's always been too dangerous."

"You didn't have much of a choice, either, to come here, so far from what you know."

"True," agreed Evelyn, thinking back to their first night on Ayda, when she and Frankie had left the boys at the beach below Seaborne's cabin. They had only walked a mile or so into the forest before Axl and Tar had found them and brought them to Tinator and Mara, and the Melorian encampment in the forest. It was strange, but in some ways, the Melorians had made her feel more at home than she had ever felt in Fells Harbor.

No, it hadn't been her choice to get shipwrecked on Ayda, sucked into her history through the fog of forgetting, and it wasn't her choice that Frankie would be captured by Dankar and poisoned. But it *had* been her choice to come back.

"You know, I could have stayed home with Frankie after Ratha sent us back through the fog," Evelyn countered. "A big part of me wanted to, but I decided to come back here with Chantarelle. He didn't force me, or Knox. We came back because we *wanted* to—because we had to. We're a part of this, and whatever happens, we are going to see it through."

Urza looped her hand through the crook of Evelyn's elbow and squeezed her arm appreciatively.

"What was it you wanted to tell me?"

Evelyn paused. It wasn't every day you asked someone for a stone of power. She was silent for a minute, then spat it out.

Urza dropped her hand from Evelyn's elbow and recoiled.

"Why?" she said, with suspicion. "For the daylights' sake, don't we have enough to worry about?"

Evelyn spilled her theory in a rush of words. She described her vision of Frankie in the fountain waters, and her idea about the stones and their ability to cancel out each other's influences.

"It makes sense," said Urza. "But why wouldn't Rysta have done this if it could be done?"

"I don't know. She had never seen a warrior being transformed, and so it never occurred to her. Like you said, few Metrians, including her, have ever traveled beyond your borders. Or maybe she thought disturbing the balance of daylights would be too dangerous for the vessel? I mean, look at the Exorians we've captured. They are so disfigured . . . And she told us that being exposed to a stone of power can damage or even kill humans, especially without the presence of a Keeper. It's risky. We may not know how it works. It might make everything worse."

"If this is so, all the more reason you should not expose yourself. Your vessel could be damaged, like the Exorians."

Evelyn thought about Frankie. The orange flecks in her eyes. Would something like that happen to her? Then she reminded herself of the little flasks of firewater the Exorian warriors had worn at their hips.

"I think exposure can be risky, but in order to make a real transformation, you need to ingest its power or absorb it consistently in some way." She shrugged her shoulders, her voice rising with excitement. "I think the daylights actually *want* to be balanced. It's their natural state. Dankar just supercharged the Exorians, so we have to use the stone of Metria to undo what he did and bring things back to normal. If it worked, we wouldn't even need the Fifth Stone. We could win on our own!"

She looked sidewise at Urza. "Besides, we have the perfect way to test it."

"With the prisoners."

Evelyn nodded.

"What if it kills them," Urza asked, "or mars them in some irreparable way?"

"More than Dankar has done already?"

Urza sighed. She looked downcast. "I wish Rysta were here; I do not know what to do. I had hoped to hear from Chantarelle by now. I had hoped there would be word."

"I know. I did too," said Evelyn, "but I think we have to act as if the Fifth Stone isn't coming back. We can't just sit here and wait for Dankar to overtake us, or hope the Fifth Stone will save us from him. We have to try and save ourselves, and if we can change the Exorian warriors back, then we'll know that the stone of Metria can be used against Exor. We can just try it with *one* of the prisoners and see what happens—"

Urza turned away.

"I'm sorry, Evelyn, but it is too dangerous. The stones of power are not to be toyed with—Dankar has made that error, and now, here we are."

Evelyn stood her ground.

"Urza, ever since Dankar killed Ranu and took the stone of Exor, Rysta and the other Keepers believed that the only way to contain Dankar was to keep the stones separate and hidden from him. They never wanted to risk exposing a stone for fear he might capture it. But it's too late for that now! He's *not* contained. The stone of Melor might be in his hands right now for all we know!" She got down on her knees and took Urza's hand with both of hers, begging. "If you tell me where Rysta hid the stone of Metria, I will die before I tell anyone where it is. I will use it to make the antidote and then I will hide it again."

Urza pulled Evelyn up from her knees. They stood in silence, eyes locked on one another's.

"It's not as easy as you think," said Urza, weighing her words. "You will discover that even if I tell you where the stone was last hidden, its power is elusive. Only a Keeper can gift the power of his or her stone to another, and I do not see how that is possible now that Rysta has fragmented. Even Dankar cannot use the stone of Metria since she did not pass it to him. I am grateful for this. For though he may overwhelm the Metrian daylights, he will never completely usurp them as he has done with the Exorians'. Even if you manage to find the stone, it will be useless in your hands."

"I understand," said Evelyn, undeterred.

"And yet you still ask to go on this quest, with no hope of its success?"

Evelyn nodded, thinking back to the golden web of light that spun between her hands and the waters in the fountain. Her daylights had spoken.

"Very well, then," said Urza, capitulating. "I will tell you what I know."

# Chapter Eight

# WORMHOLE

Frankie opened her eyes.

At first, she was aware only of her own heartbeat. It thrummed with effort, as if she had run a great distance.

"Evelyn?" she murmured, and sat up. Her mouth felt dry. She must have been sleeping for a long time. She felt a presence. Somebody was with her—or had been. Was it her sister?

Wires were connected to her head and chest; they pulled her back on the pillow. She felt a flicker of panic. She did not recognize this place. Above her head, a fluorescent light was set on dim. She saw a crack of light under the door leading out to a hall, and another outlining what must be the bathroom. Outside the window, it was dark. Inside the room, it was dusk.

"You are awake," a deep voice said from the shadows, like it came from a throat filled with stones.

"Who's there?" She traced the room with her eyes. She saw a slumped outline of a person sleeping in a chair, covered by a blanket, but she couldn't see anyone else.

"Where are you?" she asked.

"Here," said the voice.

Frankie felt fingers grab her left foot. She withdrew it in surprise and looked down at the edge of her bed, where the strangest creature she had ever seen was standing. His head barely cleared the top of the mattress. He had long, dark hair covered in a tight-fitting cap, and golden brown skin. He surprised her by slapping a gnarled walking stick on the mattress, hooking its carved knob on the opposite side, and using the whole contraption to hoist himself up on the bed.

"My name is Chantarelle. I am pleased to meet you. I know your sister."

"You know Evelyn? How?" Frankie was not entirely sure she wasn't dreaming.

The little man was dressed in greens and browns, and seemed to merge with the shadows in the room so that he was only partly visible.

"We come from the same stock," he said. "We are friends."

"Where am I?"

"You are in a hospital. You are sick with an Exorian curse, but you will not get better here. For that, you need to come with me." He smiled at her, showing brown, mottled gums and yellow teeth.

"Where?"

"Somewhere that can heal you. Somewhere you have been before."

"With Evelyn?"

Chantarelle bobbed his head. "She is already there."

Frankie understood.

For a long time she had been dreaming she was in another place—actually, more of a feeling than a place—and a woman she knew as Rysta had been there with her. She had seen Evelyn once, and only once. She had heard her sister crying from a long way off and had followed the sound. She had wanted to be with Evelyn so badly—to find out why she was crying, and to let her know it would all be okay—and then somehow, she *was* with her.

They had spoken, but it was as if a huge gulf of shadow lay between them. Frankie had barely been able to make out her sister's face. Evelyn had been kneeling in a swampy grove where strange, dead trees grew, covered with moss.

And then, just as quickly as she had appeared, Evelyn was gone, and Frankie was back in the in-between place.

She told Chantarelle she did not want to go back there.

"Why not?" he asked.

"It's lonely there."

"Tell me about it," he said, and listened to her describe this place that was neither here nor there. The place that was not really a place.

"No, child, that place is not for you yet. Your body has always been here. What you experienced was your daylights. They left your vessel for a while, lingering in the place that is in between life and death, until you became strong enough for them to return. You are lucky. Sometimes the vessel does not heal, and the daylights do not return to it. But that does not concern us today. Where I want you to go, you will not be lonely, although it is dangerous. Nonetheless, I can say with certainty that it is where you should be."

"Because I am sick?"

"Because there, you will no longer be sick."

"What about my grandmother?" asked Frankie.

"She will be fine," said Chantarelle.

"But she will worry about me," Frankie wavered. "I can't leave her."

The little man jumped off the bed and opened the drawer to her bedside table. He reached inside and retrieved a necklace. It consisted of a leather cord on which was strung a wooden bead. "Before you decide, will you allow me to show you something?"

Frankie nodded. She liked this little man. He reminded her of another life, when she was very small and nothing bad ever happened.

Chantarelle breathed on the bead, and the room filled with a rich, fertile smell—like dirt newly turned over in spring. He held it up to Frankie's nose. She inhaled deeply. A flood of memories came back to her.

She saw Evelyn sitting cross-legged, stitching a shirt in the shade of a wooded clearing, a small cabin behind her. She saw a courtyard and a fountain, and a man with small eyes and a gold crown smiling down at her. Then, she saw the face of a younger man, with blue eyes, who held her on his back and rode a camel with her across the desert. She recognized him instantly.

"Louis!" she gasped.

"Yes," said Chantarelle. "You remember him. He is in great danger still, but he does not know it."

"And you can take me to him?"

Chantarelle nodded. "I can show you the way."

Frankie began pulling off the sticky pads that were connected to the wires. The machine beside the bed went into a loud frenzy. The figure in the chair stirred.

"Quickly, now, follow me! We only have a few seconds," said Chantarelle.

Frankie slipped off the bed. She fell backwards, feeling unwell, and caught herself on the rail.

Chantarelle grabbed her hand. His palm was dry and warm.

"Follow me, and do exactly as I do," he whispered in her ear.

✛     ✛     ✛

Chantarelle led her from the room. No one noticed as they passed through the well-lit hallway and into the stairwell, on their way to the exit. If one of the nurses had happened to look down, he or she would have seen only a dusky gloom like an unlit corner.

Under this cover, they moved quickly. Once outside, they headed straight for the woods that abutted the parking lot. Frankie was weak. Rain pelted down, soaking her through the thin cotton of her hospital gown in seconds.

"I can't do this," she panted. "I'm too tired."

"You will regain your strength soon enough. Just follow me."

She did not dare take her hand out of Chantarelle's grip. He blended in so well with the ground and the trees that she was afraid she would lose him. Once they were under the trees, the rain let up a bit and she could see a few paces ahead.

"Where are we going?" She was beginning to feel afraid.

"Not far now."

He stopped before a small hill with no trees growing on it. Rain sluiced down the sides, flattening the grass. Chantarelle tapped his walking stick on the edge of the hill and a crack opened, revealing a hollow inside. It was black as a tomb, and Frankie shied away.

"I don't want to go in," she said.

"This is the fastest way. Very few have ever been allowed to travel it."

Frankie reared back.

"It is the only way now," urged Chantarelle. "There is no time to wander. Your friends and your sister need you. You must be brave."

She took a step forward. Chantarelle stepped back.

"Aren't you coming with me?"

Chantarelle shook his head. "No, I have another charge I must complete."

The dark center of the hollow of the hill appeared to grow wider, and darker, as if it were opening to swallow her. She knew what this was like. The earth opened and you disappeared.

"I don't like this," she cried. "I don't like spaces where you can't get out."

"Oh, my dear, you are going to get out. Do not fear."

As Chantarelle said those words, a knob of white light floated into the center of the cavity, like a small, spinning ball. It elongated into a line, sending out tendrils of blue and red and purple light that spiraled outward into the darkness. The interior of the cave lit up. The light spun faster. Frankie could not look away.

"You are very special; do you know that?" said Chantarelle. "This only happens once in a thousand years. If you do not go soon, the portal will close and we will lose our chance."

"Where does it come out?"

"I do not know, for I have never gone this way."

"I don't want to go alone—"

"I'll go with you," said another voice from behind them. A man's voice, awe-filled.

Alarmed, Chantarelle leapt to the top of the hill.

"It's a wormhole," Jim Thompson breathed. "A warping of space and time."

He was holding a hospital blanket over his head like an umbrella. He moved beside Frankie, transfixed, sheltering her with the blanket. He bent down on one knee so he could look her full in the face. He pushed his spectacles onto his head and smiled encouragingly.

"Hi, Frankie. I'm Jim Thompson. Chase, Knox, and Teddy's dad."

"I remember," breathed Frankie. Raindrops and mud spattered Jim Thompson's face, but its angular shape and the sound of his voice were familiar to her.

"Do you know where your sister is? Where the boys are?"

Frankie nodded.

"Are they through there?" Jim pointed at the wormhole.

Frankie looked to the top of the hill, searching for Chantarelle, not wanting to get him in trouble. She could not make him out in the darkness.

"I think so, yes," she whispered.

"I'd like to go and find them. I miss them a lot."

"Me too."

Jim cleaned the lenses of his glasses with his damp shirttail and put the glasses back on. Then he turned to stare at the nebula of color emanating from the little cave. The colors reflected off his eyeglasses, dancing across the lenses. The spinning light spread farther out, like water from a whirling sprinkler. The gravitational pull of its center was strong.

"I don't think it hurts to pass through a wormhole—I've never read anything to suggest such a thing, but it might be a little disorienting. Will you hold on to me?"

By way of an answer, Frankie grabbed Jim's hand. Jim wrapped her in the blanket, stood, and picked her up, tucking her legs around him.

"Shall we go find the rest of our family, then?" he whispered to her.

She tightened her arms around his neck and gave him a grateful squeeze.

Together they approached the light, going nearer and nearer, until they could not have pulled back even if they'd wanted to. The tendrils spun and twirled, tugging at their clothes. And then, all sense of gravity left them. Jim took another step and they fell in.

After a minute or two, the light at the center began to fade.

Chantarelle stayed hidden at his post until it, and the surrounding woods, were dark again. The crack in the hill closed.

Rain fell silently on the shallow hill, gathering into rivulets that formed small pools along the edges. The wet grass lay undisturbed. The wormhole had disappeared completely, erasing all signs of its appearance, taking Frankie and Jim with it.

# Chapter Nine

# SURPRISE GUEST

The evening sky surrounding Ratha's terrace was pink and purple. As twilight fell, a deeper blue began to overtake the lighter colors, bleeding darkness. Soon, Chase would be able to see the first evening stars, and, later, the cosmic spiral of the Milky Way. In his time here, he had almost grown used to the dizzying effects of the terrace, had even ventured to the very last step that dropped off into nothing but dark air and bruised-looking cloud. If he stood on the step and closed his eyes, he heard sounds that could have been human voices. He liked to think they were from people below brought up by the wind. He wondered what would happen if he just stepped off the staircase. Would he hurtle off the mountain and die? How far would he fall before he hit something? He pictured himself tumbling and turning through the void. Would Ratha send Calyphor and Deruda to save him? After all, what was she keeping him here for? He had been a slow student, and he would so much rather be down below, fighting for real—not in his dreams.

For at least the thousandth time, he thought about Knox and his mother and Teddy in Melor. He tried to use some of the tricks Ratha had been teaching him to conjure them in his mind—not as he remembered them, but as they were right now. Like opening a window into what they were doing. He wondered about Evelyn, too, but in a different way. He longed to see her with an ache that was physical. Only a few hours ago, he thought he might have had success trying to see her. He had focused on her face—the way she had smiled at him the last time she'd seen him on the shores of the Voss. As he was picturing her, another image burst forth into his head. He saw a tower in Metria; then the vision had telescoped so that he knew he was in a round room at the top of the tower. He saw a table and some maps, and he knew in his gut that Evelyn was there. The vision faded almost instantly. He tried to bring it back—had been trying to bring it back all afternoon—unsuccessfully. Now his head was ringing with pain.

A hand on his arm startled him and he pitched forward off the step. The hand pulled him backwards, sending him sprawling. He looked up to see Ratha.

"You are very close to the edge," she said, unsmiling, then turned and began to walk up the stairs. "Come with me. We have a visitor."

*At last*, thought Chase, with a smile. *Captain Nate.*

If Ratha was hearing his thoughts, she didn't answer. Instead, she led the way up the steps and across the terrace, past the burning cauldron and toward the other set of stairs that led down from the north side of the building.

Ratha's home was large as far as Varunan dwellings went, but smaller than the dwellings he'd seen in Metria, and far less opulent than Dankar's palace in Exor. The building was constructed of smooth round stones mortared together in sharp angles that rose several stories. The first floor was the largest, with each subsequent floor somewhat reduced, but set flush on one side, so that the other sides were stepped like massive stairs.

Chase's room was on the fourth floor, with a window that faced south. There were two more floors above his. The top story was a windowless box that he was pretty sure was Ratha's room, but he didn't know for certain. He was doubtful that she ever slept, and the idea of her pacing around the confines of a small, dark room, plotting and watching other people's thoughts and dreams, made him nervous. He didn't *want* to think about it.

He pushed past her on their way through the front door and into the main hall. A large fire burned in yet another enormous stone hearth. There was a woven rug set before the fire, and a few wooden chairs draped with furs. Chase looked around eagerly for the Captain's familiar shape.

"Where is he?" he asked.

"*He?*" said Ratha.

"C'mon, you know what I mean. Where's Captain Nate?"

"I have no earthly idea," she said, and moved toward the fireplace in the eerie, floaty way she had. "But here is someone who knows you."

Ratha lifted up the corner of one of the furs. A small form lay in the chair, barely moving.

Chase's heart leapt in his mouth. The only person he knew who was that small was Teddy. Could it be? He moved to Ratha's side and looked down. There, sleeping curled in a fetal position, her face raw and sore from the cold, was Bodi.

"What—? How?!" exclaimed Chase.

"Shhh, she is very tired, and too young to have come such a ways by herself. Calyphor picked her up a few miles inland from the Voss. She was barely alive, and he did not think she would survive the journey. But she is an Exorian, and a very strong one at that."

Ratha looked down at the sleeping girl, her expression softening a little, then turning stern again. "Calyphor tells me she came to find the

Captain. Alas, she will not find him here. Once an oath-breaker, always an oath-breaker."

"He'll come," said Chase stubbornly. He squatted beside Bodi and gently touched her shoulder.

"Hey, Bodi, wake up. It's me, Chase."

Bodi's eyes fluttered.

Chase looked her over. She was in rough shape. The sores on her face were crusted and scabbed over, the tip of her nose was turning black, and her lips were so chapped they were bloody. She looked tiny curled up on the seat of the chair. Chase stared at her, then back up at Ratha.

"How long was she out there alone?"

"At least seven moonrises, I should think, but maybe less. It is colder now. The year is turning. Plus, she is not used to Varuna. The air would have taxed her greatly."

"She helped us in Exor. She got me and the Captain into the Palace— she and her mother—and then she and her brother helped us get out. His name is Emon. He was a scribe."

Bodi stirred at the sound of her brother's name. Chase touched her shoulder again. This time, she opened her eyes. They were bloodshot and glassy; still, she recognized him.

"I saw you in my dreams," she said, with a smile. "I knew you were here. I've been looking for you."

Chase and Ratha exchanged glances. In all the time he had been in Varuna, he had not once sensed Bodi's presence, but all the way in Exor, she had sensed his. Maybe there was more Varunan in Bodi than Exorian. Maybe the same was true for all the Exorians, if they could just break free of Dankar's hold on their daylights. Chase hadn't thought about it before. The Exorians all seemed so . . . Exorian. He had never considered that their daylights might be attuned somewhere else.

"Discovering the true nature of one's daylights is a solitary journey, Chase," Ratha's voice interrupted, talking in mindspeak. "But you are right to wonder how many of the Exorians would be more at home in other lands had Dankar not corrupted their stone. And, conversely, how many Melorians, Metrians, and Varunans might be drawn to Exor. Maybe even you? Or your brothers? An interesting question."

Chase tried to shut her out by shifting his full attention back to Bodi.

"I'm not much of a dreamwalker yet, Bodi. I'm still learning, otherwise I would have visited you more."

Bodi sat up, engulfed in the fur. She caught sight of Ratha and gave a frightened yelp.

"This is Ratha; she is my Keeper." Chase tried to hide a smile. Ratha had that effect on people. Bodi leaned forward to whisper in his ear.

"She's scarier than Dankar."

Chase grinned. "Let's hope she is. She's on our side."

Ratha fluttered behind him impatiently.

"Do you think I can't hear the two of you?" she said. "I am on no one's *side* except my own; I am here to protect my land and my people, and thereby I must do whatever it takes to guard the island of Ayda from extinction. Can you aid me in that, girl-child?" Her colorless eyes fell on Bodi.

Bodi shrank beneath the furs.

"It's okay, Bodi, she means well," said Chase, but he knew how uncomfortable it was to have Ratha prowl around in your thoughts. It was like living in a room with no door. Nothing felt secure, and every now and then, things seemed to get shuffled around.

Several moments passed before Ratha released Bodi from her mental grip. The little girl looked like she might faint. Ratha stepped away, and, uncharacteristically, went to stand directly before the fire. The flames leapt and danced with her closeness, but Ratha herself seemed diminished.

"What is it?" said Chase, alarmed.

"I have seen into this girl's mind. Some things we know: Dankar uses one arm to grab the stone of Melor, and the other to reach for the stone of Metria. He cares not for his own people. Only for war. The Exorians in Exor are starving and dying. I did not know that. He is as ruthless with his own as he is with ours."

"But maybe that could be an advantage?" asked Chase, moving toward the fire to stand beside her. "Some of the Exorians were already rebelling at the arena. If there's no food, more will fight on our side. Maybe we can switch them over?" He felt nervous. He'd never seen Ratha look worried before. When she spoke again, it was in mindspeak.

"If any are left . . . I curse the day Dankar was ever led to our shores. He has cost me too much: my father, my mother, my brother, my sister. And now he wastes his own people as if they were nothing. If he can do such an evil thing to his own, I fear we may have already lost."

"What do you mean?" asked Chase, not moving his lips.

"When Ranu surrendered his stone, he did so on the condition that Dankar swear a blood oath that no Exorian would ever slay another on purpose. That oath is now broken. Dankar has given the Exorians one choice: Fight for him or die. He has turned his warriors against his own people." Her voice dropped to a terrible whisper in Chase's mind. "This is what that poor child showed me—"

A vivid picture blossomed in Chase's head as Ratha shared her thoughts with him. It was of the rock spires on the outskirts of the Dwellings. Small dots littered the upper ledges. It took Chase a moment to realize what they were. Vultures. He focused more intently on the image, and it grew larger and more grisly, as if it were responding to his attention.

He could easily make out the bodies of Exorians, hung like pendants on a necklace around the lower foundations of the spires. Scribes, women—even children.

His mind went blank.

"What about Bodi's mother and her brother?"

Ratha shook her head, her lips a tight line.

Chase buried his face in his hands. It was unthinkable. How could this be happening? Emon's face swam before him, as he'd last seen him, holding the camel's reins out to him after the explosion at the arena. He remembered what Emon had said about Dankar.

*He is very angry. He does not like disobedience.*

He remembered how young both Emon and Bodi had looked. And then he remembered their mother. She had risked everything to smuggle him and the Captain past the pit-houses and into the tunnels beneath the Palace. And now she was gone. Bodi would never see either of them again. A flash of rage coursed through him. Where the heck was Captain Nate? And where the heck was the Fifth Stone?

Ratha turned her pale eyes on him.

"Once an oath-breaker, always an oath-breaker," she repeated, out loud.

"Chase," said Bodi, sitting up under her fur.

He pivoted and took the few steps toward her.

"Yeah, Bodi?" He had never seen a person look so small or as fragile as she did right now. Her eyes protruded from her face, and her skin, normally a healthy umber color, was now yellow beneath the scabs and sores. He wondered when she had last eaten anything.

"Will you tell me again about your brother's turtle? What was his name . . . Bob?"

Chase nodded. "That's right, it was Bob. You have a good memory."

He dropped to his knees and, before he realized what he was doing, grabbed Bodi in a big hug. She weighed less than his robe.

Bodi pulled away after a few moments and patted his face with her hand, amazed.

"Your face is wet with body water," she said.

Chase scraped his face with his sleeve. "Yeah, Bodi. It sometimes happens when I get sad. I'm so sorry about Emon and your moth—"

Bodi looked away, clearly uncomfortable. Her lower lip quivered, but she did not cry.

Chase stopped himself, took a few breaths, and sat back on his haunches.

"Don't worry, okay? I'm gonna take care of you now. You're safe."

Ratha still had her back turned, facing the fire, but she was listening.

"So, you want me to tell you about Bob?"

Bodi nodded slowly.

"Well, he's about this big—" Chase began.

The outside door to the hall swung open and crashed against the stone wall, sending a sudden wind through the room. The fire leapt in the grate.

Ratha whirled around in alarm. Chase scrambled to his feet, reaching for his sword, which happened to still be in his room.

"Are you on again about that turtle?" exclaimed a gruff voice from the threshold.

It was Captain Nate, looking the worse for wear, frost-covered, and not a little bloody.

"I'm sorry I'm late; but I had some trouble getting here—in case you both forgot, up here in the middle of nowhere, there's a war raging down below you."

Chase felt all the tension he'd been storing flow out of the bottom of his feet.

Captain Nate was here. The world that had felt so dangerously off-keel only moments ago tipped back on its right axis.

"Thank the daylights," he said out loud.

"No, thank Varunan Airlines," said the Captain. He entered the room with Calyphor and Deruda following behind him. He made a beeline for the fire and held his hands out to warm them. He cast a sideways glance at Ratha.

"You've got me here now. You can leave the boy alone."

*Chapter Ten*

# ENEMY LINES

Louis monitored the progress of his warriors as they dragged burnt tree trunks toward the moat and laid them across its mouth. His battalion had joined forces with a sortie party laying siege outside the deathfield, and he had assumed control. It had taken some time, but they had managed to find several whole trunks that would serve as a bridge over the moat. He called a halt and ordered the battalion to drink from the flasks at their hips. Louis took a slug of firewater, himself, enjoying the bitter taste and the tingle of energy that always accompanied the drink. With a full flask of firewater, an Exorian warrior could go without food for several days.

His right hand was throbbing. He resisted the impulse to take it out of the sling and rub it. It was hard getting used to using his left hand for everything, but he was not going to reveal his arm and hand at this moment, on the verge of attack. He was ashamed of the puny, pink appendage on his right side. It felt unbefitting to a warrior of his stature, and Dankar's favorite soldier. He far preferred the thick, scaled appearance of his left hand. Now *that* was a hand that could deal a mighty blow.

Louis flexed it. He thought again about Dankar's words of parting: the ones that had been for his ears only. He wondered if the Melorians had any idea what was about to happen.

He made a fist with his right hand. His weakness was also his strength. He was unique among the Exorian warriors, with his blue eyes and malformed shape, and this gave him advantages. Dankar had praised him as the first of his kind; once an outlier, now with the strength of an Exorian warrior. Dankar had not known—or particularly cared—if Louis's vessel would survive the transformation, but since it had, Dankar was hopeful that those who lived beyond the fog would be able to do the same. Louis's right arm was a reminder that the process was not foolproof, but his continued existence was proof that it could be done. Because of this, he had earned the respect of his men, and the trust of Dankar. He would lead them from Ayda when the day came and the curse of the fog was broken.

The trials beyond the fog were off in the future, however; today was the day that his strength would be put to its first real test. Today, he would face the Keeper of Melor, and try to take his stone. Dankar had assured him it would not be as hard as legends would have him believe. Melor was a waning power, its stone and its Keeper weakened by the growing power of Exor and the loss of Rysta. One glimpse around the charred husk of the forest revealed as much.

Louis waved his battalion over the makeshift bridges. He was happy to have sent the *tehuantl* back to the Broomwash. It was a difficult task, keeping the cats under control this far into the Wold, and *tehuantl* would not have entered the deathfield anyway. It was one less moving piece for him to worry about.

Once all of the warriors were over the moat, they crashed en masse through the scrim of flowering bushes, moving swiftly into the spring-time glen.

Upon entering the oasis, their spears went dark. No flame would reignite them; this they already knew from past excursions. They had tried more than once to burn this glen. Nothing came of it. Their spears sparked and fizzled, and a few leaves of grass turned brown, but before they advanced another step, new grass was already growing. Life clung to this meadow and was not easily dampened.

Louis was not immune to the power of the glen. He felt a lightness in his step as he moved through the high grass. It was pleasing in a more satisfying way than firewater. He took in the soft light falling on the last remaining copse of green meadow left in all of Melor. The air in the glade felt clean, and was filled with the scent that was most alluring to a desert dweller: moisture. He knew it was dangerous for Exorians to breathe the water scent in for long. It tempted them to sink into the grasses. Those who did, never got up. This meadow was under a strange spell, and Louis knew better than to allow his troops any quarter in it.

He urged them onward.

They marched quickly, crushing small violet-colored flowers under-foot and low-hung berries that turned the soles of their bare feet blue. A sudden sound, like laughter, caught his attention and he whipped his head around. He saw nothing except the grass bending in the wind, revealing the lighter color of their underleaf.

Ahead lay a granite outcropping marking the boundary of a large bog. He himself had never been this far into the Wold, but scouts had told him it lay just beyond the sweet meadow, and was filled with stinking mud and moss-covered trees. No Exorian had been able to penetrate it—until today. Whatever Melorian forces controlled these parts, Louis was to put an end to it. He would not be turning back.

They crossed the rocks and strode down into the marsh. The wind ceased and the air became thick and sulfurous. Swarms of mosquitoes flew up with each step, attacking the bloody cracks between the scales in their skin. Mud from the bog clung to their bare legs, coating their calves in gray-green slime. Dread crept into Louis's heart, as if it were seeping in through his skin with the mud. He told himself it was not real. It was just another spell that came from the bog. This was how the Melorians trapped their prey. But this time, he was prepared.

He signaled to the warriors to chug from their flasks as he removed his and took a glug. The firewater hit him, spreading warmth through his veins and easing the dread. He took another hit, and signaled for the others to advance. Most of the battalion moved ahead. Louis did not concern himself with the few who could not—they were already dead. Their own thoughts would leave them mired here until a Melorian arrow found them.

They slogged ahead, moving slowly but with determination, reaching the first stand of dead trees when a volley of arrows rained down on them.

The Melorians had spotted them.

"Now!" cried Louis, giving his men the signal to hit the ground.

The Exorians dropped into the mud, digging and rolling so that the foul-smelling slime covered their entire bodies—a simple but effective camouflage. They crawled on their bellies, dragging themselves through the mud with their elbows. Arrows rained down over them. Some found their mark, but many fell harmlessly in the mud.

The Exorians moved with no rhythm. They crawled a few feet, then stopped, waited, then crawled an inch. Every warrior was to head for a rally point that lay on the other side of the bog, under the shelter of the moss-covered trees. Once there, they would wait, hidden by mud and tree foliage, for the rest of the battalion. It was a mission where any amount of losses was acceptable, as long as some made it through. Rothermel's hold would be breached at long last, or they would all die trying.

Louis crab-crawled his way slowly through the bog, not daring to lift his head farther out of the mud than it took for his nostrils to breathe. Another volley of arrows fell behind him. He did not look back to see how many had been hit. He kept his eyes focused forward, letting a mouthful of firewater slowly trickle down his throat. He had armed his men with as much firewater as they could carry, and his plan was to stay in the bog—or at the rally point, if he could make it—for as long as it took. He would stay motionless and hidden until the Melorians thought all the Exorians were dead.

And just when the Melorians thought they were safe, Louis and any surviving troops would attack.

*Chapter Eleven*

# THE WEIGHT OF WATER

E velyn paddled her kayak closer to the eastern shore of the Hestredes. She was alone, and it felt better to stick close to the eastern side of the river. Exorians might have crossed over from Melor, and she was barely armed. She would not be able to fight with the throwing knives she'd inherited from Mara, which were the only weapons she carried. In better times, when Chantarelle was with her, she would never have risked open water. She would have taken the tunnels north from the city. Evelyn was not sure if the Exorians went underground, but she didn't want to run into a pack of them below the surface and find out the hard way.

Evelyn wondered if Chantarelle would ever return. Her heart traversed the familiar back-and-forth bridge between the hope that he had delivered his message and that he and the Keeper of the Fifth Stone would come back to save them, and the fear that Ayda had been abandoned. She slipped her paddle through the black surface of the river. The air was cold and she shivered to keep warm. A waning moon loomed overhead, orange and smudged, as if someone had taken an eraser to its upper edges. Her father had a word for that kind of bloated autumnal moon:

half-bitten. In Haiti, it rose above the water and hovered for half the night, like a lantern. One time, when she was very little, soon after her mother had passed away, her father had taken her up one of the hillsides outside of town to watch it rise. They had lain on their stomachs in the soft darkness, smelling the warm earth. As the moon had inched up against the horizon, enormous against the flat edge of the sea, her father had sat up and pulled her into his lap.

"It's a very big world, isn't it, *ma chérie*?"

Evelyn remembered nodding, scared speechless by the sight of the huge moon.

Her father had hugged her closer, sensing her discomfort. She remembered the bristle on his chin against her neck.

"Do not worry anymore. Your papa is here, and the moon is very far away. Nothing will hurt you ever again, if I can help it."

Evelyn smiled a little at the memory, thinking about how much she had believed him then. She had never feared anything when her father was alive. After he died, most of what she had felt since was fear—like a cold snake coiled in her belly. There were only two people who made her forget the feeling for a little while: Frankie, and her grandmother, but thinking about them was like thinking about her father. Too painful. It reminded her of how alone she really was.

As if to disagree, an owl hooted suddenly, somewhere from the shore, reminding her of Teddy's signal. Her heart beat a little faster. If only he, Knox, and the Melorians were there, hiding in the jungle. She paused, mid-stroke, ears alert for any signs of activity. After several minutes of quiet she gave up and dipped the paddle back into the water, using the J-stroke that Hesam had taught her. She needed to get to the relative safety of the cavern before sunrise. Exorians moved faster in the sunlight; their daylights thrived on it.

A battalion of Exorians had been sighted earlier that day marching south through the western reaches of Melor; another smaller force was seen attempting to pass the lowlands of Varuna to take positions in the north. According to the scouts, the colder, glacial flatlands were waylaying them, but, if they weren't stopped soon, they might descend into the marshlands of northern Metria. It would not take long for either branch to start burning the jungle. Dankar would then be able to herd all remaining survivors into the city. From there, escape was only possible underground, or by sea, in boats. The battle for Ayda was coming to the city, of that every Metrian was assured. Even now, every precaution was being taken to fortify and protect the last refuge on Ayda.

*Not the last*, said a voice in her head.

*True*, she thought to herself. Varuna seemed immune from Dankar's advances, at least for now; but Ratha had not lifted a finger as Melor burned—and she seemed to not be worried about Exorians on her lands. No Varunan had stood in their way—if they could. Evelyn was not sure what Varunans could and could not do. Her only exposure to them had been the strange, winged creatures that took Chase away. Perhaps they were all like that. Pale and fragile-looking. Creatures of the air with little substance to hold them in a fight.

*No*, she reminded herself, it was better to prepare themselves as if they *were* all alone. If the Varunans showed up, great; in the meantime, Melorians and Metrians had to save themselves. Besides, it was more than likely that Chase, and Captain Nate, were securely in the grip of Ratha's mind-control even now. When—or if—they did come back, what shape would they be in? Evelyn was convinced of it: Ratha was just a different kind of *bokor*; not as deadly as Dankar, but still willing to play with people as if they were toys. Her desire had always been set on the Fifth Stone's return to Ayda. If the downfall of Melor and Metria helped to advance that purpose, she would let them both burn before she lifted a finger.

As if to remind Evelyn of what was at stake, the scent of burning leaves drifted across the water from the west. It spurred her into paddling faster. It was all a race against time now.

✛　　✛　　✛

She reached the cavern an hour before dawn. The air was still, disturbed only by the sound of her paddle lifting in and out of the water. The mouth of the lagoon was just visible in the dim light. She headed straight for it and paddled into the cavern. She knew it must be the same, but in the shadowy dark it felt entirely different: empty and abandoned. Somewhere, deep inside the cavern, thirty Exorian warriors were being held against their will. Evelyn had not seen them since the battle at the Voss when the decision was made to take them back to Metria and try to reverse their transformation.

It had been several weeks now, and despite daily baths and draughts of the waters of the Hestredes, Dankar's spell had resisted the Metrians' efforts. The Exorians had been somewhat positively affected by their captivity, but not truly changed. Now, Evelyn hoped to fix that.

She turned the kayak toward the far wall of the cavern and headed toward Rysta's island. The sky above was lightening, becoming purple and pink. The lagoon mirrored the sky so that Evelyn felt as if she were paddling through the soft, shimmering interior of a shell. It was difficult to continue paddling. Evelyn just wanted to stop and stare at the beauty unfolding before and around her. As beautiful as the luminescent water had been in the moonlight when she'd last seen it, Rysta's island at dawn was something else entirely. Gentle, and somehow unearthly.

Urza had told her the stone was in Rysta's enclosure, but she did not know where. She had advised her to trust her instincts. So Evelyn did.

She beached the kayak and walked through the vegetation toward Rysta's pool. Her steps whispered in the sand. From a few yards away, the pool glistened pink. Evelyn stooped down and cupped a handful of sand in her hand. She closed her eyes, reaching out with her other four senses, trying to divine where the stone of Metria might be. Then, she made her way slowly to the pool. Her daylights were activated now, glowing through her amber skin, and her surroundings felt hyper-real. She could see the fretwork of dew shining like diamonds on the undersides of the leaves that hung over the enclosure. The air smelled rich and green with life. She let the sand gently drain from her hand, feeling each granule as it fell from her fingertips. She tasted a subtle flavor of salt, perhaps from her own sweat, or from the sea, carried all the way up the Hestredes. She licked her lips, and knelt by the pool.

"*Show me, please,*" she whispered, and then, as if drawn by another hand, she reached into the pool. The waters turned gold and began to spin, as they had for Rysta the first time she had shown Evelyn and the Thompson boys its magic.

Evelyn withdrew her hand. The waters spiraled like a whirlpool made of a pastel rainbow. They narrowed into a column, at the center of which spun a radiant line of gold. The center grew and took on form until it began to resemble a familiar shape.

"*Rysta,*" Evelyn breathed out loud.

"Evelyn," said Rysta's voice. She moved out of the spinning rainbow and hovered above the pool, a ghostly, golden hologram of herself. "I sense you have learned a great deal since I left you. Your daylights are stronger."

Evelyn was shocked into silence. She hadn't known what to expect, but this was beyond any of her imaginings.

"You seem so surprised to see me, but is that not why you are here? Did you not call me? I have not been gone so long, have I, that you would forget?"

"No, no, of course not," Evelyn stammered. "Urza told me to come here to find answers, but I did not think I would find you!"

"What answers do you seek?"

Evelyn blurted out the whole dilemma in one long stream. It seemed to her simultaneously impossible and the most real thing she had ever done, to be talking to Rysta's shimmering ghost in the middle of her abandoned enclosure. But if anyone could tell her what to do next, it would be Rysta.

"So, it is your belief that the stone of Metria will cure the daylights of the Exorian warriors?" Rysta repeated. "And you wish for me to give it to you?"

"Yes—well, I mean it might not cure them, but it could balance them out, right?"

Rysta did not respond for what felt like several long minutes. All sense of time telescoped inside the enclosure. It felt to Evelyn that she had been there only seconds and, simultaneously, her whole life. When Rysta next spoke, it was as if her voice had retreated far away—as if she were speaking to Evelyn from deep within a long tunnel. Her golden hologram began to fade.

"Some things are much clearer to me from here, while some are yet a mystery. I do know that there is little hope of stemming the tide that is rising. It is not only Ayda that suffers. For some time now, I have watched as the seas and the rivers of your world diminish, their creatures hunted and mutated into oblivion. I fear you all may be beyond hope. Perhaps it is wisest to let the daylights return to their source and to not interfere."

"No!" cried Evelyn.

Something in Rysta's tone reminded her of Rothermel: a weariness. Like the battle was already lost.

No answer.

"Please! Don't give up on us! We'll do better. We'll fix it. I'll fix it! First I'll heal the Exorians, and then Frankie, and then I'll find the Others who are doing all the bad things and I'll fix them, too—but I can't do it alone." Her heart was thumping in her chest. She was practically sobbing. "Help me, please. I want to make it better."

This time, when Rysta responded, her voice came from above Evelyn's head. Her image was strong and shimmering again. She was back.

"Do you remember the Melorian legend of the creation of the *atar*?" she asked, as Evelyn rose to her feet. "How the Watcher struck desire against the limitless void and forged the divine spark—the energy that is contained in all things?"

Evelyn nodded.

"I have since learned a secret that only the dead understand: The *atar* is all around and within the living, binding them to one another and the Weaver, but it is a *finite* energy. It can neither be created nor destroyed. It may evolve but it cannot be made anew, for it was created by a source so much bigger than we—human or Watcher—can comprehend."

"Are you saying it's running out?"

The golden ghost that was Rysta shook her head. Tiny shimmers of gold fell around her.

"I am saying it is like the sea. It ebbs and flows. Just as a human who is struck blind will find his or her other senses growing more sensitive, so it is with the *atar*. As it flows toward one manifestation, it ebbs from another. My stone is only as strong as the essence of the *atar* it contains, and that strength diminishes as the power of the stone of Exor grows."

Evelyn shook her head. "I still don't understand."

"There is no guarantee that what you propose will work. If I give you the stone and you fail, or if the stone of Metria is taken from you, its power might be wasted or fully absorbed by the stone of Exor. If this occurs, its energy will never be restored."

"So you mean I could make it all worse?"

"That depends."

"On what?"

"On you. On how well you are able to contain the stone's energy. You must become its Keeper."

Evelyn's mouth fell open.

"How do I do that? I'm only human."

Rysta's ghost smiled at her. "With your daylights, Evelyn. Yours are bound to the Fifth Stone; the ability to balance the *atar is* the power of the Fifth Stone. It is your calling. It is how you are going to fix things."

Rysta's voice seemed to be receding again. Her ghostly form faded. The pool was quiet once again, reflecting the morning sky.

"I don't understand! How do I become a Keeper? Where is the stone?" Evelyn yelled to the sky. "Rysta!"

Silence.

The air around the enclosure felt vacant. Rysta was gone for good this time.

Evelyn rocked back on her heels, defeated. What was she supposed to do now? She couldn't try anything; she couldn't fix anything, even if she wanted to. All her daylights had helped her to do was talk to the dead.

She bent over the pool and looked at her reflection. Her cheeks were thin and her brown eyes stared out from them like a sad, forgotten puppy.

"Not good," she said to the reflection. She dove her hands into the pool and splashed some water on her face, then dried it with the hem of her robe.

"Okay, then, what next?" she said aloud. Her words fell flat in the empty air.

The absence of Chase and Knox and Teddy and Frankie—of Urza and Hesam, even of Captain Nate—hit her so suddenly and forcefully that it made her wince. She wished more than anything that they were all together now. Safe. But they weren't. She was all alone, with no one coming to rescue her. This time, there would be no one to pull her out of the wreckage like her neighbors had done after the earthquake; like Fanny Dellemere had done when she and Frankie were in the orphanage in Haiti; as Mara had done after Frankie was taken by Dankar; as Rysta had done when they escaped Dankar; as Chantarelle had done when she was paralyzed by fear in the underground tunnels; and as Chase had done when they were running for their lives across the desert.

No. This time, she really was all alone. Whatever happened next, she would have to rely on herself—and only herself—to manage. She reached down for the hilts of her throwing knives for reassurance.

Somewhere in the distance, she heard a howler monkey caterwaul. It made her smile, despite her predicament. She wasn't *entirely* alone after all. At least she was still in a world where there were monkeys.

Nevertheless, everything Rysta told her had begun to sink in. If she was right, and Metria and Melor were losing their power to Exor, nothing would ever be the same. It would all look like the Broomwash: deserted and dry and dead. Not even the ocean would be alive.

Her heart sank. The problems felt so big.

She took one last look at her reflection, and stood up. This would be her last time in this enclosure. She might as well honor it—and the woman who had brought her here. Rysta had come back to tell her something important, but that was all. Her plan had failed; Rysta did not want to give her Metria's stone. So now it was time to take matters into her own hands and fight with tools she knew she had. She quickly resolved to visit the prisoners one last time, and then she would move north to meet Letham and help him to hold off the attack from the north. She bent her head, and pressed her palms and fingertips together.

"Thank you for all the lessons you have taught me, Rysta. I am grateful for my Metrian daylights, as I am for all the daylights. I will use mine to protect Ayda for as long and as well as I am able," she said. Then, for some reason, she added, "*Éclaire-moi, dirige-moi, et gouverne-moi aujourd'hui.*" It was a fragment of the bedtime prayer she used to say when she was a little girl. It reminded her of her mother.

As she spoke, the waters in the pool began to spin again within their confines. They spiraled faster, then rose into a vortex—like a small, fluid hurricane—stretching far above her head. It whirled faster and faster, narrowing and condensing. As it spun, it produced a brilliant light that grew in intensity. Evelyn shielded her eyes. The vortex stretched even higher, and then, with a flash and a sudden shock wave that sent Evelyn sprawling on the ground, it was over. The enclosure grew still, and when Evelyn got on her knees to look, the pool was entirely empty, revealing the rocks and tunnel that lay beneath it. There was no sign of water anywhere except for the slightly damp edges surrounding the pool—but then she saw it: a perfectly oval stone, sitting on a ledge just under the lip of the pool. It was the size of a grown man's palm and the color of a ripe plum. Tiny, hairline cracks pierced its surface and shone with a metallic substance, like golden thread.

Evelyn crawled toward it. She felt the pressure of her own daylights building, responding to the stone, stretching out to meet the energy it contained. She reached for the stone and, upon touching it, felt a sensation that was heavy but not unpleasant—like the true pull of gravity. She felt more solidly on the earth than she had ever been before, and at the same time acutely aware that her own body was mostly fluid: pulsing and rippling, rushing beneath her skin.

For a moment the feeling threatened to pull her under completely. She felt the tremendous call of the stone of Metria. It was like the call of home, but from a far deeper and older home than she had ever known. It spoke to her of contentment, and of a time before time, when she did not have a name or a body of her own.

"Take it if you are able, do with it what you will, for the good of all," Rysta's voice said, but it emanated from somewhere inside her.

Evelyn lingered for some time in the pull of the stone's power, somehow resisting the urge to give in to it fully. She bit down hard on her lip and the pain helped her to concentrate on her own edges. The feeling of her skin on the ground. She bit down again, drawing blood. The sweet-and-bitter metallic taste grounded her even further. She saw the green fronds of the plants again, the sky above them, and knew where she was. And then, like a ladder being spun out of the depths, she felt her own daylights surge, giving her something solid to hold on to as she came back to herself again.

When she was sure her legs were strong enough to hold her, she stood and tied the stone in a light green scarf, stowing it beneath her robes. She took one last look at Rysta's abandoned enclosure and now-empty pool. Then she retraced her steps back to her kayak.

It was time to heal the Exorians.

*Chapter Twelve*

# HEARTWOOD

"W here'd they go?" cried Knox.

He'd been outside one of the row houses talking with his mother when the alarm was raised. He knew immediately that it was the Exorians that had followed him from the beach. He wondered why it had taken this long for them to attack.

He saw his mother's face out of the corner of his eye. "Don't worry, Mom. It'll be okay. They've tried this before, and they never get very far. The deathfield is the best fence anyone could have."

"Isn't Teddy at the wall?" said his mom, in agitation.

"He knows what to do, Mom. I'm more worried about you. You haven't been here long enough to know how to defend yourself."

His mom nudged him with her shoulder. "Well, then, it's a good thing I've got you."

Knox grinned.

A second alarm bleated out from the direction of the wall. This time, it got Knox's full attention. And Seaborne's, who emerged from the doorway of the row house with his sword in one hand and his machete in the other.

"You coming to work, lad?" he barked at Knox as he passed.

"Yes," said Knox, "in a second."

His mom put a hand on his arm; she was staring at Seaborne's weapons. "No, Knox. No." She shook her head.

"It's what we *do*, Mom," said Knox, adjusting his harness and gently removing her hand.

"It's too risky. Let the Melorians handle it. It's their fight. You're just a boy. *My* boy," she stressed.

"I am a Melorian, Mom, don't you get that? And it is *my* fight. It's yours, too. My daylights have spoken. I'm a warrior and we are at war. If we don't do our part, we lose."

Grace looked back over her shoulder at the row house behind them, as if she expected some kind of wisdom to come from there.

"I don't understand how it came to this," she said.

"How doesn't matter anymore. It just is. I've been in a lot of battles already. Try not to worry until you have to." Knox gestured at the door to the row house. "Stay here with Calla. She needs somebody right now. I'll get Teddy." Then he fell into step beside Seaborne. "We'll be fine!" he called back over his shoulder.

Seaborne looked sideways at him. "Likely story that, Knox. We're mere sacks of bones and some spit at this point."

"We just have to stick it out. Captain Nate will get a message across. He'll get the Fifth Stone back here. It'll happen."

"Maybe, but in the meantime, Mara is gone, my belly is aching, and I still have to fight off these blasted fireworms. I'm not in a pretty mood, I will tell you that much."

Knox fell silent. When Seaborne was like this, it was better just to follow orders. Together, they retraced Knox's steps from earlier until they came to the wall. Hide-strung ladders were perched every ten feet along the inside wall of the ledge, and they each used one to scramble to the top.

There, they were met with confusion. A band of Exorians had been seen coming through the bog, but then they had vanished. It didn't help that the smoke from the burning forest hung low to the ground and made it hard to see from above. Melorians were arguing among themselves about what to do.

"What's all this now?" cried Seaborne. "Isn't it enough that we have a fight down there? Do you need to make one here?"

"We don't know where they went. They might have retreated, but I don't think so," said a hooded Melorian woman Knox knew as Sera.

"Neither do I," agreed Duelle, who was standing apart from the rest. "We need to go out and check."

A few feet behind him, farther along the wall, Teddy sat cross-legged, sorting stones for his slingshot. Bob, the turtle, was out of his pouch, resting on a small pile of stones. His head was fully extended and Knox could see his orange-brown eyes. Rothermel took a great interest in Bob, and the turtle was thriving. His shell was thick and crenellated and highly domed. His skin was healthy and he had grown to be the size of a brick.

"They could be hiding," said Sera, following Knox's gaze. "Like a turtle in its shell."

"Well, if they're hiding, the bog will do its work, won't it? All we have to do is wait. They've never passed it before," argued Seaborne.

"How long do we wait, though?" asked Duelle. "Our meat is gone, except for what Knox brought in. We need to clear them out so we can hunt."

"I agree with Duelle," said Sera. "I say we go down and clear them out. I won't be penned up and left to starve."

A small cheer of support went up from the other Melorians on the wall.

"What does Rothermel advise?" asked Seaborne.

No one answered.

"Have you not sent someone to consult with him?"

"No," said Sera, "he has been occupied with Mara's passing. We did not wish to bother him. We can handle a few rogue Exorians."

Seaborne looked exasperated. "I'll go find him myself then. Do me a favor and don't do anything rash while I'm gone. You two"—he looked at Knox and Teddy—"stay put until I get back. I won't be long." He cast a parting look at Knox, then slid down the ladder and sprinted toward the pile of boulders at the far edge of the Keep.

Knox moved closer to Duelle, on his way toward Teddy.

Duelle stopped him.

"There is something funny about this incursion, Knox—something feels different."

"What?"

"I can't say yet, but my daylights are sensing it. Something is off—"

His sentence was cut short by a spurt of blood erupting from his mouth. He fell against Knox, an Exorian spear lodged in his back.

In seconds, several other Melorians had fallen. Six were thrown backwards off the wall. Knox leapt the intervening feet between Duelle and Teddy, landing on top of his brother. Before Knox could look up, he sensed, more than saw, that the Exorians were scaling the far side of the wall, using one another's shoulders as braces to haul each other up, forming a human pyramid.

Without thinking, he grabbed Teddy and rolled with him to the other side of the wall. He looked down. It was at least a twenty-foot drop, but a few broken bones was better than death. He was about to push Teddy over the side when an Exorian head, green-gray with dried mud, popped up directly opposite them. Knox could see the orange flecks in the warrior's eyes, his murderous intent. Knox threw one of his knives, but it was at an awkward angle, and only hit the Exorian in the shoulder. Knox stood up, but before he could throw another blade, the Exorian swiped at his knees and pulled him off the wall. He tumbled and hit the far ground hard.

He heard Teddy yell from above.

"Leave my brother alone!" Knox screamed, but even as the words came out of his mouth, he remembered what Mara had said to him.

*You must let him be taken.*

Knox was floored. *Is this what she'd meant? Was he supposed to let his brother be taken?*

Why? What could Teddy possibly have to do with this?

He shook his head. No. It was not possible. Mara was wrong. Besides, his mom would never recover if he allowed Teddy to be taken prisoner by the Exorians. He jumped up, grabbed onto the nearest Exorian's waist, and scrambled up the revolting green-gray muck covering the man's back, using the human tower to his advantage. They smelled like a sewer, but at least he couldn't feel their scabby hides.

"Get your slimy hands off my brother!" Knox screamed. He grabbed the back of an Exorian's bald head as a handhold, trying to edge his way up the wall.

A hard tug on his poncho sent him tumbling back onto the ground again. He landed on his spine, all the air in his lungs vanishing with an *ooomph*.

He lay there for a few moments, unable to think or breathe. When he recovered enough to move, he found he couldn't. The tip of an Exorian spear was only three inches from his eyeball. Knox fingered a throwing knife in his harness, weighing his odds.

"I wouldn't do that if I were you. We have your brother," said a voice that sounded all too familiar.

Knox looked past the spear tip to its owner: a mud-caked face indistinguishable from the other Exorians, except for his eyes, which were a deep blue.

*Louis.*

Knox's heart sank. His poor mom. He held his hands up in surrender.

"Get up," said Louis.

Knox did as he was told, noticing that Louis had his right arm wrapped in a sling and was holding the spear awkwardly in his left.

"Right-handed, huh?" asked Knox.

"Be quiet, outlier."

"Yeah, well, it takes one to know one."

Louis whipped his human-looking hand out of the sling and used it to hook Knox around the neck, pulling him close so that he could hold the spear tip to Knox's throat.

"Shut your mouth now, or I will do it for you," said Louis.

Knox swallowed hard. This new Louis was not at all like the old one. There was no trace of warmth or familiarity in his voice. Knox knew that this Louis would never have helped them, as the old one had. This Louis was going to kill them all—unless he could somehow figure out how to remind him who he really was. Once again, he thought of his mom. Would Louis recognize her?

A shout came down from the wall. Several of the Exorians had made it to the top and were fighting with the Melorians. It was too high for Knox to see well, but he heard the unmistakable sound of machetes meeting shields.

"How do we get through the wall?" said Louis, threatening Knox with the spear tip again.

Knox did a silent count of the number of Exorians left on the ground. At least forty. Plus another six or eight climbing up the wall. Enough to put up a decent fight, especially with the Melorians so weak from hunger.

"Tell me!"

"You told me to shut my mouth, so I'm shutting it."

Louis swatted Knox on the side of the head. His ears rang.

"Do you want to live to see another day? Or are you trying to have me fragment you?"

"I don't care what you do to me, Louis. But you should know, I'm your nephew. If you kill me, you're killing your own family. And my brother up there? He's your nephew, too, so you should tell whoever is up there to lay the heck off!"

Knox waited to see if his words had any impact. He couldn't tell without looking at Louis's face, and Louis was standing behind him, arm crooked around his throat.

"My Exorian brothers are my family," Louis hissed in Knox's ear.

"Yeah, keep telling yourself that. Keep drinking that firewater. But just remember, you hurt me, you hurt your own blood."

Louis kicked Knox in the back of the knees. Knox flew forward, landing on his face. Louis put a wet foot on his back and leaned over him.

"If I were you, I would not move." He gestured to another warrior, saying "Watch him."

Knox lifted his head enough to see Louis approach the wall and bang on the rock with the butt of his spear, shearing a blanket of dank moss off the wall. Then, he felt a rumbling in the earth that made his heart sink again. The Exorians must have broken through and were opening the door.

A crack in the wall before Louis widened, and then split apart. A brilliant light spilled into the mist, alighting on the drops of moisture in the air and transforming the marsh into a glittering, golden hall. Louis and the rest of the Exorians crammed through the aperture. Rough hands pulled Knox to his feet and pushed him along.

Once through, his eyes fell on a scene so at odds with everything he knew about the Keep that his insides rebelled, as if he were suddenly on a roller coaster. He leaned over and retched.

Golden light spilled through the high branches of the massive grove of trees, as always, but it fell on the scattered bodies of dead Melorians, including Sera, who lay still, an Exorian spear twisted in her chest. The rest of the village had been rounded up and disarmed, including Teddy, Knox's mother, Adhoran, and Calla—but not Seaborne. Knox could not—he would not—let his mind even consider that Seaborne had been killed.

The Melorians were being made to kneel in a line at the center of the massive grove of trees. Exorians stood over them, wielding the machetes and axes they had taken from their prisoners. There were so few Melorians left. Maybe twenty.

Knox hung his head. Whatever happened next, this much was true: Dankar had succeeded in wiping out or displacing a whole tribe of people. He was grateful that Tinator and Mara had not lived to see this day.

The light in the grove dimmed, eclipsed for the moment as if one of the ancient trees had freed itself from the ground and begun to walk among them. A long shadow fell across the grove, and revealed itself to be cast by the helmeted figure of Rothermel, bearing a great sword. The buckle in his belt shone a deep amber.

"Who is it that comes to my home bringing such ill will?" he roared, in a tone so deep and growling it seemed to come up from the bones of the earth itself. His eyes raked over Louis's face. He stood a full head above the Exorian.

Louis was stunned into silence, then recovered himself.

"I come on behalf of the lord of Exor, Dankar, Keeper of the sacred fire and father of all true Aydans. Come with me now and no more of your people shall suffer. Refuse, and you shall watch them perish in front of your eyes."

Rothermel cocked his head, and then, unexpectedly, burst into great, booming laughter. It rolled up into the uppermost branches of the trees and seemed to reverberate back, mocking the Exorians.

Knox's heart leapt with joy, despite their predicament. He had never heard his Keeper laugh. Suddenly, he was no longer afraid.

"That is so very like my cousin to call himself the great lord and overseer of Ayda," chuckled Rothermel. "But I have only one father, and one mother, and one vow, and I do not recognize the mewling claims of a forsaken cousin." He lowered his voice. "Go now, and tell that murderous accident of nature that I refuse his request."

Louis pulled a small knife from his sling. It looked like it was made of black glass. He strode over to Knox and pulled his head up by his hair. He pointed the tip of the knife at Knox's throat.

"Then you will watch as I fragment this one."

"No!" Knox's mother yelled out. She scrambled to her feet. An Exorian pushed her roughly back down to the ground. They struggled. The Exorian used the butt of his spear against her face.

"Mom! Don't!" yelled Knox. "They'll kill you!"

A wild fear crashed over him now, intense and animal. He used all of his newfound Melorian strength to try and break free from Louis and protect his mother. He almost succeeded, but Louis had the knife. He used it to secure Knox in his grip once again, signaling for one of the Exorians to bring Grace over to him.

She glared at Louis, one side of her face already swelling into a vivid bruise.

"Don't you dare hurt him!"

Knox watched his mom closely. Would she recognize her own brother? And what about Louis? Would he have any clue he was staring at his sister? He tried to clear his mind and let Rothermel know what he was thinking. Maybe his daylights could communicate with him the way Chase's could with Ratha.

"This is your child?" Louis asked Grace, indicating Knox with a squeeze of his elbow.

She nodded.

Louis was quiet for a moment, his eyes raking the kneeling Melorians until they fell on Teddy. He chucked his chin in Teddy's direction.

"And that one?"

Grace dipped her head once.

"What if I told you that no more harm would come to them?"

"I would say, *Good.*"

"Then I will make you that promise in return for a favor."

"Mom . . . don't . . . ," whispered Knox, trying to shake his head.

Louis tightened his grip.

"Ask your Keeper to save them. If he agrees to leave this place with me, I will take my warriors and leave you all in peace."

Grace turned to face Rothermel. She did not speak, but her eyes implored him.

Rothermel studied her face, then Louis's, then Knox's, and finally, Teddy's. As he did, his expression changed. The gold flecks in his brown eyes shone with sudden comprehension. He raised an eyebrow at Knox and said, "The blue-eyed warrior."

Knox nodded.

The thick creases in Rothermel's face deepened; his shoulders rounded as if he had suddenly taken up a heavy load. His belt buckle dimmed.

"I see," he said. Then, without another word, he lowered his sword in surrender. "I will go with you."

"Over my dead body," cried Seaborne, lunging out from his hiding place behind one of the trees, machete and swords swinging. He drove the machete straight into the back of one of the Exorians. The rest responded by turning on him, leaving their prisoners unattended. The Melorians rose up, en masse, attacking the Exorians with whatever weapons they could find: rocks, fists, teeth.

Louis tightened his grip on Knox, scraping his knife's edge along Knox's cheek. Knox felt pain as it cut into his skin.

"ENOUGH!" roared Rothermel. The earth beneath them shook and the trees seemed to bend inwards. Everyone, including Louis and Knox, fell to the ground.

"*Enough*," Rothermel repeated. The earth stopped churning. The trees straightened. He took off his helmet and unhooked the buckle of his belt. He threw them on the ground beside Louis. "I go willingly to meet my enemy, fragmenter of my blood. I do not fear him. Take me to him."

Knox stumbled to his feet, free of Louis's grasp, helping his mother.

Louis swept up the helmet and the belt and rose to his feet.

"This is madness!" cried Seaborne, making his way to his Keeper's side. Blood poured from a gash on his forehead. "Do you not see that your sister did the very same thing? We cannot lose you, too. Please, don't do this. Do not go with them. We can *fight*."

Rothermel patted his shoulder. Then, he put his hands out, palms up, to be bound.

"No!" implored Seaborne. His eyes cast around, searching for support, and landed on Knox. "C'mon, lad, speak up. Tell the man. You were there, at the arena. You saw what Dankar is. He won't stop until all the Keepers are fragmented."

Knox opened his mouth to speak, only to hear Mara's last words echo in his head again.

*You must let him be taken.*

Finally, he understood. She didn't mean Teddy would be taken. She had never meant Teddy. She had been talking about Rothermel.

Knox stepped aside to allow Louis to bind Rothermel's hands behind his back.

"No," Seaborne groaned.

"You will lead in my absence, seafarer," Rothermel said. "Be good to my people, and have no regrets. I go willingly. Enough blood has been shed. Enough families forsaken. It will end, one way or another."

Louis shouldered the belt, gesturing for Rothermel to lead the way out of the Keep.

"There is one other task I have for you," he said. "And that is for you to show me where the stone of Melor lies hidden."

Rothermel stopped in his tracks. He shook his massive head.

"I will not do that."

"Ah, but I think you will," said Louis, "if you want the last remaining members of your tribe to survive."

"It matters not; how long would they last if I surrendered my stone? Tell me! I know what Dankar would do to them. Those he has not killed, he would poison, as you have been poisoned. You have my belt, you have me; it is enough."

"I have my orders."

Rothermel whipped out an arm and grabbed Louis's right hand from the sling. He pulled Louis close. The Exorians rallied, raising their spears.

"Look at your hand, man. Think! Dankar has changed you into something unnatural." He lifted the hand and shook it. "*This* is you, not the rest of it. You are not a slave."

Louis looked at the small pinkish-white hand engulfed in Rothermel's larger, tanned one. He used his left hand to withdraw the obsidian blade once more from the sling he wore, and grimaced.

"You have no idea who I am or what I am made of," he said. "You are not my Keeper. I listen to one voice, and one voice alone."

Then, he plunged the blade straight into Rothermel's heart.

*Chapter Thirteen*

# BEYOND HOPE

"She's not one for creature comforts, is she?" griped Captain Nate, looking weary after spending the night locked away with Ratha. His eyes were bloodshot and his jaw was still spasming from being clenched for so long.

Chase cracked a grin. They were in the same room as the night before, huddled around the large fireplace. A good night's sleep had done Bodi right. She was still frail and windburned, but her face had lost the hunted expression it wore when Chase first saw her.

"Not really. It's all pretty cold and stony up here—at least from what I've seen."

"I'll say. Makes me feel more than a little uneasy—that, and having her digging around my head all night. I don't know how you stand it. My melon feels like someone's driven a pickax through it."

"Varunans are scary," Bodi added.

"And Exorians aren't?" asked Chase, grinning again. He couldn't help it. Despite everything that was happening, he felt weirdly happy. He knew he had been lonely in Varuna, but now that Bodi and the Captain were here, he was realizing just how much.

The captain paced the room, stopping in front of Bodi. She was sitting in the same chair as the previous night, only this time she was wrapped from head to foot in a gray fur-and-feather robe, similar to Chase's.

"My, aren't you a sight," he said, stifling a yawn. "I could do with a few pillows and a hot meal, for starters, should *anyone be listening.*" He emphasized the last part, knowing full well Ratha had her spies all over the residence. He moved in front of the fire and stretched his hands out to warm them.

"Ratha says you bring in to Varuna what you take out," said Chase. He tapped his own head with his finger. "She doesn't plant anything in there."

"Well, that's a small mercy," the Captain sighed, squatting by the fire, "but I have brought in a great deal after five hundred years."

Chase took this opportunity to ask him about Evelyn and Metria. He'd been waiting all night.

"So, she's safe," he said, relieved after hearing the Captain's account.

"For now, yes. Dankar's forces have yet to break through the Metrian borders."

Bodi shifted uncomfortably at the sound of Dankar's name.

They kept talking, the Captain filling Chase in on the plight of the Exorian prisoners who'd been shipped to Metria, and Evelyn's attempts to cure them.

"You can't stop him, you know," Bodi cut in. "It doesn't matter what you do." She pointed at the flames leaping in the fireplace. "It's like that. Dankar will keep going until he burns everything up."

"Strong words, Bodi," said the Captain.

She hopped off the chair and came closer, dragging the weight of her robe. "It's the truth. I know. He put my mother in the dungeons with all the other mothers and their babies. And the rest of us—" She shuddered. "He doesn't care about us. Why would he care about you?"

Chase bent down so he was face-to-face with her. "He doesn't need to care. In fact, the less he thinks about us, the better. Because that means he's not thinking... but we *are*. After all, what puts out fire? Water—and that's the power the Metrians have. Their daylights are very strong. They might be able to make him stop."

Bodi thought about this for a minute, then asked, "If they can stop, why didn't they do it before?"

Chase looked sideways at Captain Nate. It was a good question.

"Uh, I dunno. Maybe, at first, they thought the Melorians would stop him, and then when that didn't happen, Rysta tried to, but she was taken prisoner before she could do anything—"

"Interesting theory, Chase," interrupted Ratha, from the back of the room.

Chase wondered how long she had been listening.

She moved to the hearth and began layering kindling and logs on the fire. It began to sizzle and spit, the flame licking all the way up the back wall of the fire surround, and still she continued to pile on fuel. The fire roared, leaping higher up toward the mantel and threatening to roll out into the room. The captain reeled backwards on his heels so he wouldn't get burned.

"Are you mad?" he shouted. He jumped to his feet and put his hand up to stop her from adding another log. "You'll burn the place down long before Dankar gets a chance!"

Ratha turned on him, her pale eyes colored with emotion for the first time ever. She shook the log at Captain Nate. Her mouth twisted; her lips moved without sound. Her long, black hair, usually kept so neat in the topknot on her head, was loose around her shoulders. She looked unhinged.

"What? What is it?" Chase cried in alarm.

"We've all been fools!" She glared at Captain Nate. "I should have ripped the answers out of your brain long before this. Now it is too late!" Her expression was so fierce it sent Bodi scuttling backwards to hide behind the chair.

"Tell me, Chase, what makes a fire blaze out of control?" She shook the log at him, now. "Fuel! And what lies between Exor and Metria? The stone of Melor, and its Keeper—my brother!"

She paused to let this sink in. Chase's brain churned to process what she was saying. "The Melorians have been under attack for a long time," he said.

"Yes, but now, with my sister gone, the stone of Exor is gaining strength. My spies tell me that Dankar's forces have broken through my brother's enchantments and entered the Keep. All who lie within are in mortal danger, including my brother and his stone."

"How close are they to gaining the stone?" the Captain asked, beginning to pace.

"Very close. I feel it. The balance is shifting. Melor has fallen."

"What?" cried Chase. "What about my brothers?" He swallowed hard. "And my *mother*?"

Ratha gave him a cold glance, then turned on the Captain.

"I wonder, Caspar, if your delay was worth it? It cost my brother and his people everything. As for the rest of us, the usurper will soon have two stones! He will advance on Metria like a conqueror, and how long do you think they will they be able to fend him off without their Keeper? How soon before he has their stone, too?"

In a sudden explosive move, she threw the log across the room. It hit the opposite wall and broke in half.

Bodi whimpered.

Chase felt the hair on his head crackle with sudden static electricity.

Ratha's eyes were locked on the Captain.

"And YOU—through it all—have sat on the other side of the fog and done *nothing*!"

Blood spurted like a geyser out of Captain Nate's nose, splattering on the stone floor. He held his hands up as if to defend a blow, but whatever was happening came from the inside. His knees buckled. He fell to the ground.

Ratha stood over him, seething.

"Your stupidity has cost me my siblings! Now it will cost you your life."

Blood dripped out of the Captain's ears. His body convulsed.

"Ratha!" shouted Chase. Then he did something he had never dared to do before. He took hold of Ratha by the shoulders and shook her—hard. He was surprised by how real and solid, and *human*, she felt.

Ratha recoiled, startled by the static discharge from his touch. For a moment, Chase thought she might strike him, but he did not let go.

"He has brought nothing but destruction to my family. He deserves to die," she said to him in mindspeak.

Chase tightened his grip, and shook his head.

"No. He doesn't," he answered, also in mindspeak. "Dankar is the one who destroyed your family, not Captain Nate. He didn't have to come back. He stayed away a long time; he could have evaded you forever. But he didn't. He came back. For me. For Rysta. For you. For Ayda. He *is* a man of his word. Everything he does—everything he has done—is about trying to protect Ayda. He's not the enemy."

Ratha blinked, breaking the spell. The electric charge in the room became palpably different.

The Captain struggled to his feet. He wiped the blood from his face with the back of his hands, glowering at Ratha.

"Do you know for certain that the stone of Melor is now in Exorian hands?" Chase asked, out loud, moving so that he blocked the Captain from Ratha's immediate view.

"No, nothing is certain."

"Then maybe there's still a chance that they don't have it. Melorians are tough. They will not give up."

"There are barely any left to fight, Chase. They have been overpowered."

"What about my mom? And Knox and Teddy?" he asked again.

Ratha shook her head. "I do not know what has happened to them. I cannot see that far."

Chase felt all the air in his lungs evaporate.

"How can you not know?"

"My sight is not as strong now." She hung her head. "The balance of the *atar* is shifting in Dankar's favor. My power is waning as Exor's rises. I can only tell you what I have heard, and I have not heard anything about your mother and brothers."

A chasm opened in Chase's stomach. He could barely form his next words.

"Does that mean they are dead?"

"It is possible," she said simply.

Chase rubbed his face with his hands, trying to take in this fact. Everything in him rebelled against the idea. It just couldn't be true. The chasm grew wider and he felt a grief grow up and out of it that threatened to overwhelm him. His mind flashed back to the dream.

The lifeless bodies of everyone he loved floating around him in a fathomless sea.

"Can't you, like, travel into their minds or something? What's the use of all this training, and the stone of Varuna, if it doesn't work?"

Ratha stepped away from him, staring into the fire.

"It does work, Chase, but not how you think. I don't create the *atar*—it simply is, and it flows between the stones, like a circular river. A Keeper's duty is to maintain the balance between the exchange, to keep it fluid. If the exchange grows unbalanced or stagnant—if one stone takes too much of it, or combines the energy of their stone with another—then the balance is disturbed. The flow of the *atar* begins to pool in one direction, streaming away from the others. This is why the stones on Ayda were given Keepers; without the Fifth Stone, we ensure that the flow of the *atar* remains even and stable. I am having difficulty because the energy is moving away from me."

Chase pictured the map of currents on Ayda that Hesam had shown him back when he was in Metria. She had revealed how the snows and ice of Varuna fed the waters of Lake Voss; from there, the three rivers flowed into the sea, where the freshwater evaporated back into the air, only to fall again on Ayda in the form of snow and rain. A self-sustaining system. If one part hoarded its energy or did not perform its role, the system would collapse. Every part relied on the others.

"Do you see it now, Chase?" asked the Captain, having regained his composure. "Dankar may soon have two stones, and will become twice as powerful, but it's still a standoff as long as the stone of Metria stays out of his hands. Ratha is weakened but still in the game if this is the case. If he gets his hands on the stone of Metria, then the flow of the *atar* will shift completely into Dankar's favor. He'll use the power of all three to pull her remaining strength toward him; he'll melt the glacier and come marching in here. She won't be able to fend him off."

"Do you know if Rothermel is alive?"

"I don't know," said Ratha, in a terrible voice. "He is cut off from me. I cannot feel him."

Chase buried his face again in his hands. It all seemed so hopeless. But there was one thing he knew beyond a doubt. He looked up, his eyes on Captain Nate.

"I don't know about you, but I'm leaving. You can't make me stay, Ratha. I have to find out if my mom and brothers are still alive. I have to warn the Metrians."

"I have not *made* you do anything, Chase," Ratha objected. "I have given you choices. I am your Keeper, not your jailer. But you should know that there is little we can do. An army of Exorians lies between us and Metria."

"So?"

"You will be of little help to anyone if you are dead," Captain Nate admonished.

"Are you agreeing with her?" said Chase, taken aback. "Are you saying we should just sit up here and drink tea and watch as Dankar rolls over all of Ayda, grabs up three stones, and sets everything on fire?"

"No," said the Captain.

"Then what?"

"I am saying that I should go fetch the Fifth Stone myself. It is time."

Chase reeled back, hearing this information. His temper rose. "You can do that?"

"I might be able to, yes."

"Then why the heck didn't you do it in the first place? Why did you put us through this?"

"Because, Chase, it is not *mine* to bring anywhere. I explained that to you. I am its protector, not its Keeper, and I swore an oath to keep it safe. There are some forces of creation that are cataclysmic—and the Fifth Stone is one. If I go now and compel its Keeper to send it back, it means that the four stones and their Keepers on Ayda have utterly failed. It means that whatever the consequences turn out to be, we are willing to accept them, for better or worse. Do you understand?" He looked meaningfully at Ratha. "You saw into my memories. You know what I speak to be the truth?"

Ratha remained silent.

"So the Fifth Stone's Keeper just has to *decide* to bring it back?" Chase asked. "That's it? What's stopping him? Maybe it's already on its way!"

"Perhaps. Perhaps not. I do know it is not an easy decision. Many outcomes must be weighed. This is why I sent Chantarelle back to send a message. I was hoping that he would be enough—or that we might gain an advantage in the meantime to make the return unnecessary. But I know now that it is." He looked to Ratha again.

Ratha met his gaze.

"It is."

"Then, I will see to it that it is brought here, come what may," he sighed. "Can you get me safely to Metria? I will need my boat."

She nodded. Calyphor and Deruda appeared almost instantly at the door.

The Captain clapped a hand on Chase's shoulder.

"I hope I see you again, boy." Then he nodded toward Bodi. "But if I don't, take care of what's in front of you. Let others do the same. If your brothers and mother are alive, they'll look after themselves."

"What about Evelyn?"

"The battle is coming to her. If you want to help, I suggest you go straight to Metria."

✛    ✛    ✛

Chase sprinted up to his room, gathering his sword and the few belongings he'd collected during his time in Varuna, including the kaleidoscope that Ratha had shown him the first time he had come here. Bodi followed him.

"Take me with you," she pleaded.

"I can't. You're too little; you'll slow me down. Besides, you almost froze to death once already."

"I don't want to stay here with her. I want to be with you."

"It's okay, Bodi. She's not so bad once you get used to her. I've been here a while. There's some cool stuff. You can see all the stars."

Chase whirled around the room, taking a final inventory. His mind was racing. Evelyn was alone in Metria, with the Exorian army headed straight toward her.

"I don't care," Bodi said, pouting. "I won't stay here without you."

"And I will not keep her here against her will," said Ratha, from Chase's doorway. "You are both free to go to Melor or Metria, as you see fit."

"I need to get to the border of Metria and Varuna as quickly as possible," said Chase.

"I thought you might," said Ratha. She gave him a penetrating stare, then walked toward his window. She looked out at the view of the mountain range, and beyond, toward the veil of pink borealis light flickering in the eastern sky. "I will take you as far as Lake Voss. Without Calyphor and Deruda, it is not so easy to leave my abode. It is very high up."

Chase hadn't thought about how he might get down from the mountaintop. He'd always been flown there. This time, he would have to climb down. He would need Ratha to show him the way.

"What if we run into the Exorian army at the Voss? We can't risk them taking *you* prisoner!"

Ratha's expression might have been a smile.

"I may be weakened, Chase, but I'm still the Keeper of the great stone of Varuna . . . I should like to see them try."

*Chapter Fourteen*

# SPLIT

"Noooooo!"

Knox heard his own voice as if it were far away.

Behind him the Melorians all cried out at the same time.

Rothermel wheeled backwards, the hilt of Louis's blade protruding from his leather undervest. He put both hands on the hilt and pulled, yet it remained firmly embedded in his chest.

"Your daylights—strong as they are—cannot withstand the sacrificial blade of Exor for long," said Louis. "Show me where your stone is, and I will remove it so you may heal."

Rothermel shook his head again.

"Then you will fragment, and take all your people here with you. In time, Dankar will come to this place and tear it from its roots. He will find the stone eventually, so why not just give it to him now and spare the lives of the last remaining members of your tribe?"

Several seconds passed in tense silence. Rothermel cast his eyes over the last of the Melorians, Exorian spears pointed at their hearts. His gaze landed finally on Grace and Teddy.

"You are their Keeper. Are you going to protect them—or let them all die for your pride?"

Rothermel bowed his head, then stumbled and fell to his knees. He looked up at Louis and nodded once, consenting.

"Take it out!" Knox wept.

Louis pulled the black blade from Rothermel's chest.

The Keeper fell forward.

Louis leaned in. Rothermel murmured directions to him.

"Thank you," said Louis, but he did not stow the blade. Instead, he wavered, a strange look in his eye, as if he were weighing whether or not to plunge it into Rothermel's back. Before he could decide, the blade flew out of his hand with a sharp ringing sound and fell to the ground.

"Leave him alone," growled Knox, aiming another one of his throwing knives at Louis's head, "or I'll kill you myself. I don't care who you are, or what you are, you miserable excuse for a human."

Louis shot a dark look at Knox and stooped to pick up the blade.

"Your master has not told you everything," panted Rothermel, struggling to rise. "You think that if you steal my stone you will unlock its secrets, but you are wrong. You need me alive to wield it. I have not granted it to you and have no plans to. You are to take me, and the stone, to Dankar. If my people are left here, unmolested, I will reconsider—" He lost his footing, dizzy from loss of blood. Knox leapt to support him.

Louis hesitated; but then, with no further word, he headed straight for the grove of trees. He pushed past the kneeling Melorian prisoners to stand at the foot of a tall, full-branched tree that grew heart-shaped leaves the color of copper. He surveyed the tree closely, using Rothermel's belt buckle as a guide. When he came to the place where the buckle began to glow, he drove the blade deep into its trunk. The tree groaned and shook, and then split apart, falling to either side with a deafening thud. As it fell, its roots tore from the ground, revealing a shallow bed of earth, at the center of which was an oval-shaped stone the size of a man's palm. It was the color of honey, and streaked with black lines. The golden light in the grove intensified, and a hum of energy passed between the stone and its Keeper.

Rothermel basked in the light, drawing the energy toward him, using it to heal himself. Within seconds, he was able to stand on his own again; the wound in his chest stopped bleeding. Knox, too, felt his daylights cross the distance between him and the stone of Melor like a wave of energy that fueled and strengthened him. Suddenly, the thought of fighting off forty Exorians felt easy. He recognized this feeling from his first full day on Ayda, in the duel with Tinator. And he was not alone. The Melorians recovered from their shock, and rose up to challenge their captors once again.

Knox gripped his last throwing knife and advanced on Louis. He didn't care anymore if Louis was his uncle. Louis deserved what he was going to get.

Rothermel stopped him with one hand.

"The deal is done," he said.

"It's not fair," whispered Knox.

Rothermel's forehead crinkled. "Not much is, Knox, but I meant what I said. The outlier may take our stone, but he cannot wield it without my permission—nor can Dankar. I intend to follow my stone into the heart of my enemy—and I will see for myself what he is planning."

Knox felt the wave of energy dip.

Louis had taken off his sling and thrown it over the stone.

Rothermel visibly bristled. Knox squinted to take a closer look at the sling. He realized, with a sudden churning disgust, that the sling was actually made from the pelt of a *tehuantl*.

"There are no words for this kind of evil," said Rothermel, low but loud enough for Knox to hear. "The *tehuantl* are descended from the ancients. Dankar has made a grave error."

"What do you mean?" whispered Knox.

"He has turned on those who have protected him. He thinks fear and butchery will rule them—but they will turn on him, in time. You'll see."

"We don't have that much time."

Knox watched as Louis wrapped the stone in the pelt, added the belt, and shouldered it.

"We split ranks here," Louis said, signaling his troops. "I will take Rothermel and our prize to Metria, where Dankar should be waiting." He motioned to a few of his warriors. "You, come with me. The rest of you, stay here with the prisoners until we are safely away. If any of them try to come after us—you know what to do."

"They shall not be harmed—that is our agreement," said Rothermel, falling in line with Louis, his injury almost healed.

Louis nodded once, cast his blue eyes over the scene, and marched out of the Keep.

The remaining Exorians rounded up Knox and the rest of the Melorians and herded them into one of the row houses.

"What happens now?" Knox whispered to Seaborne.

"We lay low," said Seaborne, "until we can rid ourselves of the fire-worms; then we'll go after him. They have to cross the Hestredes to get to Metria. That will slow them down."

The now-familiar scent of smoke drifted into the grove. It came from beyond the wall, and smelled fresh.

"Now what?" cried Knox.

"I think they're burning the glen," said Calla, stricken. "They have Rothermel and our stone, so there's nothing to stop them—and once

Dankar gets ahold of him . . ." She put her head in her hands. "It's over. We're done for."

"It's never over," said Seaborne, throwing his arm around her shoulder and pulling her close. "Not as long as I'm breathing."

Knox turned to his mom and Teddy.

"Are you guys okay?"

"I lost Bob," Teddy gulped.

His mom stroked the back of Teddy's head. Her cheek looked sore, but Knox thought that her daylights must be growing, because the bruise didn't look so bad.

She leaned in to whisper to Knox. "Who was that awful man?"

Knox's brain sputtered, trying to think of what to say. He couldn't think of a nice way to tell her, so he just blurted it out.

"*That* was your brother—that's Uncle Edward."

✝     ✝     ✝

Seaborne hatched a desperate plan.

It would mean taking the long way around the Voss, and heading into Metria via the north. But if the rumors were true about the Exorians—that they were most fearful of the cold, and Varuna—the Melorians could be assured that few, if any, of them would be taking that route. And the southern route would slow the others down, since they must cross both the Vossbeck and the Hestredes to get to the city.

The bridge across the Vossbeck would aid them, but no such thing existed at the mouth of the Hestredes. It was Seaborne's hope that the Melorians, with their ability to swim, and the speed and resilience granted to them by their daylights, could cross the Hestredes and descend on Louis and the Exorians from the north as they reached the city. They would rescue Rothermel, and their stone, before the enemy had a chance to give it to Dankar. It was a gamble, but, as Seaborne said, it was the only hand they could play.

"We've got the short end of the stick, there's no denying it," he grumbled to Knox, as he sharpened his machete blade with a whetstone. Around them, the Melorians were packing what they could into baskets, rolling up their hammocks, and preparing to leave at nightfall. Outside, the Exorians were quiet. They had gathered the fallen bodies of their brothers to burn them. The bodies of the dead Melorians they left obscenely in the open.

"What about Teddy and my mother?" Knox whispered.

He was worried. He knew that his mother's daylights must be getting stronger on Ayda, as everyone's did, but he had yet to see any sign of them being overtly Melorian. And, of course, Teddy was a Metrian. He was doubtful the two of them could keep up the pace Seaborne wanted to set.

"Do you think they can come with us?"

"Aye, I would not leave them here. The place will be overrun with Exorians and *tehuantl* before long—and I wouldn't wish that on anyone. If only that wee bugger Chantarelle were here. I'd like to take a shortcut underground if there is one."

"Not one that goes under a river, sadly," said Knox, thinking back to the tunnels he had traveled in Melor. "Besides, the Exorians know about the tunnels now. It's too dangerous."

The Melorians, and Grace and Teddy, were silent as they ate a quick meal made from the fish that Knox had caught and dried. Several volunteers, including Adhoran, chose to stay behind and distract their captors so that the others might escape unnoticed. The parting was brief and final. There was little hope that anyone left behind would be seen again, and equally little that the party that set out would succeed. Yet there were no words of good-bye, no lingering looks or outward displays of grief.

Seaborne pocketed some coals from the fire in his ember-chamber. He alone had his sword, which he removed from its scabbard. He had taken it off out of respect for Mara's last moments, and it had remained hidden from the Exorians in the row house during the skirmish. He raised it to give Adhoran the signal.

Adhoran and five Melorian soldiers raced outside, armed with hoes and shovels from the garden. They ran fast, drawing the Exorian troops away from the door.

Seaborne and Calla led Knox, Teddy, Grace, and eight other Melorians across the clearing. They were practically invisible in the dusk under their hoods, and walked without sound. Adhoran had led the Exorians to the jumble of rocks at the other side. Those who were staying were now taunting the Exorians from higher ground, keeping them occupied.

The rest walked silently past the smoldering burial pyres of the Exorians, and the cold bodies of their fallen kindred, through the passage in the wall and into the deathfield. They skirted the churned lumps of stinking mud and upturned swamp grasses and passed under the moss-bearded trees, looking more forlorn and rotten than ever before. The company fell into dark thoughts, unbidden and uncomforted, even as they passed into what had been the sweet meadow and grasses of the springtime glen—now black and smoking. Its loss was felt by every Melorian, a weakening blow. One by one they filed across it, and came to the ravine that marked the edge of the Keep. Seaborne paused to let the whole company assemble, taking count.

"Where is Knox?" he whispered.

"He was right behind me," said Teddy.

A shudder of anxiety passed through the group.

"I'll double back," said Grace. "Maybe he's stuck in the bog."

"All respect, but I doubt that very much," said Seaborne. A look passed between him and Calla.

"I'll go," said Calla, slipping to the back of the group, just as Knox appeared, panting and stuffing something under his poncho.

"I'm here . . . I'm all right. I just got delayed for a second."

"Don't ever do that again," she hissed.

"Now that we are all accounted for," said Seaborne, swinging Teddy up on his back, "we run." He leapt effortlessly over the width of the ravine. The rest of the Melorians followed suit, then found a tree-length to lay across the mouth so that Grace could cross. Once she was over, Knox tossed the tree-length down into the ravine and jumped across himself.

Not a single Melorian looked back.

There would be no return.

# Chapter Fifteen

# CONVERGENCE

Chase and Bodi stood with Ratha at the bottom step at the edge of the terrace. Below them, dark clouds swirled, lit from within by electrical charges. Behind them, the purple flame of the cauldron danced in the winds that emanated from the four-sided building. Ratha's hair lifted and spun as the winds tossed it. Bodi clung to Chase's hand, terrified.

Ratha looked sideways at Chase.

"Do you trust me?" she said in mindspeak.

"Do I have a choice?" he replied, similarly.

"You always have a choice," she said.

He gripped Bodi's hand more firmly and nodded yes.

The winds behind them howled. The doors to the building rattled against their hinges. The clouds before them spun wildly, throwing off lightning. Chase tasted metal in the air.

Ratha held her arms up and, without warning, dove headfirst into the broiling, dark storm that lay before them.

Chase shouted after her, but his voice was drowned out by the raging wind. Bodi buried her face in his robe. For a moment, he panicked, thinking that Ratha had left them. It was not beyond his imagination.

But then, like a missile shooting up through the clouds, a giant bird burst through the storm and circled high above them. She was beautiful in her transformation: sleek and black and powerful, with her talons fully extended.

"RATHA!" Chase cheered into the wind.

He clutched Bodi to his chest just as the bird swooped down and caught them in her talons. Her wings pushed against the air and they hovered for a moment, and then, with a stomach-lurching jolt, dove straight down.

Chase felt the pressure slap his cheeks back. This was unlike any flying he had experienced before—in his dreams, or with Calyphor and Deruda. This was more akin to falling straight down, like he had jumped out of a plane without a parachute. He clamped his lips shut so he wouldn't choke on all the air being forced into his mouth.

Bodi clung to him, terrified, burying her face into his neck. He held on to her with everything he had. He closed his eyes, hoping he wouldn't lose consciousness and drop her.

The bird that was Ratha wrapped her talons around them, and pulled up just as they broke through the clouds. The mountain peaks of Varuna zoomed into focus as their velocity slowed. The eastern flank of the mountain range was already in darkness; its high peaks were covered with snow, while its skirt and feet were brown. Running through it, like a vast, tumbled white river, was the glacier where Evelyn and Seaborne had once fallen into a crevasse. From the air, Chase could see how expansive it truly was. Ratha dipped them lower, then, catching an air current, swooped them back up, flying over the lower peaks that marched south and west.

As they flew south, a bitter taste hung in the air. It was familiar to Chase from his dreams. Soon enough he realized what it was: ashes. The taste of Melor burning. He twisted his head to the right. A blanket of thick smoke lay over Melor, hiding what lay beneath from view. Knox, Teddy, and his mom could be out there somewhere. And Seaborne and Calla. Every instinct told him it was where he should be headed—but Ratha's wings thwacked and thumped the air, flying south with determination. Soon he saw the shining disc of Lake Voss, turning from dark purple to silver as the sun descended.

Captain Nate's words rang in his ears.

*Take care of what's in front of you.*

He turned his sights beyond the lake, and set them on the still-green jungle canopy that lay beyond it.

✚    ✚    ✚

The warrior who was once called Louis kept his prisoner and guard on a steady pace, heading southeast through the remains of the Melorian forest. He saw little of his surroundings, content only when they were moving. It was lucky for them all to be traveling with a Keeper. Rothermel's stamina was not dependent on a steady supply of firewater—as theirs was—or food, which was nowhere to be found. The Keeper's strength came from within, or perhaps from the stone that was so carefully wrapped in a *tehuantl* pelt. Dankar had told him to be careful handling it, and not to touch it directly.

The belt was a different thing altogether, and Louis grew increasingly aware of its heft as they marched. The belt was cool and smooth on his shoulder, and its amber-colored buckle seemed to glow despite the permanent smoke-filled dusk of the forest. His right hand, the defective one, often found its way toward the buckle.

The smoke was an unanticipated hazard—one they had not prepared for. It lingered along the ground at eye level and was thick and bitter-tasting. It made it hard to breathe and slowed their progress. Only Rothermel seemed unaffected.

As night fell, Louis contemplated retreating underground, to the tunnels, but he had never traveled them in Melor, and even in Exor they had made him uncomfortable. He preferred being able to see what lay ahead. What they gained in speed, they would lose in their ability to defend themselves out in the open. Who knew what lurked in the tunnels of Melor? The idea of living underground, away from the life-sustaining warmth of the sun, seemed like a nightmare to him. Although, to be truthful, nightmares and dreams had both left him. Since his transformation, sleep was just a blank space of emptiness that he and his fellow Exorians fell into for short periods of time. He had the sense that at one point the experience had been different, but he could not remember enough of it to say how. Instead, it was the firewater that refreshed his spirit now. Sleep was merely a physical necessity.

He and his troops drove Rothermel hard, passing over the Vossbeck and most of Melor through the night. As they marched, the ground grew mossier and damp. It became a burden to trudge through, yet they persisted. Each step took them closer to their prize. By the end of this day, they would finally be in Metria. Another day's march and, barring any serious skirmishes, they would soon be within sight of the city itself, ready to welcome Dankar and present him with their prisoner and his mighty gift.

✛      ✛      ✛

The Exorian grimaced, his mottled skin twitching, as Evelyn made him swallow another mouthful of the potion. She poured some on a broad sponge and used it to wipe the cracked areas on his arms and chest. He beat his chained wrists against the cavern wall with each of her strokes. They all did. Evelyn hadn't wanted to keep the prisoners shackled, but Hesam had made her do it for her own protection. Hesam had recently arrived on her ship, now at anchor in the bay just outside the lagoon. Everyone else had been relieved of their duties and told to return to the city. Evelyn and Hesam were left alone to effect the cure. It was safer that way. No one had any idea if—or how—it would work.

Evelyn had spent two days dunking the stone of Metria into different vats of water, then feeding the treated water to the Exorian prisoners and bathing them in it. So far, she could see no difference in their appearance or attitude.

"What do I do now, Rysta?" she whispered to herself, watching the Exorian before her. Both she and Hesam agreed that the prisoners were calmer, but maybe that had nothing to do with the treatment. They hardly spoke, and ate very little.

They were, however, always thirsty. At first they hadn't liked the treated water, but now they seemed to be tolerating it well, asking for it, even. The sponge baths were another story. Evelyn hoped that their skin would react to them soon, maybe even soften and start to look more human.

"It won't matter much if their minds aren't changed," Hesam had remarked.

"I guess not, but it would show us that it's working. Maybe it just takes time."

"How much time?"

Hesam was itching to get back to the city. Scouts brought word of what was happening, but only rarely. Exorians had made their way to the southern shore of the Hestredes, below the city. They were making large encampments there.

The Metrians used the cover of night to move all the boats to the main harbor, which faced east, directly out to sea. They removed any piers or pilings in the river that could be used by the Exorians to gain entry, and stockpiled the rubble along the southern wall.

It was evident that Melor had been overrun by the sheer number of Exorians amassing on the shore. Dankar had emptied Exor—or so it seemed. It appeared now that the skirmishes in the north had been a decoy to allow the Exorians time to move south.

This was helpful to Evelyn's plan, since, for the time being, she and Hesam were free to conduct their experiment. But time was running out. Already a scout had brought them news of a band of Exorians that had been seen moving into Metria near the southern border of Lake Voss. They were following the path she and the Thompson boys had taken on horseback the first time she had come to Metria, and would be near the caverns in two moonrises.

Both she and Hesam were worried about the safety of the stone of Metria. Now that Evelyn had it in her possession, she knew it was up to her to keep it away from the Exorians as best she could.

But she also needed to use it. If she could cure the Exorians, then she could use them to convince the others to drink the antidote. She couldn't imagine that any of them actually *wanted* to be what Dankar had turned them into.

She dipped the sponge back into the bowl of water, and moved on to the next prisoner, repeating the treatment. She would do this thirty more times this evening—once for each remaining prisoner—until every prisoner had been soaked in the healing water. Then she would go back to the gathering room she had once shared with the Thompson boys, light a candle, and make more of the cure. Once she had enough of the treated water to perform a day's worth of treatments, she would wrap the stone and hide it in the bow of the small dory that Hesam kept hidden and well-stocked. If they were attacked, it would be up to her to take the boat out into the river and throw the stone of Metria overboard. It wasn't ideal, but it was the best plan they could think of.

Evelyn spoke gently to her prisoners as she bathed them, apologizing for any pain she was causing. When the last warrior had been soaked in water, she left them. As a group, the Exorians were grim and silent, their dark eyes and closed expressions revealing little.

Tomorrow at sunrise she would start again, treating the prisoners three times a day, and she would keep doing it until they were cured, or she was captured—whichever came first.

*Chapter Sixteen*

# ECHOES

Chase lay with his eyes closed in the cave by the Voss where he and Captain Nate had first encountered Ratha together—and almost died. Bodi lay beside him, asleep, wrapped tightly in Chase's Varunan fur-and-feather robe. Since they had left the mountain range, he had not needed its warmth, but Bodi was different. She was cold in these parts. Chase could feel her breath rising up and down through the robe. He was surprised to admit to himself that he was happy she had come with him. He was grateful for the company—plus, he would not have liked to think of her all by herself in Varuna.

As for Ratha herself, Chase had no idea where she was now. She had deposited him and Bodi on the edge of the lake, releasing them from her talons and then shooting up into the sky. When he had next seen her, she was back in her human form, washing her hands in the lake. Chase thought he had seen blood, and wondered if she had decided to visit the Exorians they had heard about from Captain Nate. He could only imagine how shocked they would have been to be swooped down on and picked up by a giant, black bird. Chase thought about those powerful talons, and shivered. Even Exorian hides would not be thick enough if she had used them as weapons. He decided not to ask.

He and Bodi had made a quick meal from the supplies he had packed in Varuna. Ratha did not join them, but instead stood quietly watching the water as they ate. It occurred to Chase that he had never seen her eat. Perhaps she lived on air. At some point in the night, she had left them again, with no word of where she might be going.

Chase could not sleep, so instead he used a trick that Ratha had shown him, a kind of half-sleep where you let your mind wander wherever it wants to go, without judgment or direction. She called it *reverie*.

His mind took a path into the caverns in Metria, where he and Evelyn and Knox had spent such a relaxed time under Rysta's care. He saw the wall of water cascading into the lagoon; he heard the dip of the oars as they rowed, turning over the phosphorescence so the water was as starry as the sky. Memories. There was Evelyn, smiling at him in her new Metrian clothes, a sparkling diadem on her forehead. The gathering room at night, flickering in the candlelight. The image deepened. His mind dropped further, on the edge of sleep. The orange glow of the cavern wall grew brighter and he began to lose consciousness, into real sleep.

A man's scream made him sit bolt upright. He opened his eyes, but the dream-vision remained, as if he were watching a screen that could not be turned off. There was another scream and a banging of metal against rock. He heard Evelyn's voice, soothing and comforting. His mental vision sharpened and he saw the gathering room anew: bare and cold, with a single candle lit on the low table beside an assortment of water pitchers. He saw Evelyn enter the room, weary and frightened-looking. She was carrying something—something valuable, by the way she was holding it. She did not linger in the gathering room, but picked up a pitcher and headed in the direction of the bathing area.

He watched her retreating back with a growing sense of foreboding. Something was happening, or about to happen. He tried to warn her, but couldn't speak. And then, in a flash, the vision shifted.

An Exorian warrior stood on top of the ledge above the caverns, looking down at the shadowy bay from the same ledge that he and Knox and Evelyn used to jump from during their time together in Metria. This warrior had blue eyes and a human-looking hand. It was Louis—his uncle Edward. And beside him, to Chase's dismay, was a bound-and-shackled Rothermel watching a host of Exorian warriors, their spears ignited, advancing on the cavern. Just below them, nestled in a crook of the bay, lay Hesam's ship.

Chase watched the scene with rising panic. He saw no sign of any other Metrians. If Evelyn had sailed Hesam's ship there all by herself, she would certainly be captured—or slaughtered. He forced the panic down and willed himself to stay with the vision, flying out over the bay with his awareness, snaking it into the cavern and the gathering room, through the hall and into the bathing room, where he saw Evelyn kneeling by the water, placing something into the tub. He called out to her, repeating the same phrase.

*Get out, Evelyn! They're coming!*

Evelyn's back stiffened.

Had she heard him?

"I see her, too," said Ratha, from somewhere behind him. Her voice reeled him out of the vision and back into the cave at the Voss.

"We have to get to the caverns in Metria!" he gasped, trying to rise and get his footing. He was dizzy and disoriented by how quickly he had shifted from one place to another, like getting off a ride at an amusement park.

"I know—"

"*What?*" cried Chase. He did not like her tone.

"It is the stone of Metria. Evelyn has it. My sister must have given it to her. It is the only way a Keeper can truly pass on their stone—as a gift. But she is inexperienced. The blue-eyed warrior will take it from her. We cannot let that happen."

"I have to warn her!"

"It is too late. These things we have seen, they are occurring as we speak."

She moved out into the open mouth of the cave. Beyond her, a shrouded half-moon hung low in the sky. The lake was calm and glowed faintly silver. Not a breath of air stirred in the cave. For a moment, all was deathly silent.

"Even if Caspar returns with the Fifth Stone, it is too late now. Tonight will be the last night we shall know Ayda as she has been. By tomorrow, Dankar will have three stones in his possession, and the power of Varuna will not be enough to sustain the balance."

Chase remembered a vision he had seen in what felt like a long time ago: an army of Exorians marching toward them, setting ablaze everything in their path, led by a pillar of fire.

"It gets worse, Chase," she said to him, in mindspeak. "Dankar will destroy us—and then he will set his sights—and his warriors—on your lands. *Your* home. My father foresaw this. It is why he created the four stones in the first place, and sent the Fifth Stone away. He knew that the day would come when Ayda might fall. It is a day I have spent much of my life trying to avoid. It is why I brought you all here in the first place. I thought I could change our destiny.

"But it is not in my power anymore, Chase. Ayda is finished. The next battle will be for your world. I only pray that your kind has the strength to fight it."

Chase hung his head. It all felt too big. What was he supposed to do now? He'd always believed Ratha could beat Dankar. She was the most powerful Keeper on Ayda—but he hadn't taken into account that she could be weakened. Maybe it really *was* over.

He went to stand beside Ratha. The lake spread before him, calm, and as unchanged as the first day he had seen it. How often had he felt hopeless since they'd first come to Ayda? All the way back to the beginning, he realized. When they first saw the cliffs below Seaborne's cabin, those great sucking mouths of water pulling them in. He had believed at that moment that they would all die.

But they hadn't. Frankie had been kidnapped and Teddy almost drowned. Ratha had almost killed him in this very cave. He had crossed over the Exorian desert, first with Captain Nate, and again, with Knox and Evelyn; they had fought back an army of Exorians in the arena and escaped from under Dankar's nose. They weren't hopeless. They just had to keep going. Ratha had to keep going.

He turned to face her.

"Dankar hasn't won yet. Evelyn won't give up the stone of Metria. I know her. She may be inexperienced, but she's smart, and she's tough. She would never give it up, so we aren't going to give up on her—"

"You have a soul connection with this girl, do you not?" asked Ratha.

The memory of Evelyn's wide brown eyes flashed at him.

"I do."

Ratha was silent. A loaded silence. Chase wondered if she had seen something more that she was not telling him.

"Don't give up," he pleaded with her in mindspeak. "Fight for us. Fight for Ayda—"

He was interrupted by a scuttling sound outside the cave. Running feet, moving fast across the beach, getting closer. Could they be Exorians?

"Go," said Ratha, retreating toward the cave, and Bodi.

Chase reached for his sword.

+ + +

Evelyn knelt over a deep basin filled with water from the sunken tub where Chase, Knox, and Teddy used to bathe. Her attention remained wholly focused on the stone of Metria, which she held submerged beneath the surface of the water with both hands. The pull of energy that the stone emitted was like a magnet drawing her own daylights to the surface. She could feel them rising, answering the call of the stone. Her skin grew translucent; the golden web of the daylights made itself visible beneath her skin, and then, as the two streams of energy met, she felt a wave of contentedness, and the same liquid calm she felt in Rysta's enclosure.

The stone began to glow, its cracks and seams glittering from within. The water shimmered in the basin, blue and purple as if lit by the moon. She held the stone in the water for several minutes, allowing its essence to wash through her, flooding her with a sense of blankness. Peace.

When she judged it had been immersed long enough, she lifted the stone from the water and wrapped it in a hammock of Metrian scarves. The waters in the basin continued to glow. She got busy filling and stoppering bottles for tomorrow's treatments. After all, if she felt this way when her daylights communed with the stone of Metria, then maybe, with time, the treatments would have a similar effect on the Exorians. It was proving harder than she had anticipated.

*Maybe I'm not strong enough*, she thought to herself.

A sudden gust of wind came into the small room through the crack in the rock face that served as a window. The candle at the side of the tub flickered. She heard a voice say clearly: *Get out!*

Evelyn whipped around, looking for the source.

*They're coming!* the voice said again, clearly. This time she knew who it came from. Chase. A warning. From Varuna.

*Get out, Evelyn!*

Evelyn grabbed the stone of Metria and the bottles of treated water and stuffed them in her robes. She raced into the hall and through the gathering room, snuffing out candles as she went. She had to find Hesam and make it to the beach where they had stashed the dory. She heard heavy footsteps above her, and realized that the intruders—Exorians, no doubt—were on the roof of the cavern itself.

She heard several *thwacks* outside the larger openings in the rock face of the cliff. Exorians were lowering themselves from the ledge along the outside of the cavern walls, toward the windows. They would be inside any second now.

She sprinted through the narrow hallway, using memory to guide her in the dark. There was no sign of Hesam and no time to look for her. She made straight for the beach and the dory they had prepared for escape. As she crossed the few open yards, a robed figure rushed out from the shadows.

"Hesam!" she yelped in surprise and relief.

Hesam put her finger to her lips, and gestured for Evelyn to get in the dory; then she pushed it out into the lagoon.

"Row out to the cavern entrance and wait for me there," she whispered.

Evelyn did as she was told. Beyond the mouth of the cavern, the bay was dark and quiet, lit only by the dim glow of a rising half-moon.

Evelyn held her breath. She heard the steady stroke of a paddle, and soon Hesam was beside her in another dory.

"We need to change course—the stone is too important. You must get it to safety. I'll lead the Exorians as far away as I can. When it's safe, take your dory up the Hestredes and into Varuna. Get the stone to Ratha. She will know what to do."

Hesam plunged the paddle into the water. Her dory lurched ahead into the narrowing mouth of the cavern, its bow pointed toward her ship.

"Wait!" cried Evelyn, forgetting about the echo in the cavern. Her own voice came back at her, high and terrified.

*Wait . . . wait . . . wait.*

Shouts came from beach. A few torches burst into flame, shedding more light across the water.

Hesam stopped. Evelyn came up beside her. Their only protection now was the darkness of the mouth of the cavern, and the water.

"What about taking the stone and throwing it in the river?"

Hesam shook her head. "We need the stone if we are ever going to have a chance at rebalancing the daylights. We can't throw it away. We must get it to Ratha."

"But . . . the Fifth Stone. It'll be here soon—"

Somewhere behind them, they heard the whistle of a spear, and then a splash.

"GO! Hide yourself!"

Hesam took a few strokes and separated from Evelyn, moving through the mouth toward the bay.

"We will see each other again someday, if the daylights are willing."

The Exorians were lighting their torches and fussing with the remaining dories stored on the beach, readying themselves to go after them. They were clumsy and inexperienced, and Evelyn had time to paddle back into the lagoon and cross along the far reaches. She passed into Rysta's enclosure before they could give chase.

Once she was safely there, she heard Hesam yell.

"You!!" The echo repeated and repeated. "Who goes there!"

Hesam's shout echoed throughout the cavern.

*There . . . there . . . there.*

Evelyn dug in with her oar and did not look back. By the sounds of shouting and grunting on the beach, the Exorians were shoving the leftover dories into the water and going after Hesam, who was paddling with all her strength toward the bay and her ship. With any luck, they would not notice Evelyn at all.

Evelyn stowed her paddle, trying not to make a sound. The voices inside the cavern were moving out. Hesam must have led them into the bay. She thought about what Hesam had said at their parting as she looked up at the open sky, grateful for the dark night and smallish moon. She would very much like to see Hesam again.

Evelyn floated in silence under the shadowed sky. Rysta's island was a darker hump a few yards to her left. Whatever undercurrents there were in the lagoon began to slowly pull her toward it. Her heartbeat began to even out, and with a greater sense of calm came another feeling: She realized how terribly vulnerable she was. She wondered how long she should wait.

A distant shouting brought back her alarm. She strained her ears. Reflections from a blaze of torches flickered along the cavern wall behind her. She could hear the dip and splash of several paddles approaching. The Exorians were coming back—and this time they were coming back for her.

In a split second, Evelyn decided to stash the dory and head for the tunnel beneath Rysta's pool. With any luck, she could put some distance between her and the Exorians before they discovered it.

She might be alone and vulnerable, but she had to protect the stone of Metria. Rysta had given it to *her*. Evelyn hastily stowed the dory on the beach, hiding it as best she could under the bushes, and sprinted for the tunnel.

It was up to her now.

# Chapter Seventeen

# LOSSES

"They are too light and regular to be Exorians—unless it's a trick," Chase called back to Ratha.

She reemerged from the cave and cocked her head in that strange, birdlike way she had. Her shoulders softened, and she gestured to the sword. "You will not need that."

A band of people traveled swiftly, single file, down the beach. There were two in the lead, one carrying a large load on his back. And some yards behind them, eight more, and then some yards farther, two more—a slower runner being urged on by a young Melorian. And behind them all ran two extraordinarily large hounds.

Chase grinned so hard his face hurt. He would recognize that loping stride of Knox's anywhere.

✦ ✦ ✦

"It's so good to see you, Mom," said Chase, from the depths of her enormous hug. She smelled uncharacteristically like woodsmoke, sweat, and dirty fur, but underneath it was her own mom smell. Like grass and lemons. He would recognize it anywhere.

He smiled at Knox from over her shoulder.

Knox held up his palm, fingers splayed.

"Yo, bro."

Chase laughed and met it with his own, before his mom buried him in another hug.

She held him close, then pushed him away so she could look at him, then grabbed him close again. He was sinew and bone beneath a layer of feather and fur.

"You're so tall," she murmured. "How is your asthma?"

"There's no such thing on Ayda, Mom," he laughed. His purple eyes were shining at her.

Teddy pushed between them and suctioned himself to Chase's waist.

"Hi, Tedders. You've grown, too. " Chase pulled back the Melorian hood and ruffled his little brother's hair.

"Chantarelle brought Mom and me back to Ayda through the tunnels. I missed you and Knox. We came to find you."

"I missed you, too, Ted—and I knew you were here. I saw you both in the tunnels. I'm fine. I've been with Ratha in Varuna."

He looked around for her so he could introduce her, but the Keeper had vanished.

"Knox told us. He told us everything."

Chase cocked an eyebrow at Knox.

"Everything?"

"Yeah, Mom knows," Knox said. "She saw Louis—er, Edward—herself. Let me tell you, that guy has turned into the world's biggest jerk."

"It's not really his fault," said Chase, thinking back to the arena. Dankar had made Louis drink firewater, which had never before been drunk by an outlier.

"Yeah, maybe," said Knox, "but he's taken to it just fine. Being a murderous Exorian loser is right up his alley." He shot a look at his mother. "Sorry, Mom, but it's true."

"I can't believe that's really him," said Grace, shaking her head. "The Edward I remember was funny and kind—"

"That's not Edward." Knox cut her off. "Edward's dead. That's just some freak in a firewater suit."

Grace's face fell.

"Kind of harsh, Knox," said Chase, thinking of the conversation he'd had with Ratha, back at the aerie, when they both looked out the window of his room at the sunrise. "He's not all gone, Mom," he explained. "Somewhere underneath it all, he hasn't changed. It's just that his daylights are messed up."

Grace gave him a little smile.

"Well, at least we're all together again."

"Yeah—barely. That was a close scrape," said Knox. He quickly filled his brother in on what had happened in the Keep.

As he was talking, a small voice called to Chase from the mouth of the cave. It was Bodi. She had woken up with all the excitement.

"It's okay, Bodi. They're Melorians. And this is my mom and my other brother, Teddy."

Bodi came out into the open, dragging Chase's fur-and-feather robe behind her.

"Bodi! How did you get here?" Knox cried, holding up his palm in greeting. He took in her outfit with an amused look. "And what the heck are you wearing? A bearskin?"

"It's a long story," Chase cut in, not wanting to talk about Ratha's giant bird alter ego. It was a new feeling, but he felt protective of Ratha now. He didn't want to reveal her secrets unnecessarily.

Seaborne and Calla watched as Bodi dragged herself and the robe to where Knox was standing. Chase could read their baleful expressions: Here was yet another child to keep alive.

"How's Dad?" he asked his mother.

She shook her head. "I don't know. I didn't have time to tell him anything. Teddy and I just followed your trail through the cave in the woods and into the tunnels."

"Trail?" Chase shot a questioning look at Knox.

"The pinecones," said Grace. "We found one of your necklaces on a branch outside the cave, and then there was a trail of pinecones that went pretty far into the tunnels. Teddy was sure it was yours."

Knox shook his head. "That was Evelyn."

Chase smiled to himself. It was just like Evelyn to think ahead like that.

"Either way, we found it, and we just . . . left. No chance to get Dad, or let him know. At the time, all I could think of was you boys. I just wanted to find you. I thought I would go crazy if I didn't. It wasn't until we were lost in the tunnels that I thought about Dad . . . " Her voice trailed off. She paused a moment, then continued.

"When Chantarelle left us here, I asked him to go back, to get word to Dad, but whether or not he did is anyone's guess. I—I feel so terrible about it."

The look on her face was so guilt-stricken that Chase felt compelled to weigh in.

"It's okay, Mom. I bet Chantarelle told him," he said, but even as he spoke, he doubted it was true. "Even if he didn't, he's with Frankie."

"Yeah," Knox nodded his head. "He's probably showing all the doctors his weird lab stuff at the hospital. Maybe he's cured Frankie with it."

Grace brightened a little. "I didn't think of that."

"Plus," said Knox, "can you imagine Dad *here*?" He waved his arms, taking in the ragtag Melorians, the vast lake, the empty cave. "He's better off at home."

"Or better off than we are right now," agreed Chase.

"Well, that's not saying much," said Seaborne, who had been listening. "He must be frantic with worry."

"I'm sure—but what can we do about it?"

"That is the question of the moment, isn't it?" said a high, eerie voice. It was Ratha, coming toward them. "What to do."

It had the effect on the Melorians of a cold shower.

Axl and Tar whined.

"Tell them, Chase. Tell them what we have seen," she commanded.

Chase related his vision of Evelyn in Metria.

Seaborne fiddled with his sword and began to pace.

"This *is* a fine kettle of fish," he ranted. "That abomination of Dankar's on the loose with the stone of Melor, and the stone of Metria with no one but Evelyn to fend off a pack of Exorians. I'd say our goose is fairly well cooked, wouldn't you? We might as well go to Metria and have it eaten." He stopped directly in front of Calla. "I am sorry to have brought you to this."

Ratha followed him with her colorless eyes as she spoke to Chase in mindspeak.

"I have contemplated your words and found them sound. All is not lost until it is lost. I wish for you to go with these Melorians into Metria. Find Evelyn and my brother. Bring them and their stones to me—if you can."

"And if we can't?" Chase asked, also in mindspeak.

"Do your best. I will do what is possible from here. We are all Aydans now, and I will use whatever power remains in Varuna against our enemy."

"Where will you go?"

"That is not your concern. But be assured: I will not desert you. I promise you this, and I never break promises."

✢     ✢     ✢

They left the cave—and Ratha—before daybreak and headed straight south. Axl and Tar took the lead, scouting their path.

Chase and Knox had tried to convince their mother to stay in Varuna, with Teddy and Bodi, under Ratha's protection, but there was no arguing with her.

"We go where you go," she stated. "I won't lose you again."

"Okay, Mom. Just don't get mad at me if I have to kill somebody," grumbled Knox.

"Knox," his mom admonished, more out of habit than feeling.

"Seriously, Mom? Do you know what we do here?" He whipped out one of his throwing knives. "I can't wait to bust some heads, so you'd better prepare yourself." He sprinted ahead to catch up with Seaborne, Calla, and Teddy.

Chase kept pace alongside his mother, with Bodi on his back.

"Knox is in his element here, isn't he?" said Grace wistfully, watching as her middle son raced down the lakeshore, trying to beat Axl and Tar. "You are all so changed. It's like you are all grown up already. Even Teddy seems older."

"It's the daylights. Ours have spoken to us," agreed Chase. He noticed that she did not mention her brother. He wondered what she was feeling. What if Knox disappeared one day and he didn't see him again for thirty years, and then, when he did, Knox was a raging lunatic, bent on burning everything and everyone. Chase shook his head. He'd want to kill him. Is *that* what his mother was feeling?

"Mom, I don't know if Knox told you, but Uncle Edward—Louis, that's how we know him—saved our lives once. He was a really good guy before Dankar changed him."

"I'd like to believe it. I only have one brother, and it feels like he's still lost. You said it was his daylights. Mara told me about them, but I'd like to hear you describe them. You are a Varunan, correct? What does that mean?"

Chase struggled to answer.

"It's hard to describe. It's like things just click into place—and it all just flows easily, and then you find yourself doing stuff you never thought you could do, but it's not a surprise. It's like it was always there, just waiting for you to tap into it."

He scooched Bodi up on his back. "Have you felt anything yet, Mom?"

Grace paused for a moment. "I'm not sure. Maybe. Back in the Keep when Ed—," she corrected herself, "—Louis had your brother, I thought I could fight all of the Exorians bare-handed."

Chase clapped a bemused hand on her shoulder.

"I'm glad you didn't. One thing Seaborne always says about the daylights: You'll know them when you feel them."

"I look forward to it . . ." Her voice trailed off, and then she added, "I am happiest being your mom. Is that my daylights speaking?"

"I don't know. Maybe."

They walked on in silence for a while. And then, Grace began to talk. She told him how Knox and Seaborne had found her and Teddy in Melor, after they had crawled up from the tunnels. She told him about Mara. He could tell that, despite what she may think, his mother was also changed—stronger from her time on Ayda. Her stride was long and energetic, her eyes bright.

Bodi remained very quiet. Occasionally, Grace would pat Bodi on the back as she spoke to Chase. It was an unconscious, motherly gesture. Bodi did not openly respond, but suddenly Chase felt a damp spot between his shoulder blades. He stopped mid-stride and shifted her to the front so he could look at her.

"Oh, my," said Grace, seeing Bodi's tearstained face.

"Dankar killed her brother, Mom, and put her mother in the dungeons. He would have done the same to her if she hadn't run away."

Grace held out her arms in Bodi's direction. To Chase's surprise, Bodi dove straight into them. No shyness or fear. Maybe his mother did have some kind of mom-daylight thing going on.

"It's okay now," she soothed, hugging Bodi close. "I'll take care of you. I lost my brother, too, and I am not going to let anything else happen to you."

Chase wanted to tell her not to make promises like that on Ayda, but a low hooting from Teddy at the front told him they were passing the border into Metria. He pulled his sword from the scabbard and closed his eyes, reaching out with his awareness. He tried to catch a glimpse—a fragment, even—of what might lie ahead, but his mind remained as dark as the path before them.

"Stay close," he whispered.

"Always," she whispered back, lowering Bodi to the ground and taking a firm grip on the girl's hand.

✛    ✛    ✛

They reached the caverns at daybreak. The sun rose, pale and washed out, slowly gaining height in a gray sky. A low mist lay on the river. Seaborne, Calla, Knox, and the hounds took point, leading their small tribe down and across the shoreline toward the beach that lay across the bay from the cavern's main entrance. It was impossible to know what lay inside the cavern, and they did not want to walk into a trap. The mist shrouded the entrance, and the dim silhouette of Hesam's ship was barely visible.

Evidence of the giant turtles was everywhere—shallow bowls in the sand, trenches that led to the water—but no turtles themselves. Axl and Tar nosed their snouts into the sand, delighted by the strange new scents.

The beach was deserted. Seaborne and Calla set out to check the area. Grace and the remaining Melorians stood watch.

Teddy sighed.

"I wish Bob were here. He would like this beach."

Knox bustled up to him, brimming with a secret.

"You think so?"

"Yeah, it's, like, his place," said Teddy. "It's where turtles live." Then his face fell. "I feel bad I brought him here. He'd still be alive if I had left him at home."

"Don't feel too bad, Tedders," said Knox, his mouth ticking up. He reached inside his fur poncho and pulled out Bob, with a flourish.

"I went back to get him on the wall before we left the Keep. I didn't expect him to be there, but he was, all tucked up tight in his shell. The Exorians probably thought he was some strange rock."

Teddy grabbed Bob by his shell. It was shut tight as a drum.

"He's there all right! Do you think he's alive?"

"I don't know," said Knox. "Maybe."

"Bob! Come out," Teddy coaxed, lifting the shell up to his mouth.

Chase joined his brothers, Bodi at his side, and saw what they were doing. He examined the shell, then gave it back to Teddy.

"Even if he is alive, he might not want to come out, Ted. Why come out when everything here is so bad?"

Teddy frowned. He put his mouth up to the shell again.

"Bob, please. Come out. It's Teddy. Everything's okay."

Nothing happened.

"He's probably dead," said Teddy, stricken.

"Can I see?" asked Bodi, reaching for the shell.

Teddy pulled back, clearly reluctant to let Bob go to some stranger.

"There's a creature in there?" she asked.

He nodded. "Yeah, he's kind of like a lizard, but with a shell. And he can swim."

Bodi's eyes widened. "A lizard with a shell?"

"Yes," Teddy said, gratified by her amazement. "His name is Bob. He's really cool and brave, but he's little compared to the other turtles that live here. And he's slow. He mostly likes to get his feet and shell wet and then sunbathe."

"A lizard that swims; I can't even imagine such a thing," Bodi said, eyes wide.

"You can look at him, but be careful," he admonished. "Just don't drop him."

She examined Bob's shell gently and stroked its hard surface and white underbelly. Then, she traced with her eyes the trails that led across the sand, saying, "His kin have gone to the water. Maybe he would like the same? Maybe he would come out if he could feel the water."

"You know, that's not a bad idea," said Knox.

"Try it, Ted," said Chase.

Teddy crossed the few yards of beach to where it met the lapping waters. He knelt in the shallow water and placed the turtle at the waterline. A few minutes went by. Bob stayed snug inside his little fortress.

Teddy moved the shell closer to the water, letting the river lap its edges. The motion rolled the shell over on its back. Teddy righted it. It rolled over again.

"Please don't be dead, Bob," said Teddy. He stroked the now-glistening shell. "You're safe now." He put the turtle back in the water, right side up.

One of the hounds barked loudly. An alarm bark. Not ten feet from shore, a giant turtle head had broken the surface of the river and was staring at him with its snake-like face.

Teddy lifted Bob up to look.

"See, Bob. A friend!"

Bob's head emerged suddenly from his shell, orange eyes blinking. He stretched out his neck and legs and arms.

"BOB!" Teddy hooted, and put him down on the beach. The turtle began a slow crawl into the water.

"All right!" crowed Knox. "I knew it! I knew that old turtle still had it in him!"

Teddy got on all fours, crawling beside Bob.

"Whaddya wanna do now, Bob? Find some food?"

Bob stretched out his neck again, and crawled deeper into the water.

The giant turtle sank silently below the surface. Then, with no warning, Bob dove under.

"Wait!" cried Teddy, in alarm. "Where you going, Bob?" He thrashed around in the water, trying to grab the turtle, and came up empty. He looked at his mother, bewildered.

"He's gone!"

Grace moved to comfort him, but Chase and Knox stopped her.

"He's where he belongs, Teddy. He'll be okay," said Knox. "He has a tribe here. They belong together. It'll be too hard for him where we are going."

Teddy looked down at the water, blinking back tears.

"But he's supposed to be with me," said Teddy. "He's *always* been with me. *I'm* his tribe." He stared out at the water for a moment. "I hope nobody eats him. He's so small compared to the other ones."

"Nobody'll eat Bob," said Chase. "He's too tough."

"Yeah," Knox agreed. "Besides, he has all those other big guys looking out for him. He's in a turtle posse now, Tedders. He's happy."

"Yeah, maybe you're right," said Teddy, but his voice sounded like he didn't believe it.

"I'm always right," said Knox.

Chase slugged him halfheartedly on the shoulder. "No, *I'm* always right."

"Well, I'm glad to see some things haven't changed," said their mother.

Chase smiled at her, then tensed. Out of the corner of his eye he saw Seaborne and Calla gesturing toward them.

"We gotta go. Something's up," he said, nodding to the Melorians down the beach.

They sprinted the quarter-mile or so and caught up to where Seaborne and Calla were standing. They were at a juncture where the jungle crowded into the shoreline and a shallow inlet had been created in the sand. A small dory was lodged against the opposite sandbank, and inside it was a hooded and robed figure, slumped over the paddle, an Exorian spear lodged in her back. The robes were the kind worn by Metrian women. The figure was not moving.

Chase swallowed hard. He had seen these robes before—in his vision of Evelyn the night before. Axl and Tar began to whimper.

"Oh, no," he breathed. "Evelyn."

Chase felt the sand beneath his feet turn to liquid. His head filled with recriminations: He should have done more to warn her. He should have paid more attention to what Ratha was trying to teach him. Heck, he should never have left Evelyn in the first place. It was all his fault.

Seaborne reached the dory and pulled the figure back off her paddle. He dislodged the spear and threw it on the ground, then he carried her across the inlet toward the others.

Chase closed his eyes. He couldn't bear to look.

"She's gone." Seaborne's voice broke.

Knox swore.

Calla turned away.

Seaborne pushed back the damp folds of the scarf covering the girl's face. He made an unintelligible sound.

"Who is it?" asked Grace.

Chase opened his eyes, surprised at his mother's question. He saw a familiar face, now white and cold.

"She was our friend," croaked Knox. "Her name was Hesam."

*Chapter Eighteen*

# DIFFERENT PATHS

Seaborne, Calla, Chase, and Knox and the rest of the Melorians did a quick search of the caverns, which were deserted. Empty shackles, burnt candles, and the remnants of a few meals were all that was left behind. To their relief, they saw no evidence of violence. Either Evelyn had escaped, or had been taken prisoner herself.

"How far ahead are they, do you think?" asked Chase.

Calla picked up a candle and sniffed the wick. "A day . . . maybe a little less."

"We have the two little ones," said Seaborne. "I don't see how we can catch up with them, even if we run."

"And my mom," added Chase.

"She's faster than you think," said Calla. "But I agree." She threw a loaded glance at Seaborne. To Chase, it felt like he had just witnessed a full conversation but heard nothing.

"What?"

"Your mother should stay here with Teddy and Bodi," said Calla. "It is the best plan, and the surest bet for their survival. Axl and Tar can stay with them for protection."

"How do you figure that?" cried Chase. "If we leave them here, they'll be defenseless. My mom can't protect them by herself! Who knows how many Exorians could still be coming through? Besides, Mom won't stay behind. I know it."

"She will if I say so, lad," said Seaborne, raising an eyebrow. His tone reminded Chase of how he had spoken to them their first day on Ayda.

Chase shook his head. "You don't know my mom—and anyway, she might be the only one who can get through to Louis, now that Dankar controls him. He might remember her. She is his sister, after all."

Seaborne was silent for a few moments, contemplating their next move. His eyes raked the confines of the cavern. Exorians had swept through here by the looks of it: turned-over pitchers and bowls of water, the pillows and bedding thrown to the floor as if they were looking for something. He spoke to Calla.

"I may be off my chump, but I think there has been enough division among us. I tend to agree with the boy. It is best that we stick together, no matter what may endanger us—"

"But—" Calla objected.

"We are in new territory now, Calla," said Seaborne, making a calming gesture. "The old ways were carried away by that blasted envoy of Exorians when they took our stone. Nothing is as it was, nor shall it be again. As for the little ones, their daylights have spoken. They are older than they look and have seen battle before. We cannot protect them any more than they can protect themselves. It has moved beyond us now." He lifted one of the shackles and let it drop. It clanked heavily against the rock wall. "Sadly, I cannot say what might have befallen Evelyn and the stone of Metria."

"I saw her here. I told you," said Chase.

"Well, she is not here now, that much is certain. She might have escaped—or she might have been captured. Either way, we have no way of knowing if she still has the stone. There are signs of a search here. Maybe she hid it."

They swiveled their heads around, as if the stone might magically appear somewhere in the room.

"What do you want to do?" asked Knox, finally.

Seaborne leaned against the wall. His long hair was curled into grizzled ringlets by the humidity. His eyes were sunken into his skull. He looked thin and exhausted. So did Calla. Her poncho hung on her shoulders like a shirt on a hanger, as if there was nothing of substance under it.

Chase kicked himself mentally for not feeding them all back in Varuna. He was so used to relying on Seaborne to take care of everything, it hadn't occurred to him to ask the Melorians if they needed anything. He wondered if there was still food in the holds of the cavern.

"Maybe we should eat?" he ventured.

"Aye, if we can find any provisions, we should do that at least." Seaborne's voice was weary. He inched his back down against the wall into a squatting position and hung his head. Calla moved to his side and laid her hand on the back of his head. They were quiet together for many minutes. When he next spoke, it was with grim resignation.

"We must follow the Exorians into the heart of Metria, and fight to regain anything we can. Rothermel is still out there." He reached up to squeeze Calla's hand and she pulled him up to standing. "But first we will see to Hesam."

�﹢   ✚   ✚

They buried her in a shallow grave by the inlet, using rocks and shells to dig. They covered her body with sand and drove a branch into the ground to mark the spot. Teddy spelled out HESAM in the sand with small, white river stones. Grace tied Hesam's scarf to the branch.

"I will return to do this properly, my friend," vowed Seaborne.

"Aren't we doing it properly?" asked Knox. He was coated in sweat from digging.

"Not for a Metrian," said Seaborne. "They are usually buried at sea. It is not right to leave her here like this. It is not where she belongs."

Calla pushed her hood back with a sandy hand.

"It is no shame to let her rest here for the time being. Should we live to see better days, I will come back with you to see that she is properly honored."

"So will I, Seaborne," said Teddy.

Seaborne chucked Teddy's chin and gave him a sad little smile.

"I will hold you to that, my lad. Did you know that Hesam and I met in Metria when I was not much taller than you? Back then she would race me up the Hestredes with nothing more than a floating log and a sheet." His eyes lit up with the memory. "She could harness the wind like Ratha herself."

As if on cue, a gust of wind picked up from behind them and caught the scarf that had been hanging limply on the branch. It lifted and fluttered in the breeze, like a blue-and-purple flag.

"Speak of the devil," Seaborne mumbled.

Grace was staring at the scarf, watching it billow in the wind. She turned on her heel, her eyes landing on Hesam's big sailing ship, lying dormant on its anchor in the bay. Her countenance changed.

"Seaborne, does that ship have a sail?"

"Aye, ma'am, it does—or did," said Seaborne, his eyes skipping from her to the ship and back, catching her drift. "And if it doesn't, I bet I could fashion one! I'm not such a bad deckhand, either, when all is said and done."

"What are you thinking, Mom?" asked Knox.

"I'm thinking that I didn't take all those years of sailing lessons in Fells Harbor for nothing. I'm thinking we should use that ship to take us all downriver. We are safer on the water, right?"

Knox's eyes widened, then he pumped his fist. "Yessss!" he shouted, and made for the dory that had washed up on the beach carrying Hesam's body. He could use it to ferry everyone—and the hounds—to the ship.

The Melorians and Bodi went aboard in shifts. Grace, Teddy, and Chase were last. As they waited on the beach, Grace studied the scarf marking Hesam's grave. It tugged and unfurled, then fell flat, then billowed out again with each shift in the wind. Her brow furrowed.

"Chase, your Keeper—she can control the wind?" Grace asked.

"Pretty much. Why?"

"When we hoist the sail, do whatever you need to do to get Ratha to give us a northwesterly wind the likes of which you've never seen before. Strong and steady. Okay? We want to go downriver: south and east."

"You bet, Mom. I'll try."

She crossed the few steps to where Teddy was standing, searching the bay with his eyes. She pulled him to her.

"Are you looking for Bob?"

He nodded, eyes welling.

Teddy, who had been so brave through the fight at the Keep—who had walked all the way to Varuna without complaining, watched his best friend Bob swim away, and seen Hesam get buried, all without crying—finally broke. He fell into his mother's arms and sobbed like the six-year-old boy he was.

Chase's heart hit the back of his throat watching. His brother was still so very young. He thought of his father. He wished now, more than ever, that they were all together again. He didn't know if this was selfish—there was a part of him that was grateful that his dad and Frankie were safe beyond the fog—all he knew was that he felt it. And suddenly, he was deeply homesick for Summerledge, for the summers they had had there as a family when no one knew anything about Ayda, or Uncle Edward's fate, or the fog. He'd had thirteen of them: blissful, ignorant, wonderful summers, where the worst part of a day was not getting to go out on the boat, or coming back from Secret Beach empty-handed. *Poor Teddy*, he thought to himself. *He's only going to remember this.* His next thought left him cold. *If he lives to remember any of it.*

✢     ✢     ✢

Evelyn plunged through the pitch-black tunnel, trying to stem her rising panic. She had no idea if she was headed in the right direction, and had no torch or lantern to help her navigate. So far, there were no signs she was being followed, but how long would that last? And how was she supposed to get to Varuna from here? As far as she knew, this tunnel only went one way: to the city of Metria.

She slowed her pace, worried she might fall and break something in the dark.

Hesam had told her she must go to Varuna—but how? Should she wait here and then go back to the cavern? Try to find her dory? How long would she have to wait? The darkness pressed in on her, bringing back all the old fears. She heard a rumbling above her and cried out. But was it real? Or was her mind playing tricks on her in the dark? How she hated being underground!

She laid down the bundle she was carrying and tried to catch her breath. She had to calm down and think. She tried not to imagine the walls around her caving in and burying her alive. She thought about Chantarelle. He *lived* down here; surely, she could make it through a swift journey.

She remembered the last time she felt this way, on the journey back to Ayda with Knox when she had passed out in the tunnel. Knox had dragged her all the way to an underground lake. When she had woken up, Chantarelle had been there. He had shown her how to sense her own daylights and find her courage.

She pictured the little man's face. His earth-colored skin and gray and green clothing. She had known instantly that he was a world-walker, known to her from the stories her mother had told her when she was very little.

In those stories, there were three worlds: the one that humans lived in; the one where souls and gods lived; and one in between, where humankind and gods could meet. Many of the stories she was told as a child were about those who could visit this in-between world. Chantarelle was such a creature—not a god, not the soul of a dead person, and not a human, but something else. A world-walker.

Sometimes, Evelyn knew from what her mother had told her, if a human was very special, or if they were very sick, or they had suffered a terrible shock, he or she would be called to the in-between world and see and hear things that no normal human was allowed to witness. They might see the future, or talk to the dead, or learn a great truth. When they returned to the human world, they were never the same. They were called priests or shamans, and revered, or they were called crazy, and persecuted. And Evelyn knew—beyond a shadow of a doubt—that these worlds existed. Frankie had spoken to her from this in-between place, and Rysta had been there with her before she had fragmented.

Evelyn comforted herself, imagining a healthy and happy Frankie and Gran Fanny sitting in the living room in Fells Harbor, surrounded by her grandmother's collection of found treasures. Maybe they would be playing cards on the squeaky old card table, or Monopoly. Or maybe they would be watching TV. For all she knew, they could be there right now, talking about her. How much they missed her. How much they loved her. How happy they would be when they were all together again.

Evelyn could almost *feel* herself there, in some wonderful future time. The room would be warm and cozy. Her grandmother would laugh in that way that made everyone join in. They would drink hot tea with milk and honey, and everything bad and scary that had happened would be forgotten. She smiled in the dark at her future, happy self.

And then, as if brought to the surface by her thoughts, she became aware of her daylights. Her arms were glowing, the arteries and veins becoming visible like amber-lit meridians. The glow spilled from her hands into the surrounding blackness, creating an aura that surrounded her and spread out several feet, taking in the bundle on the ground. As the glow touched it, the stone hidden inside also began to glow, as it did underwater in the bath. Aboveground, the light it shed was more like moonlight: a silvery, lavender radiance.

Evelyn lifted the stone from its folds of fabric and held it in front of her. The tunnel revealed itself before her. The light pulled her forward, beckoning her to follow, to Metria. She took a deep breath. It was not what Hesam had told her to do, but it was what her daylights were insisting upon. She had never felt so certain of anything before. All her fear dissipated, and she knew what she had to do.

"Okay, then," she breathed. She locked her fingers around the stone, took one last glance backwards into the pitch black behind her. "Lead the way."

# Chapter Nineteen

# COMPROMISE

The jungle was harder to burn than Louis had expected. It didn't help that the Keeper under his control just smirked at the efforts of the Exorians—their numbers now healthy, expanded by the thirty captives they had freed—to set it alight. The vegetation that crowded around them like a hostile web seemed to pull back only to make way for Rothermel. He strode calmly through, despite the weight of his chains, never breaking stride.

Louis had put the Keeper at the lead after leaving the cavern, hoping to take advantage of his gifts, but it did little good. The plants were too quick: Roots would pop up out of the mossy earth to trip the Exorians; dense vines snaked around their ankles; and the glossy leaves of one plant would give way to the vicious spikes of another. And despite their increased numbers, the Exorians were losing strength with each step they took into Metria. Rations of firewater were dangerously low, made more so by the fact that it now had to be shared between the newcomers, who were greedy for it. And they still had the width of the Hestredes to cross.

All in all, it was a disaster. When it became clear that they would not make the city by the middle of the following day, as Dankar expected—despite having a Keeper and a stone of power in their midst—Louis decided to set fire to the jungle and clear their way.

But it wasn't working. The plants were too green and heavy with sap to burn. The troops had been trying for some time now, and their torches simply flamed out, like wet leaves. Exasperated, Louis threw his own torch onto the ground where it, too, sizzled and went out.

"How do you do it?" he shouted at Rothermel, who stood apart from the Exorians, amused.

The Keeper raised his bushy eyebrows and shrugged.

Louis had a sudden urge to take one of his men's still-lit torches and press it against Rothermel's bare flesh, but a new aversion to causing pain stayed his hand. It was a feeling that grew stronger the longer he carried the stone of Melor. His heart felt heavy, all the more so since one of his men had killed the Metrian woman.

She had emerged from the entrance to the lagoon in her dory, rowing quickly. There was enough moonlight to see the phosphorescent trail of her boat from where they were perched, and before Louis had had the chance to give an order, one of his warriors had thrown a spear. The figure slumped forward, and the hand dropped the paddle. It had found its target, dead-on.

Louis's right hand immediately begun to tingle at the memory. The sensation shot up his arm and penetrated his heart, doubling its weight; since the death of the Metrian, he had not been able to shake the feeling that something terrible was happening, and the semi-regular slugs of firewater no longer eased his anxiety.

The presence of Rothermel made it worse. Every time Rothermel looked at him—with a strange mix of sympathy and contempt—his anxiety flared. The only time he felt better was when they were marching. If he could just get his men and the stone to Dankar, hear his Keeper's voice, answer his commands—all would be set right. He was out of his depth . . . unfit to lead. Anyone would feel strange under the circumstances. At least, that was what he kept telling himself.

As if in agreement, another torch flared and fizzled to the ground. The jungle pressed in closer. At this rate, none of them would be going anywhere. They had underestimated Metria profoundly.

" 'Tis a wonder," mused Rothermel, his first audible words in more than a day.

"What?"

"It is a wonder that you were sent on such an important mission with so little knowledge."

Louis was struck by the fact that the Keeper had captured his thoughts so accurately.

"You don't need knowledge if you have superior strength."

"Really?" said Rothermel. "When all this time I had been under the impression that knowledge *is* strength. Ah, never mind. But I will tell you, it gives me more than a little hope. My cousin must be denser than a tree trunk not to have predicted this."

He laughed, and the sound rumbled up and got caught in the canopy above them. The whole jungle answered. Birds trilled more loudly, and the thick, humid air lifted—if only for the length of time that the laugh lingered in the air.

The Exorians who had been held captive in Metria responded, too, breaking out in strange choking sounds that might be described as chuckles.

"Stop it!" Louis shouted, alarmed at the effect the laugh was having on him. It was like a tickle in his chest that he had to swallow hard not to set free.

Rothermel laughed harder. All of the Exorians joined in, their scaled skin rippling and shaking as they convulsed in the unfamiliar reflex. Here they were, stuck in a jungle, as far away from home as they could get, with the Keeper of Melor. It seemed hysterically funny for some reason.

Louis stared at Rothermel, laughing despite himself. When had he last laughed? He had no memory of laughing. But as he chortled and shook, the heavy feeling he'd been dragging around began to lift. His right hand felt warm and healthy, and he was overcome with a desire to give Rothermel back his stone and forget the whole mission. He went as far as to reach for the *tehuantl* pelt that wrapped the stone. When he touched the animal skin, the laughter died inside him. He became aware that Rothermel was watching him.

He returned the stare. He did not blink, or look away, and the longer he stared at Rothermel, the more aware he became of the weight of the belt he carried across his shoulder, and the stone he bore on his back. The buckle of the belt began to glow faintly, as if it were responding to Rothermel's attention.

Before Louis knew what he was saying, he blurted, "What is happening to me?"

Rothermel's tone was serious, all trace of humor gone.

"Son, you are meddling in forces far too complex to be trifled with. Do you really think they are so easily perverted? The ground you walk on is deep and old. It has endured heat a thousand times greater than any you or your tribe might threaten. You have no idea what you are doing. And when one has no idea what one is doing, it is wiser to stop and think than to do."

Louis's right hand began to throb. The weight of the stone on his back was becoming unbearable. It was as if the ground itself were pulling on the stone, demanding its return. He felt as if his feet and legs were being pulled down, as if they might sink into the spongy ground beneath them.

He was once again aware of wanting to give Rothermel the stone. It was a powerful desire, as elemental as thirst. His right hand went again to his shoulder.

"What would you have me do?" he asked, in a voice that came from a different place inside him. A deeper place.

"*Stop*. Turn back before you claim another life or further risk your own. Take your brothers and return to your native lands. Rise up against Dankar. Refuse to do his bidding."

In his mind's eye Louis saw the limp bodies of the Exorians who had disobeyed Dankar hanging from the ledges of the rock spires, eyes eaten out by vultures.

"I can't. He'll kill us," said Louis. "He's already killed so many. He does not forgive disobedience. I must do as he says."

"Ah," said Rothermel, his voice kinder.

He stood up, his form towering over Louis.

"I think, then, that it is best you give me back my belt, at least, and with it, I shall ensure that your passage through the jungle is easier. If I am brought to my cousin with my stone, you shall all be greeted as great heroes, am I correct? Your lives will be celebrated, not ended? He will not care about the belt."

Louis lifted his shoulders. "I don't know."

Rothermel laughed again. "At least you are honest."

Louis fingered the belt. The desire to hand over the burden of the stone was still strong, but his fear of Dankar was stronger. The belt was a compromise. And how much damage could the Keeper do, chained, with spears pointed at him? He shifted the belt off his shoulder.

"If I give the belt to you, do you swear on pain of death that you will use it only to aid our passage to the city?"

Rothermel nodded.

"I'm not afraid to kill you, you know," he said, but even as he was saying it he knew he didn't mean it.

"I understand."

Louis threw the belt to Rothermel. The instant it touched its Keeper's hands, it radiated an intense, warm glow. Above them the jungle canopy drew back, and the light of a clear, high half-moon fell down around them.

"Shall we proceed, then, to fame and ruin?" mused Rothermel, stepping lightly into the bush. With each step the ground before him evened out, the tangle of vine and leaf retreated, and the way forward became clear.

✝   ✝   ✝

Louis and the Exorians followed Rothermel through the night without rest, moving southeast toward the southern shore of the Hestredes. The sun rose accompanied by screeching monkeys, who flung themselves from branch to branch above their heads. To the Exorians, the small, furred creatures sounded like *tehuantl*—a reassuring sound. They paused to rest, and restore themselves with the last remaining dregs of firewater just as, to the north, Teddy spelled out the last letter of Hesam's name beside her grave. Then they threw themselves on the ground and slept, knowing that the encampment opposite the city was within half a day's march.

Rothermel did not sleep, however, and so Louis, too, was forced to keep his eyes open. The sun felt good on his scaled flesh, streaming down through the jungle canopy. It made him drowsy. He must have dozed off, because when he opened his eyes, the Keeper was gone. The air beneath the jungle canopy was still, but Louis could sense a shift.

Something had changed.

He patted the bundle beside him, reassuring himself that he still had the stone, then leapt to his feet. He thrashed around the bushes for a moment and let loose a frustrated curse.

From above his head, Rothermel said, "Quiet down. A good leader lets his people rest when they've walked as far as we have."

Louis looked up. There was Rothermel, sitting in the crook of a sprawling tree surrounded by several monkeys. He was petting them with his chained hand. One had a tiny baby monkey clinging to its back. Far above the Keeper's head, the uppermost branches of the canopy rustled and swayed wildly. Rothermel seemed impervious to the bending and swaying above him. A small monkey leapt on his head, then used his beard to climb down onto his chest. He stroked the monkey's white face. The monkey chittered happily.

"What are you doing up there?" Louis said, more harshly than he felt. He would have liked to be up there with Rothermel, petting the fur of a monkey. His right hand reached upward on its own, toward a tree limb.

"Getting the lay of the land. Visiting with friends."

Rothermel stroked the face of the monkey with the baby once more, then jumped down, landing easily. His eyes were shining. How he could maneuver so well with his hands chained was a mystery to Louis.

"I am happy to see my sister's lands," he said, in a low voice. "It has been ages since I walked through Metria."

"And what do you see?"

"We turn east here, where the land slopes. The Hestredes lies not too far beyond, and then, it is a short journey to the shore; that is, if we do not meet any . . . *resistance*."

He looked sideways at Louis, but Louis was too busy thinking about how they would cross the river to hear the meaning beneath the words.

"Good, good," he said. "We'll be there before the day is wasted, then."

"Yes," said the Keeper. "Before it is wasted."

*Chapter Twenty*

# BRISK WINDS

Chase prowled the front deck of Hesam's ship. It was the same ship they had sailed on when they had first come to Metria, but it had been worked over by the Exorians. He took note of the scorch marks on the planking and found a stray spear. He broke it over his knee and threw it into the river, watching as it sank below the surface. He couldn't help but hope that it was a symbol of what would happen to all of their spears.

By the looks of it, the Exorians had halfheartedly tried to burn the ship as they retreated from the bay, but no real damage had been done, and none below the watermark. The ship was still sound, and would carry them downriver swiftly with the right wind. His mother, Knox, Calla, and Seaborne had rigged the sail in no time at all; now it was Chase's turn.

He went alone to the prow of the boat and cleared his mind as he had been trained by Ratha to do. Axl and Tar watched him from the beach, sitting beside Hesam's grave. Knox had begged to bring them but Calla had refused. Seaborne agreed, saying, "A ship is no place for the hounds of Melor. They stay on land."

Chase quieted all thought of the hounds, of the ship, of Evelyn, and closed his eyes. He brought to the forefront an image of a simple Varunan shelter he had stayed in during his time with Ratha. He pictured himself there, on the floor of a small stone hut, lying on a straw pallet, covered by his fur robe. He heard the wind shrieking outside the stone walls, over the roof, and entering the shelter through the lone hole in the roof: the *vindauga*, the wind's eye. It poured over him, bathing him in fluid, cold air. And then, as Ratha had taught him, he let it lift him—or more precisely, his awareness—and send it up and out, traveling high above the mountains.

He felt a leap of joy as the snowy peaks unfurled below him, a carpet of white more substantial than clouds but just as untouchable. He flew with purpose, and found his way back to Ratha's terrace. She stood there, as he had seen her so many times before. Chase understood now that this was not the *real* terrace or the *real* Ratha, but a projection: a place in both of their minds where they could meet.

"I am impressed, Varunan," she said in mindspeak. "Your daylights have become strong."

Chase couldn't help but smile at the praise, but wasted no time in telling Ratha what he needed.

She nodded once, and two of the doors on the square building burst open. A gust of cold air from the north rocked Chase backwards on his heels, followed by a dry, hot wind from the west. He felt the two currents whip around him, rise, and speed off toward their target. It was still strange to him to feel how substantial wind was—as steady and strong as water or sand. How could it be possible that he'd never noticed this before?

"Now, follow it, and get back to the ship."

"What about you?"

"I am not far behind," said Ratha. The flames in her cauldron leapt higher, and another rush of the two winds blew down the terrace. This time, Chase was ready. He turned his back to them and leapt, catching the crest of the wind as it spilled off the steps and into the great, swirling nebula of color that surrounded the terrace. He rode it all the way through, slowly bringing back his awareness into his body, to the present. And when he opened his eyes, he saw the river glistening before him. He heard the rattling cry of a high-crested bird, and stared as it dove into the water and came out again with a small fish in its beak.

Behind him, the sail luffed and slapped against the rigging; Seaborne tightened the line, and, like a miracle, the wind picked up strength, stretching and filling the sail. The ship bolted forward. Seaborne let out a whoop of delight, and the ship began to tack out of the bay and onto the open river.

"You did it, Chase!" hooted Knox, springing up to the bow and clapping his hand on his brother's back. "We'll be there in no time!" He had to yell to be heard above the rising howl of the wind.

"Careful!" he yelled, catching Knox as the wind blew him forward. "Ratha always goes big!"

Chase's hair was so long now that it lifted and blew around his face in a tangle. He scraped it back and held on to his little brother. Despite everything that had happened so far, it was exhilarating to stand there together, whipped by the wind, and feel the power of the daylights coursing in and around them. He looked back once at the empty bay, the entry to the caverns—golden sandstone lapped by clear blue water—and across the way to the sand beach where Hesam lay. He caught a glimpse of his mother in the ship's cockpit: one hand shading her eyes, the other on the wheel. He saw Teddy and Bodi, crouched alongside Calla and Seaborne in the lee of the ship, and he felt his brother's arm wrapped around his waist, leaning into him. Grace tipped the wheel and adjusted course, and in seconds, they were on the open river, sailing east.

Chase watched as the river curled around the bow in frothy ringlets, lit pink and silver by the sun. The crested bird was flying ahead of them, low on the water. He could not hear anything because of the wind, but he knew that somewhere along the shore were monkeys, howling, and below them, fish and turtles swimming with Bob in their midst. He took this all in, and for a moment that would stay with him as long as he lived, he truly understood that they were fighting for more than each other. They were fighting for everything.

✛　　✛　　✛

Evelyn came out of the tunnel short of the city of Metria by a few miles, on the southern shore of the river. The sun was directly overhead, and was so bright to her unadjusted eyes that it sickened her. She quickly stowed the stone of Metria back under her robes, not knowing who or what might be about. Her spirits soared as she tucked the stone in its pouch under her belt. Her daylights were responding to bringing it so near its home. She had never been in more danger, yet she had never felt so calm.

"Thank you, Rysta," she murmured to herself, and did a full circle to get a better idea of where she was.

The jungle was more manicured this close to the city, but was still a confusing tangle of vine and bush for those who did not already know their way. Luckily, she had passed this way before with Urza, Captain Nate, and Chantarelle, after the fight on the shores of Lake Voss. How long ago had that been? She could not say. It might have been a month, or a year. Time passed differently on Ayda.

Out of the corner of her eye she spotted a signpost used by the Metrians: a vine twisted into a large loop, indicating she should not go that way. It was like a stop sign, but only a Metrian would know it. Hesam had shown her. She felt a pang at the thought of her friend and wondered if she was all right.

She turned around to see yet another sign. The pale, large fronds that grew straight up from the jungle floor had been notched, and beyond was a moss-covered tree with small strips of moss removed. It was a green light, telling her to walk in that direction. She sprinted forward, feeling relieved to be out of the tunnel and in the open air.

Before long, she caught sight of the Hestredes, dappled and brilliant under the sun. The gusting wind was strong enough to kick up small whitecaps and spray. Evelyn paused to get her bearings and make a plan. It would be easier to approach the city from the banks of the river, but she needed to stay under cover of the jungle. She decided to stick to the edges of the jungle and head southeast, keeping the river on her left. She knew this was the proper direction, because at low tide, the ocean's pull acted like gravity, pulling the river forward vigorously, like now. At high tide, its currents meandered and looped around one another.

She raked her eyes over whatever open territory she could see, keeping alert for any Exorian activity. She saw nothing ahead, but when she looked back, a flash of something caught her eye. Silver? Something metallic was catching the sun and reflecting back. In moments, she was able to make out a Metrian ship under full sail. Her heart leapt. It was Hesam's ship! She would recognize it anywhere! She had made it! The Exorians wouldn't know how to sail a ship.

Evelyn scrambled down to the open bank of the river. The ship was moving fast. She had to be quick to signal it, or it would fly past her. For a second, she was stumped; then she remembered the flash she had just seen. She pulled out one of her curved hunting knives and held it up, catching the sun's beams. She angled it at the ship, and used her other hand to break the reflection in what she hoped was something like Morse code. At first it didn't seem to be working. The ship sped on, sailing swiftly downriver, oblivious to her. She continued to signal until the ship disappeared around a small peninsula in the river. Discouraged, Evelyn retreated back toward the sheltering scrim of the jungle and proceeded south, thinking hard about what the presence of the ship might signify.

She decided to take it as a sign that it was safe to walk on the relatively open stretches of shore that formed the southern bank of the river. It felt good to walk in the sunshine, the river rushing by her.

Voices in the distance brought her back to the present. She heard a male voice, then a softer answer. She was immediately on guard. Staying low, and retreating into the cover of the jungle, she made her way to the tip of the peninsula that created a bend in the river. Directly downriver was the ship, lying at anchor like a docile beast close to shore. There were at least two people on land and more climbing down into a dory from a knotted rope thrown over the side like a ladder.

Evelyn couldn't see clearly enough to make out who it was, but it only made sense that it was Hesam. *Who could be with her?* She wondered. She took note of the scorch marks on the ship's hull: Exorian calling cards. Had the Exorians attacked the ship? She only had her two hunting knives to defend herself. They would be no match for Exorian spears.

More voices carried over the water—vague murmurs, and then, clear as a bell, she heard a very familiar voice saying "Blimey!"

Evelyn crashed out of the jungle and hit the shore at a dead run. She didn't stop until she had thrown herself at a flabbergasted Seaborne.

"It's me, it's me!" she yelled, not knowing whether to laugh or cry.

"Aye, it is," cried Seaborne. "I can scarcely believe it. What in the devil's business are you doing here? Don't you know these shores are crawling with fireworms?"

"I could ask the same of you," she said, wiping her eyes.

"We saw a flash over there," he nodded upriver. "We thought it was them. We're looking for a particularly nasty pack of them." His voice dropped. "They took Rothermel and the stone of Melor."

"Oh no," gasped Evelyn.

Before Seaborne could tell her more, another voice called her name.

She turned to see Chase wading onto the shore, carrying a robe made of fur and feathers and his sword. His eyes looked strange. It took Evelyn a moment to realize that they were now almost entirely purple. She felt shy all of a sudden. He seemed so different.

"It's about time!" cried Knox, splashing up behind his brother. He pushed past Chase, who seemed frozen, and threw his arms around Evelyn. "Hey, stranger! You forget your way to Melor? Just had to make us come visit you, huh?"

Evelyn grinned at him. "Yeah, that's right."

Within minutes, Calla, Bodi, Teddy, and Grace had disembarked from the ship and made their way over to Evelyn. She greeted them with joy and looked expectantly at the ship. Her eyes searched the deck. She saw more faces—but all of them were Melorian.

"Where's Hesam?"

A shadow passed over the small group on the shore.

"She's not here," said Chase, with his strange purple gaze. "She was fragmented back at the caverns."

✠   ✠   ✠

"How can she be dead?" Evelyn wept. "And Mara, too?"

Chase stroked her hair; the others had retreated a discreet distance away, giving the two of them space for a moment before they had to return to the ship.

Evelyn repeated the words to herself silently, as if it would help make them sink in. She felt as if she were splitting in two: There was the one Evelyn who was sitting listening to Chase as he told her everything that had happened since they'd last seen one another, but there was a second Evelyn who was watching the scene from somewhere deep and dark, like a prisoner in a cell. That Evelyn did not register the bright sun overhead or the faces of the ones she loved who were finally here with her again. The prisoner Evelyn felt only hollow loss: first, her parents, then Rysta, now Mara and Hesam. Would it ever end? Would the Ghede, the Haitian gods of the dead, ever give up her scent? Or would they not rest until everyone she cared about was taken away?

She drew her knees up to her chin and put her hands over her ears.

"Stop," she whispered. "I can't hear anymore."

Chase remembered the day when he thought this same river had swallowed up his brother Teddy. It hadn't, but the memory of how much that hurt gave him some insight into what Evelyn was feeling. He tried to put his feelings into words.

"Do you remember what Rothermel said when Tinator died?"

Evelyn rubbed her face back and forth in her hands, saying nothing.

"He told us that Tinator could never be lost—that he would always be with us—and everything I've learned here makes me think it's true. All of this right now—you, me, our vessels—it's just temporary; it's the daylights that live on. It has to be that way, don't you think? I mean, when a tree gets old and dies, it falls over and crumbles into the dirt, which gives life to more trees. It's a big circle, and humans are a part of it. The same has to be true for Hesam, and Mara, and for Rysta, and for your parents, and every person who dies. Their bodies pass away, but their energy gives life to new things. Just like ours will someday. It never ends . . . it just *changes*."

Evelyn was silent for a moment, listening. "It's not really the same though, is it? I'd rather have Hesam here, not just her energy."

"Yeah, me too. But when I was in Varuna with Ratha and you weren't there with me, I still knew you were *with* me—you know. And Knox, and Teddy. And I think that, back home, Frankie and my dad, they know . . ."

He shook his head. He was having a hard time expressing what it was he wanted to say.

"I dunno, Ev, this is so much bigger and more complicated than we think it is. Nothing is black-and-white anymore. It's not about you and me, or any one person living or dying. It's so much more than that."

Evelyn nudged him with her shoulder.

"You've gotten deep, Varunan." Then she sighed, and added "*Dèyè mòn, gen mòn.*"

"What does that mean?"

"It's something my mother used to say: *Beyond the mountains, there are mountains.* It means that there is no end, only the journey. It's what you are saying."

"Who's the deep one now?" said Chase. He touched her arm, and felt that same flutter he'd felt before when she was near. He remembered the way her lips felt on his cheek when she kissed him. He wanted her to do it again.

"Ev—" he started, turning to face her.

Evelyn looked sideways at him

Chase felt his face flush. She was so pretty, and so close. And they had come so far together.

"Yes?" She leaned toward him.

*Where is the stone of Metria?* interrupted a high-pitched voice in his head.

It was like a slap in the face. *Ratha.* The moment passed.

"We need to get you on the ship," he blurted. Whatever was between him and Evelyn would have to wait.

# Chapter Twenty-One

# STANDOFF

The Exorian encampment was abuzz in preparation for Dankar's arrival. The advance guards that had been sent to clear the jungle along the southern shore had done their job, though no one knew how Dankar planned to cross the river. Despite being far from their homes, the Exorians were in a good mood. They had met little resistance once the Wold had been subdued. *Tehuantl* now patrolled the wasteland of Melor, so no surprises would come from that direction. The warriors had set up base camp on a spit of sand directly across the mouth of the wide river, facing east. From there, the tall towers and blue-domed roofs of the city loomed like a great treasure rising through the fog and sea mist. Only the waters of the Hestredes lay between them and their conquest.

On the other side of the river, Urza and her advisors watched the enemy's activities from their vantage point at the top of the tower. Earlier, they had sent those inhabitants—including the Melorian refugees—who were too young or too weak to fight into the secret hiding places that lay at the foundations of the city. The rest were armed and waiting for the battle yet to come. It still seemed improbable that it would be staged from the southern shore, for everyone knew that Exorians could not cross water, and they did not possess the knowledge—or the time—to build ships or bridges.

"It must be some other diversion," said Letham, who had just barely returned alive from Varuna. His troops had been surrounded in the low-slung hills that bordered their homeland, many of them never to return. The few that were saved would not talk about how it had happened, even among themselves. One moment they had been fighting for their lives; the next, some kind of immense winged creature from the ancient times was carrying off the Exorians in its lethal-looking talons. Letham remembered it as a kind of dream or hallucination brought on by battle fatigue. As he looked down upon the growing Exorian encampment, he could not help but wish the creature would make another appearance.

"I am perplexed by our enemy's strategy," said Urza, silently making her own wish: that Rysta were here to guide them. "You are convinced Dankar's main assault will not come from the north?"

A flashback of the wide-winged creature and the startled screams of the Exorians caused Letham to shake his head and say "No." He could not explain further. The words tangled and flew out of his head every time he tried to describe what he'd seen. "We still have friends in Varuna."

Urza frowned. She crossed the octagonal floor of the tower and looked out to sea. Somewhere, beyond the fog, was their salvation. If only Captain Nate would return with the Fifth Stone and its Keeper, Urza could lay this burden at their feet.

From across the river came the roar of a *tehuantl*. It sent shivers up her spine. The Exorians were too close. She pictured the large cats prowling the alleys and walkways of Metria as the buildings burned. She could not let that happen.

"We must hold them off as long as possible," she announced. "Send reinforcements to the north, but do not take your eyes off the embankment. Canvass the Melorians and find all those who are good with a bow. Place them in the towers. If the Exorians move to cross the river by some artifice or trick, we will pick them off."

"Urza, come, look!" Letham exclaimed.

Urza wheeled around. Across the river, a path of flame burned a line through the jungle. It blazed all the way through the encampment, bright enough to send an orange glow across the mist where the river met the sea.

"What does it mean?" she gasped.

Letham rubbed a heavy hand across his chin.

"I think it means that Dankar has arrived."

✢     ✢     ✢

Louis and the Exorians sensed the heat of the fire before they saw it. Monkeys screeched and howled their retreat from the river.

"Not far now," said Louis. He felt a new surge of energy. Quickly he assessed the Exorians, taking stock of the ones they had freed from the caverns. Dankar would not be pleased. Their captivity in Metria had softened them, and the lack of firewater, even more so. Louis could only hope that in all the excitement of being so close to victory, his leader would not notice. He did not want them to be punished. He felt strangely attached to them, and, if he was being totally honest, to his prisoner, as well.

"I need the belt back," he said, pointing to Rothermel's buckle.

"No, you don't," said Rothermel. "You have the stone; that is all he wants. Give the stone to him, and the belt is unnecessary."

"If it's unnecessary, then why won't you just give it to me?"

"Because it is mine; I made it, and I choose not to. If you want to take it from me, go ahead and try."

Rothermel pulled himself up to his full height, standing a full head above Louis. Though he had no weapon, the power that surged off of him was palpable.

Louis backed down, rubbing his right hand. His emotions felt confused. He would be grateful when this mission was over. He had delivered the Keeper and the stone, as he had been ordered. If Dankar wanted the belt, too, he could deal with it.

"Keep it, then."

They pushed on, keeping the river in sight and following its course east.

Soon enough, the tall towers of Metria became visible, rising high above the mist that lay across the water. The jungle gave way abruptly and they found themselves on a low hill overlooking the new encampment. Hasty shelters of felled trees and tarps had been built to house the Exorian troops, and beyond them a series of more-official-looking tents. A burn trail wound up through the jungle from the encampment. Louis used it to lead his party down the hill, a freshly shackled Rothermel at the head. As they passed through camp, all activity ceased.

Two enormous *tehuantl* were pacing in front of the entrance to the largest tent. Louis brought Rothermel before it. The *tehuantl* roared, and rose up on their hind legs, ears flattened to the sides of their heads. Rothermel raised his shackled hands and made a calming sound. The *tehuantl* reacted by sitting back on their haunches. The flap to the tent drew back and Dankar emerged.

He wore a glossy *tehuantl* pelt across his broad shoulders and a gold circlet on his forehead. His black eyes roamed between Rothermel, Louis, and the Exorian troops. He bared his white teeth in what approximated a smile.

"At last, at last," he said, circling Rothermel. The two men were the same towering height; however, one was smooth and bronzed and golden, while the other was creased and weathered and gray. Dankar stopped and laid a soft hand on Rothermel's shoulder. The *tehuantl* came closer, fascinated by the scene. "Cousin."

Rothermel flinched.

"What a happy day for me—a momentous day!" Dankar's tone was light, but the menace behind the words oozed up between them. He spoke for the crowd that was gathering around the newcomers. "Not only have my lost warriors been returned to me, but my cousin has at long last come to pay a visit. It has been an age, now, hasn't it?"

Rothermel did not answer. His formidable brow was caked in jungle pitch and dust, and his long hair lay tangled across the shoulders of a Melorian poncho that had seen better days. He raised his bound hands and shook them.

"Take these off, then, *cousin*. Or are you afraid to let me loose?"

Dankar smirked.

"Afraid? I think not. Rather, I think it is the other way around." He stuck his nose in Rothermel's face and hissed. "If you do not fear me yet, cousin, you will come to." He turned his attention to Louis. "Do you have it?"

Louis reached for the pelt on his back.

Rothermel shifted uncomfortably.

Louis held out the bundle. Dankar went to take it, but Louis's right hand would not release it. Dankar tugged at the pelt. For a moment, they struggled, until Louis used his left hand to pry open the right. Dankar sneered at the sight of Louis's human hand, then held the bundle up to show the troops.

"A great weapon has been delivered to us today! Victory is at hand!"

A cheer went up.

Dankar motioned toward Louis.

"Take your brothers to get food and rest, and be sure they replenish their supply of firewater. I see that they are not themselves. Metria does not agree with Exorians. The sooner we scour this city, the better."

Louis hesitated, balking suddenly at the prospect of leaving Rothermel.

"What about the prisoner? He has not eaten the entire journey. Shall I see to him?"

"Leave that to me," Dankar said with a leer. "He is my guest of honor, after all."

He pushed Rothermel toward the tent. As he did so, his hand fell on Rothermel's belt, hidden beneath his poncho.

"What is this? A trick?" He rounded on Louis and grabbed him by the throat. "If you have betrayed me, by my lights I will feed you to the *tehuantl*."

"N-n-no!" stammered Louis, instantly afraid.

Rothermel intervened. "There is no trickery here, Dankar. The man has done exactly what you asked him to do; now let him rest. I am here. Treat with me."

"You do not give orders here!" Dankar shouted at Rothermel, He let Louis go, but not before demanding the obsidian blade.

Louis handed it over, his right hand shaking.

Dankar taunted Louis with it, then laughed and grabbed his human hand.

"What shall I take from you in exchange for allowing the prisoner in with a weapon?"

Louis's heart sank. He was defenseless. There was nothing between him and the blade. He gritted his teeth.

"Here, take the belt," said Rothermel, unbuckling it. "Leave him alone."

Dankar dropped Louis's hand and dismissed him with a wave as he took the belt from Rothermal.

Louis caught Rothermel's eye as he turned to go with the others. All the contempt was gone. Only the pity remained.

✢     ✢     ✢

"How does it work?" asked Calla.

They were aboard Hesam's ship, headed full sail toward the city of Metria. The stone of power lay nestled in Evelyn's scarf on her lap. Its striations glittered in the sun, but the stone itself was inert and smaller than anyone had expected. None of them had ever seen a stone of power before.

"It's a lot of fuss over a rock, if you ask me," grumbled Seaborne, but he didn't take his eyes off it.

Evelyn was carefully monitoring her own daylights, not wanting to inadvertently power the stone and upset everyone. She had no idea how it might affect Melorians—or Varunans, for that matter.

"I'm not really sure," she replied. "I was able to bring it to life, in a way, back at the caverns. I used it to create an antidote to the firewater." She told them all about the experiment with the waters in the caverns.

"I saw you doing that!" cried Chase.

"Chase sees a lot of things now," said Knox. He made the "cuckoo" motion with his finger, circling it by his ear.

Seaborne cuffed his shoulder.

"*Anyway*," continued Evelyn, "Hesam and I made the Exorians drink the treated water. I even made them bathe in it, but it didn't change them back. I mean, I think it was working a little. Their skin got softer and they were less angry, but it's not like it changed them back to normal." Her eyes flashed over to Bodi, who was sitting cross-legged next to Chase. "Exorians are tough."

"It was a good plan, Evelyn. It makes sense," said Seaborne.

Evelyn lifted the stone out of its nest. Teddy reached for it. Without thinking, Evelyn gave it to him. He was a Metrian, after all. He had a right to it.

"Can we save Metria with it?" he asked. His eyes were shining. His daylights were happy to be so near the stone.

"I don't know. Maybe Urza knows. I think we should bring it to her."

Chase frowned. "It has been hidden all this time. Maybe it's not wise to bring it to the city."

"What else can we do at this point?" she asked.

"Why isn't it making us all go crazy?" asked Knox. "I thought the stones were too powerful for outliers to handle."

Chase stood up. He looked down at the river passing by. He wished with all his heart that Captain Nate were here. He even wished that Ratha was with them. He thought back to what he had learned about the stones, and how things were changing.

"I think it's less powerful now," said Chase. "Now that Dankar has Melor, the balance is shifting."

Then, the sail flapped behind him as if to remind him that the wind was still active. Chase raked both shorelines with his heightened vision. A dark line of smoke rose up from the jungle. He could just make out a swathe of burnt vegetation stretching back toward Melor. It was a road. The boat tacked and they passed another small jut of land; mist was growing thicker, and he could hear gulls. They must be close to the sea.

It was then that he saw the Exorian camp.

"Bodi, come here!" he shouted.

Bodi leapt to her feet.

"Exorians can't swim, right?"

"No." Her eyes drifted apprehensively over the deck and toward the river. "Why? We aren't going in, are we?"

Chase shook his head. "No, not us, but do you see over there?" He pointed toward the Exorian camp. "Dankar has amassed a huge force. He is planning to take the city, but I don't understand how they will get across the river. Can you imagine what he has planned?"

While he was talking, Seaborne, Calla, and Knox came up beside him.

"They are moving in supplies and reinforcements," said Calla, noting the road.

"If Rothermel is still alive, that is where that blasted half-blooded Exorian and his mangy brothers will have taken him, I know it."

"Whoa, now, Seaborne—easy; you're talking about my uncle," said Knox.

"Aye, lad, but you better get one thing straight before we get any closer. He is nobody to you. Not anymore," he said.

Knox flashed a look over the deck at his mother, who was at the ship's wheel. She was wearing her poncho with the hood raised, her glance moving constantly between the sail, the river, and the compass on the deck. Knox's heart swelled for a moment. He had never seen her look so in command.

Seaborne followed his gaze. "He is no one to her, either, except an enemy. Do you understand? We are your family now, bound by our daylights, and if it comes to a choice between him and us, you will choose correctly, right, lad? Rothermel's life might depend on it. You are Melorian, and your first loyalties remain with us—with *him*. Blood means nothing here. It is the daylights that define where you belong, and whom you owe."

Knox nodded, but his heart still felt heavy. He felt sad for his mom. He hoped that when her daylights spoke to her, she would become a Melorian like him so they would always be together.

The ship tacked to port, following the graceful bend in the river. The air grew cooler and the fog that lingered along the coast began to snake up the river. To the east, Chase could make out the tops of the towers rising over the fog. He swept his gaze across the river toward the huts and tents of the Exorian encampment, clearly visible now.

Knox exhaled sharply, seeing the same thing. "It's a standoff."

"And we're sailing right into it with the stone of Metria," cried Calla. She wheeled back to shout to Grace. "We have to keep sailing, right past them, and out to sea."

"No!" cried Seaborne. We'll get lost in the fog, and we'll be no good to anyone. The current will dash us on the straits of Varuna!"

"Then what? What should we do? We can't risk taking the stone into the city with the Exorians so close."

Chase closed his eyes, trying to look inside himself for an answer. He didn't notice that Evelyn was right beside him until she spoke.

"Seaborne, do you think Rothermel is there?" She nodded toward the Exorian side.

"Most likely—unless they've fragmented him."

"Why?" asked Chase, opening his eyes.

"I think we should confront Dankar."

"No offense, Evelyn, but that's a daft plan," said Seaborne. "We'd be sailing the stone of Metria right into his hands. It's suicide."

"No, I don't think so," said Evelyn, thinking back to how her daylights and the stone of Metria had commingled in the tunnel. "We've been so busy trying to keep the stones out of Dankar's hands that we've forgotten that we can *use* them. I know that in the past, Ratha, Rothermel, and

Rysta felt that keeping the stones separate was the best guarantee of their safety—but things have changed. We need to do things differently now. I think I can manage the stone of Metria, at least enough to activate it and help us get into that camp. If Rothermel is there, I will give it to him. Then he can use it to get back the stone of Melor. We would have two stones against Dankar's one, and a Keeper."

"Or, Dankar will use his two stones to take yours, and it will be three against none," Knox chimed in. "How do we know your plan will work?"

"We don't," said Chase. "But if we do as Evelyn says, we will have Rothermel and a stone on our side, and that's a huge advantage."

Knox leaned in to whisper to Chase. "What about Mom? And Bodi and Teddy? We can't take them into Dankar's camp. It's too dangerous. Maybe they should drop us off."

"And do what?"

Chase never got a chance to hear the answer.

A thundering *boom* echoed out across the river. The trees along either shoreline bent almost to the ground, and the river in front of them rose up into a giant tidal wave. The ship heeled hard with the force, its main mast skimming the water. Five of the Melorians were launched overboard. Everyone else was thrown across the deck as the ship began to capsize.

*Chapter Twenty-Two*

# SHAKEN

A wall of water swamped the ship. Chase, Knox, and Evelyn scrambled for handholds. Grace crawled toward the wheel, which spun wildly. Bodi and Teddy had been swept into the cockpit and were struggling to hold on to Grace. Seaborne hugged the main mast and began slashing at whatever rigging he could to lower the sails.

"Did a bomb go off?" shouted Knox, as another huge wave washed over the deck. Water poured over them, pounding their backs.

"Hold your breath, and don't let go!" Calla commanded, as another wave crashed over the bow. For several seconds, the ship threatened to turn completely over. They were submerged until the wave passed on and the water withdrew.

Chase coughed and gasped, trying to catch his breath. He had swallowed some water and, for the first time in a long time, he remembered what it was like when he had asthma. The beast in his chest began to stir. He tried to take even breaths and put it back to sleep.

A giant rumble shook the river.

"I think it's an earthquake!" Knox yelled.

Chase rolled to his side so he could look at the trees on the shoreline. The branches and leaves were trembling, and the trunks swayed in unison.

Grace regained control of the wheel.

"Everyone climb to the higher side of the deck!" she shouted. "We need more weight."

They clambered up the deck, which was now almost sideways to the water. Seaborne went so far as to throw himself over the side, hanging on to a cleat. Slowly, the ship began to right itself. Seaborne walked up the hull until he was back on deck. The wet, torn sail slapped around the mast.

"Perfect!" cried Knox, sopping wet and shivering. "This is just perfect! Like we don't have enough going against us!"

There was a brief lull in the intense groaning and creaking that echoed along the river, and the enormous waves settled down. Calla took the opportunity to scramble back to the cockpit and grab some line, which she threw back to help Evelyn, Knox, and Chase. The air reverberated with an ominous groan, and the surface of the river shuddered again, like water in a glass when a truck rumbles by. The bow of the boat turned inward and the currents of the river began to swirl.

"It's a gyre!" yelled Seaborne. "We've got to beach her, NOW!"

He grabbed the wheel, and together, he and Grace cranked it hard to starboard. The hull shuddered and the bow swung right.

"Hold on!" Grace shouted, bracing for impact.

The ship met land with a juddering thud. Decking flew up from the bow as the front caved in, showering Evelyn, Chase, and Knox with splintered wood. The mast trembled and cracked, its anchors far below jolting out of their bolts. What was left of the hull rolled hard on its right, revealing its dark-stained underbelly and keel. It came to rest sideways, like a semi-beached whale.

Everyone dropped or climbed off the wrecked ship, coughing and spluttering their way onto land. The Exorian encampment was less than a mile to the east. They had barely escaped sailing right into their midst.

Before they had time to regroup, the ground underneath their feet shook again with tremendous force. It sent them all sprawling to the ground; another riot of large waves coursed up the river. The air split with a thundering *boom* and the river poured back on itself, churning like a washing machine at full throttle, swamping the beach and the remains of the ship.

They crawled farther onshore, away from the flood, scrabbling across the leaf-littered floor as the ground beneath them bucked and swayed. Another ferocious *boom* shook the air, followed by the sound of rock scraping against rock. The entire world seemed to tremble on its axis and the jungle threatened to collapse in on itself. Seaborne threw himself over Calla to protect her. Grace gathered Teddy and Bodi close, and Evelyn took shelter beneath a large plant with plate-shaped leaves. There was no sign of the Melorians who had been thrown overboard. Knox and Chase and the three Melorian soldiers who had managed to stay on deck grabbed at whatever they could find—root, tree trunk, vine—and held on for their lives.

And then, as suddenly as it had begun, it was over. The air fell still and the shaking ceased. The ground returned to solid form. The only sound came from the lapping of the river from somewhere below.

They stood, cautiously, took stock of one another, checked for bruises, and traced their steps back to the shore. They did not have to walk far.

"Holy crap," said Knox, staring.

"Crikey," echoed Seaborne.

Where the wide mouth of the Hestredes had once been there now stood a ledge of earth and granite that had not been there before—

a dam between the river and the sea. The Exorians could now walk straight into the city.

"Blast it—they made a bridge," Seaborne said.

"And they used Rothermel to do it," said Chase.

Seaborne put his face in his hands.

"We're sunk. Dankar has control over the stone of Melor, or he wouldn't have been able to do such a thing. He must have made Rothermel surrender his power, and then fragmented him. Our Keeper would never have done this of his own accord. The Hestredes has run its course since the beginning of creation. Now it's dammed like a child's bathtub. It's over. We cannot fight this."

The defeat in Seaborne's voice silenced Knox.

Chase crossed down to the shore to get a better look. Fog from the coast drifted in and out, but he could discern movement. Large troop formations of Exorian soldiers were advancing across it.

"They are already moving," he called back.

A flurry of activity brought everyone to the shore. All eyes strayed to the river, which looked more like a lake now—cloudy and unsettled, and wide. They watched as a prisoner was led at spear point across the dam. The silhouette of the prisoner was a good head taller than his guards, and he was wearing a Melorian poncho.

"Rothermel!" Seaborne pounded Chase on the back. "He's still alive!"

"Then we should stick to the plan," said Evelyn. "They won't be expecting us. We can sneak up on them from behind."

"But Dankar has both stones. We only have one—and it's an awful lot of Exorians, Ev. Only Seaborne, you, and I have weapons." Chase put his hand on his sword hilt.

"The city will not surrender without a fight," Evelyn assured them. "The Exorians will be distracted. Urza and the Tower Guard have been preparing for this. I say we follow and sneak up behind them. We'll find Rothermel. One stone is better than none."

Chase shot a questioning look at Seaborne. He wasn't so sure about that.

"We could backtrack and take it to Varuna. We could give it to Ratha," he ventured.

"That would take days!" Evelyn objected. "The city can't hold on that long!"

Calla shaded her eyes, watching the prisoner's progress across the land bridge.

"What would make Rothermel gift the stone and its powers to Dankar?" she wondered out loud. "What threat or promise was made?"

"I'd wager it's the same one the devil made to Ranu: He'd stop all the slaughtering. There are many people in the city—many of them Melorians. Rothermel is thinking of them, no doubt," Seaborne replied.

As Seaborne and Calla consulted with the remaining Melorians, Grace sidled up to Chase.

"What about the Fifth Stone?" she asked. "Why is no one talking about it? Isn't there a chance it could save us?"

"I don't know anymore, Mom. Captain Nate is out there trying."

"And what about Ratha—can she help? Instead of us bringing her the stone, why don't you ask her to come to us?"

Chase tried to picture Ratha outside of Varuna, and couldn't, even at the height of her powers—but it was worth a shot. He nodded, then closed his eyes and retreated to the shelter with the wind's eye, the *vindauga*, shutting out the chaos around him. He brought his awareness to the terrace where so often he had encountered Ratha. It was empty. He waited. Ratha did not appear. Either she was unable to meet him, or she was choosing not to. He didn't know which was more troubling.

He returned to the present and opened his eyes. Seaborne was standing in front of him with Knox beside him.

"We're at the end of the line, lad. We Melorians have decided that if we do nothing else, we will go to the city and fight for our Keeper and the last of our kin. You and your kin may come, or not, but we will not turn back."

✢     ✢     ✢

In the city, the Melorians Seaborne was talking about lay in wait, their arrows trained on the new land bridge to shoot whatever came out of the fog. All archers had been repositioned to the south side of the city. They were scattered and confused by the earthquake, the balance of their daylights as thrown and jumbled as the terrain around them.

Most managed to collect themselves, thanks to the quick thinking of a Melorian woman, Ahna, who was Adhoran's wife, left behind with their son when Adhoran went into Exor. She ordered the most agile archers to scale any rooftop or tower that remained standing. The rest joined the Metrian guard on the ground, armed with every sword, pike, and pickax left in the armory, under Letham's command.

Urza had sent all those unable to fight to the underwater caverns soon after the Exorians began building their encampment; all others were expected to defend the city in whatever way they could—including her. She donned her armor and curved blade and joined the ranks at the front. If this was to be the last fight for Metria, every Metrian who could would meet it head-on.

The first wave of Exorians emerged from the fog, their lit spears creating an orange penumbra. The Melorian archers let loose their arrows, aiming for the center. The Exorians raised their shields over their heads, but not before several arrows had found their mark, and more than a few fell from the sides and into the waters below.

Yet they advanced. The ground under their feet shook as they marched. Their eyes danced with assured victory. And, to the depleted ranks of the Melorians and Metrians, there seemed to be so many of them, these scabbed and ruined versions of their once-human selves. They descended on the city, bringing with them fire and destruction, but also something worse: an example of what might befall any survivors. The Melorians and Metrians threw themselves into battle, fighting as one for the city, and for themselves.

When the Melorian archers ran out of arrows, they lobbed whatever they could find from inside the buildings: rocks, tiles, furniture, crockery. The Exorians set fire to whatever else was left. The city, already in ruins, burned. Ground troops rushed out to fight the Exorians in hand-to-hand combat, but they were vastly outnumbered. Black smoke poisoned the air, and the troops on the ground struggled to maintain their positions. Those on the rooftops ran out of materiel. There was nothing left to do but fall back.

Ahna and Letham sounded the retreat. Survivors made for the underwater caverns, diving into the city canals that had turned orange in the reflection of the fire, the waters tasting of blood and mortar. The Exorians threw spears at them from dry land, but could not follow. As long as the stone of Metria stayed out of Dankar's hands, those who could swim would still be safe.

Urza ran through the city, taking the steps two at a time up to her watchtower, which by some miracle was still standing. She would destroy whatever maps she could, not wanting to betray the location of the underwater refuges, and then she would wait out her fate. The Exorians would find her and fragment her eventually, but she didn't care now. All that remained was honor. Better to die fully human than live and suffer as the Exorians had under Dankar.

✚    ✚    ✚

The Exorian encampment was deserted when Seaborne led their group through it. Traces of a meal were evident, and there were a few castaway flasks and broken spears among the tents, but otherwise the place was empty. Fog unfurled in ribbons along the ground, coming up from the seacoast. It flowed through the pockets between the tents and melded with the stink of smoke.

In silence, they made their way to the head of the new dam. Here, they hesitated. They could not risk being caught midway across, but they couldn't see what lay on the other side because of the fog, which was now pouring over the new ledge like the ghost of a waterfall. Beyond it, the city was on fire.

"Do you think it's a trap?" asked Knox, apprehensively. "Do you think they are lying in wait for us?"

"How could they be? They don't know we're coming," said Evelyn.

"Or they don't care," added Chase, staring into the haze. The cries and clashes of a battle carried across to them, muffled by the fog. "I don't think Dankar gives a nickel about what's behind him. He thinks it's already over, plus"—he cast a chagrined glance at Seaborne—"he's got two stones, and Rothermel."

"Well, we have one stone and all of us," said Evelyn, defiantly. "And Ratha."

Chase did not want to strip her of that hope, so he stayed silent. It could be true, but his Keeper was staying very quiet, just when he needed her most. She had told him—promised him—she wouldn't desert them. He was waiting to see if she meant it.

"We might have something else," said Grace, in a faraway voice. "Or, more accurately, some*one*."

She, too, was staring at the fog spilling over the dam, and the aura of flame and smoke that hovered above the city.

"Who?" asked Knox.

"Edward."

"Aw, Mom, I wouldn't count on it. He's one of them now. I don't think he's going to be much help to us," said Knox.

Grace rubbed her hands along her arms and caught Chase's eye. He had told her that Edward was a good man underneath it all. It appeared that she had taken that to heart.

"Maybe so; but if you can't trust your own family, there's nothing left to fight for anyway. He wasn't always like he is now. Maybe he'll change back."

"The Exorians *are* his family now," explained Knox, echoing what Seaborne had said to him. "He has no tie to us anymore. Just them."

"Not all Exorians are bad," interrupted a quiet, little voice. Bodi tugged on Grace's hand. "My brother was good. Maybe your brother is good, too."

Grace knelt down and picked up the little girl in her arms.

"Exactly, Bodi. I am going to remind him where he came from. I'm his only sister. That should count for something."

Seaborne gave her a dubious look but remained silent on the subject. Instead, he stepped forward to give orders.

"We'll enter the city. We"—he gestured at Calla and the Melorian soldiers—"will draw anyone lingering around away from you, and steal as many spears as we can. Evelyn, you must find Rothermel, and Chase and Knox, you must protect Evelyn and her stone at all costs. When you have found him and given him the stone, we will know it. We will find you. Then, and only then"—he looked pointedly at Grace—"may you look for the other outlier. Evelyn and the stone remain the highest priority at all times. Once we have Rothermel, he will know what to do."

"What about me?" asked Teddy.

Seaborne ruffled his hair and knelt down so he could talk to him, eye-to-eye.

"You, little man, must stay with your mother and Bodi at all times. You lived in this city. You know it. Take them to a safe place, and guard them both. They are brave, but they have not fought as you have. They will need your guidance. Do you accept your charge?"

Teddy raised his right hand to his chest, palm up, fingers splayed.

"Yes."

Seaborne touched Teddy's fingers with his own, lingering on his knees, straightening Teddy's poncho, pulling up his hood, taking more time than he had to.

"I am glad you came to my door, small one," he whispered, spontaneously hugging the little boy to him. "You make me so very proud."

Teddy hugged him back.

Seaborne stood, taking a minute to collect himself before addressing Evelyn.

"You have passed many moonrises in Metria most recently, and know the city better than I do. You take the lead once we cross the dam, then we will go our own way."

She nodded grimly. More than any other good-bye, the exchange she had just witnessed showed that Seaborne did not think they would ever see each other again.

They all paused together on the brink—outliers, Melorian, Exorian, Metrian, Varunan—understanding that from here on out, anything might happen.

Seaborne took his sword from the scabbard strapped to his back. He stepped out first onto the dam, then turned and lifted the sword in salute.

"Whatever we meet on the other side, my friends, fight with honor— and may your daylights preserve you." Then he sprinted ahead of them into the fog.

*Chapter Twenty-Three*

# LANDING

Frankie and Jim passed through the opening in the hill and into the shifting lights, so bright and disorienting after being outside in the dark and the rain. The ground gave way underfoot, and they slid, falling, falling, falling, until all sense or notion of time stopped, and they became barely sensible of anything but the colors shuttling around them.

There was no sound—not even when they yelled out in shock as the bottom of the hill fell away. And still they kept falling. After what might have been no time at all, or all time, there was nothing, just a black void and a sense of weightlessness, until Frankie came to on a cold, dark floor inside a cave.

Jim Thompson lay on his side a few feet from her, unconscious.

Frankie sat up and began to crawl, following a funnel of light to the opening of the cave. She found herself looking at a long lake that she had never seen before. Snow-peaked mountains were visible in the distance, glinting white. The sun was high in the sky. A flock of birds buzzed the surface of the water in a V, speeding across the glittering lake. She saw a cluster of white boulders sticking out of the water, and became aware of a woman standing on the one that was farthest out.

She wore a long, white robe and a thick knot of black hair at the top of her head. She was very pale. She stared openly at Frankie, with eyes that had no color. Frankie felt as if she should recognize her. There was something familiar about her. A name popped into Frankie's head.

*Ratha.*

Jim Thompson groaned a little, and then stirred.

She took her eyes off of the woman to check on Jim. When Frankie looked back, the woman was gone.

Somewhere in the distance, a dog howled.

"Where are we?" asked Jim, rubbing his jaw and sitting up.

"I think we're on Ayda," said Frankie.

"Ayda—" repeated Jim, still in a daze.

"There was a woman, just over there." Frankie pointed to the now-empty boulder. "I saw her. I think I know her."

"So you've been here before?"

"Yes. We were here. Me and Evelyn, and Chase and Knox and Teddy. We came here on the boat. When we got lost in the fog."

Jim stood up, bewildered.

"My boys were here?"

Frankie nodded.

Jim swiveled his head, searching the lake for any signs of life. Two large hounds burst onto the shore, making a beeline for the cave. Jim grabbed Frankie instinctively and shoved her behind him. She laughed.

"It's Axl and Tar!"

"You know them?"

"Of course."

Jim stood back as the hounds, standing as high as his hip, came to a halt right before them. Frankie ran to the smaller one and began to pet her.

"That's a good girl, Axl." The other hound licked the back of Frankie's head. "Where's Evelyn?"

A large, black bird, larger and more menacing than any bird Jim Thompson had ever seen, landed on the outermost granite boulder. It stood with its head cocked, looking at them. The surface of the lake glittered in the sun behind them, making it hard to see. Jim stifled a moment of panic. Where in the heck was he? Was he dreaming?

Jim shaded his eyes, and in that moment, the bird disappeared and a woman stood in its place.

*I must be dreaming*, he thought to himself. Nothing in all of science could explain a bird suddenly turning into a woman. This must all be a figment of his imagination. It had to be. But then, how did Frankie fit in? And the wormhole?

"See? That's her," said Frankie, nodding toward the woman.

Jim wiped his lips with the back of his palm, trying to make sense of what he was seeing. The whole thing was unnerving, and the woman especially so. He rubbed his eyes, expecting to reach under his glasses—but they had disappeared. Jim did a double take. He was incredibly nearsighted. There was no way he would be able to see that far across the lake without his glasses—and yet, here he was, doing it.

She came toward them, moving swiftly, stepping easily along the boulders that studded the surface of the lake. Her robe flickered with different-colored lights, similar to those they had fallen through in the tunnel. Her expression was impossible to read, and her eyes were chilling. She reached the shore, standing only feet from Jim and Frankie.

Jim felt his insides turn over. His vision spun. The panic became more intense.

"Do you have it?" the woman questioned him with vehemence.

He could barely understand, he was so dizzy.

Frankie grabbed his hand, frightened. Her touch made him feel a little better.

The woman asked him again.

"What?" said Jim. "Do I have what?" He was suddenly afraid.

"Are you the Keeper of the Fifth Stone?"

He was hallucinating—that had to be the explanation. Or maybe he had hit his head on a rock? None of this was making any sense, yet it felt very real. His eyes skipped past the woman and out to the lake and then back to her. She did not blink, but waited for him to speak.

"I have no idea what you are talking about," he said, finally.

The woman cast her translucent eyes down to Frankie, impatient.

"Do *you* have it?"

Frankie wrapped her hand in Axl's fur and shook her head.

Ratha's eyes closed.

Jim felt the strangest sensation—as if someone else was inside his head, poking around. His thoughts became loose and unfixed, rising up and fading away faster than he could catch them.

When Ratha opened her eyes, she spoke as much to herself as to them.

"I am perplexed," she said. "I have opened this doorway so that Caspar or Chantarelle could return with the Fifth Stone; instead, they have sent you. I do not understand. What could be the meaning of this?"

"Chantarelle sent us back to help Louis," Frankie explained. "He didn't say anything about the Fifth Stone."

Jim's knees gave way. He squatted on the ground, trying to get his bearings. "I think I'm losing my mind."

"I would know instantly if you were," said Ratha, turning on him with those unearthly eyes. "You are not. Human minds are easy to read. Yours especially so. Very orderly. Your son's was somewhat more complicated. More complicated than yours, at least."

"My *son*? You know my son? Which one?"

"The Varunan—Chase. He stood where you stand not so very long ago."

Jim stood up, disbelieving.

"Where did he go? Was he alone? Who else was with him?"

Ratha dismissed him.

"You have too many questions, and we have no time to waste. I waited here, hoping for salvation. Instead, I am sent a puzzle. You said that Chantarelle sent you to help Louis? Those were his words?"

Frankie nodded.

"The blue-eyed warrior," murmured Ratha to herself.

Jim held up his hands. "I don't know what she's talking about. Where is my son? Where is Chase?"

"The path that leads to your children will also lead to Louis," said Ratha, matter-of-factly. "But we must go. Your questions will have to wait."

"*Children*?" Jim repeated. "They're all here? Have you seen a blonde woman, about this tall—" He put one hand at his shoulder height.

"They are all here."

For the first time since they had landed in this strange place, Jim felt his feet firmly connect to the ground. He stood up straighter.

"You must take me to them!"

"I must—" Ratha began, but the rest of her reply was cut off by the sound of rumbling from inside the cave. Behind her, the waters in the Voss shimmied and rippled in circular waves. The earth bucked. The opening to the cave cracked and heaved, and the mouth crashed in on itself. Another large tremor traveling up from the south end of the lake, where the Voss met the Hestredes, sent rocks flying off the mountainside. Axl and Tar sprinted down the shore to escape the projectiles.

"It's an earthquake!" yelled Jim. The ground shook again with a magnitude he had never felt. Frankie fell against him. He grabbed her. Small rocks and boulders tumbled to either side of them and into the lake. Suddenly, Jim felt two great talons dig into his back; he heard the sound of great wings flapping—and then, in a stomach-dropping *whoosh*, they were airborne.

The lake fell away, transforming into a small blue disc below them. Clouds of dust flew up from where landslides of rock landed. The promontory outside the cave, where they had all been standing, collapsed into the water with a foamy surge.

Ratha flew them southeast, following the long ribbon of the Hestredes.

Ahead, in the far, far distance, lay a thick blanket of fog, and the remains of Metria.

*Chapter Twenty-Four*

# DISASTER

C hase kept the back of Evelyn's head in view, and Knox's just ahead of hers. Somewhere beyond that, swallowed up in mist, were his mother, Teddy, Seaborne, Bodi, and Calla. They proceeded across the dam, not knowing what—or who—they might meet on the other side. The only sound was the slap of invisible waves against the eastern shore.

Fog covered the dam and spilled over the ledge. He looked to his left, toward the large lake that was now the terminus of the Hestredes. He longed to use his daylights to rise up above the blinding fog, to see how far it reached across the lake. He could imagine it—a giant tongue of white that fell off like a wave cresting—but there was no time for him to try. A chill had arrived with the fog, so he pulled on his Varunan robe. It was heavy, and he wasn't sure that he would be able to fight in it. He tightened his grip on his sword hilt, keeping it unsheathed at his hip.

Chase paused. It felt just as desolate ahead of him as it did behind him. This must be the midpoint of the dam. He wished again that he could see something beyond Evelyn and Knox's heads. He wished he had trained harder with Ratha. Had she seen what had transpired since they'd left her? She must have at least felt it when the stone of Melor was used. How could she not? And what was she doing about it?

Chase fanned a hand through the fog and moved forward. So insubstantial, and yet so powerful. It hid so many secrets. He could almost understand Dankar's frustration—*almost*—and his desire to burn it off and erase the division once and for all between Ayda and the rest of the world.

Ahead, Knox threw up a fist. Evelyn and Chase stopped in their tracks. They must be close. Even though they could not see anything, somehow the atmosphere had changed. The battle sounds had died down. Flames and heat from the fire glowed above the city. They were aware of approaching something large and imposing; and then, in moments, they were at the foot of what had once been a broad marble stairway. It was now cracked, with a deep chasm between the two halves.

"I know where we are," Evelyn whispered.

"Aye, I remember this, too," said Seaborne. "These stairs flanked the southern side of the pavilion, which means the harbor is just over there." He indicated to the right. "We are at the outskirts of the city."

Grace took Teddy and Bodi by their hands.

Seaborne held his finger up to his mouth.

Carefully, quietly, they picked their way up the broken stairs and crept out onto the pavilion. The mist lay heavy on the ground, but this time, it was an ally. They followed the perimeter of the square until they found cover in a dark alley. Bodies of dead Exorians, Melorians, and Metrians littered their path. They took a moment to collect any blade or spear to be found among the dead.

The earthquake had shaken the city, and the streets were filled with rubble. Deep cracks split the soft, golden walls of the standing buildings. Many of the blue-painted shutters that adorned the windows of the houses had been thrown loose and lay broken on the ground. Whole buildings had been ripped from their foundations; their facades tilted dangerously into the alley.

The city felt abandoned; no cries for help, and the buildings, mere shells. Fires burned amid the rubble, and smoke coated the walls.

"Where is everyone?" Chase whispered.

"Dead or buried," said Evelyn. She knew from experience what an earthquake could do to a city.

"Maybe they were evacuated in time," said Seaborne.

"Let's hope," muttered Calla.

"Where are the Exorians?" asked Knox.

"That's what I'm worried about."

Teddy put his hand on one of the building walls and pushed it. A little bit of the stone crumbled into sandy dust. "It's empty, like the sand dollars on the beach."

Seaborne halted at the top of the alley, whispering, "Evelyn, my memory is not sure enough to lead us now. Do you know where Urza might be, or where we might find what's left of the Metrian guard?"

Evelyn shook her head. She was on high alert, one hand on one of her knives and the other clutched close under her robe, protecting the stone in her possession.

"Maybe the watchtower, or the underground caverns, but I don't know for sure. There is a courtyard a few blocks from here, and beyond that are the main buildings. They might be there, too—but so could the Exorians."

"I remember that courtyard," said Chase. "With the fountain."

"That's the one," said Evelyn.

Seaborne took a deep breath. Calla gave him an almost imperceptible nod.

"Well, we haven't come here to hide, have we?" he said. "If it's Exorians we find, then so be it. Rothermel will be near. And if it is Urza and the Metrian guard, all the better. If you are ready, Evelyn, lead the way."

Evelyn picked her way through the maze of alleys. It was slower going than they had anticipated because several of the bridges had collapsed, and in some cases, the alleys were completely blocked. Her heart beat wildly. She had seen this kind of destruction before. She had heard the cries from people buried beneath whole buildings. She remembered the feeling of being trapped and hungry and afraid. The sight of Metria in a heap opened a door in her mind to the past—a door that led to a dark and unhappy place. She willed herself to walk by it and focus on the task at hand. Almost without knowing it, her hand found the stone of Metria. Its shape and weight soothed her.

She stopped, then had them all retrace their steps. Eventually, they wound their way into the courtyard. The sound of water hitting stone reverberated across the enclosed space.

A solid jet of water shot from a hole in the ground where the magnificent fountain had once stood. The statue and carvings that had so beautifully shaped and cascaded the water lay smashed on the ground, the trumpet-like shells in pieces.

"It's broken!" cried Teddy.

Calla shushed him, but the amplifying effects of the square did their job. His small cry echoed up and around them, hovering in the air.

A shout and the sound of running feet soon followed.

"Get back," urged Seaborne, too late.

Exorians flooded into the courtyard. The Melorians surged forward, with Seaborne and Calla fanning out. In the confusion, Grace slipped back down the alley with Teddy and Bodi. Evelyn went running for cover, flanked by Knox and Chase.

"Whatever happens, don't lose that stone," cried Chase, trying to push open a pair of heavy bronze doors. They were locked from the inside.

"Quick, in here," Evelyn hissed.

She threw open a side door she had used with Urza and they hurried into a dark hallway. Keeping their backs to the wall, they made their way toward the opposite end, where it opened onto a very large room, and froze.

There, standing in the center, was Louis, lit by sheets of dusky light spilling down from long horizontal openings in the wall. He was alone, and his changed state looked even more out of place set against the bareness of the room. His mottled skin was bare except for a pair of loose muslin pants and a sling around his right hand. In his left hand, he held up Rothermel's belt. The buckle was smashed and dark.

"I've been waiting for you," he said, shaking the belt in the air. He took a step toward them. "Dankar told me exactly where to find you. Did you really think you could bring a stone of power so near to him and he would not feel it?" His gaze landed on Knox. "What I want to know is why you would follow me here. I told Rothermel you would be left in peace—and you were."

"Do you think I'd let you waltz off to Dankar with my Keeper?" hissed Knox.

Louis held the broken belt up. "He is no longer your Keeper."

Chase and Knox moved to a defensive position, blocking Evelyn from view.

Louis eyed their movements, a vacant look on his face.

"He has great plans for us all."

"Get back," Chase whispered to Evelyn.

Evelyn slowly pulled back. Chase and Knox closed the distance between themselves and Louis. Chase raised his sword; Knox aimed a Metrian blade at Louis's chest.

"You know, Louis, you are related to us," said Chase, in an even tone.

"What are you doing?" hissed Knox.

Chase raised his palm to calm his brother, and said to Louis, "You're not a true Exorian. You're an outlier, just like us. Look at your hand! Doesn't that tell you something? You don't belong here. You belong with your *real* family. With your sister."

Louis took a flask from the side of his hip and swigged from it. He looked at his right hand in the sling, and then at Chase, his eyes devoid of feeling.

"I don't have a sister. And I don't know you," he said. "The only family I have is them." He pointed with his thumb over his shoulder. Out of the shadows at the corners of the room emerged a mass of fully armed Exorian troops. They slammed their spears on the ground. The tips erupted into flame.

"Take them," ordered Louis.

The Exorians descended on Chase and Knox. Knox ran full tilt into the fray and, using one of their shields as a launching pad, somersaulted over their heads. He landed on the other side of the room. Chase's sword flashed as he fought back their torches. He smelled the sickening odor of singed fur and realized his robe was burning. He threw it off, narrowly avoiding a spear tip, and blocked another with his sword. Then he heard Knox yelp.

"Ratha, help me!" he said in mindspeak, over and over, hoping she was listening again.

Whether it was a coincidence or an answer, Chase would never know, but a sudden gust came through the horizontal windows and extinguished the Exorian spears. Even with this small advantage, though, he and Knox were outnumbered and cornered. He lay down his sword.

Louis kicked it away.

"Why are you doing this?" Knox shouted, surrounded by Exorians. "We're your nephews! You're just gonna turn us over to Dankar?"

"Take them outside," Louis said to his men.

They shoved Chase and Knox roughly into line, and began to bind them.

"Stop!" came a voice from the hallway. It was Evelyn. She was holding the stone of Metria. A purple glow emanated from it like a tide. It swept the room and hit Louis and the Exorians like a shock of cold water.

"You will not be taking my friends anywhere." Her voice was eerily calm, and seemed to come from far away. She had activated the stone of Metria.

"Evelyn, no!" said Chase, under his breath.

Louis hesitated, rubbing his right hand vigorously. He looked momentarily confused. "The stone . . ." His left hand groped for the flask at his hip. He took a swig, and then stepped toward Evelyn, gesturing for his men to back him up. "If you come with me, your friends are free to go. We will take the stone to Dankar."

"No need; I am already here," said an oily voice snaking across the room.

Dankar strode into the hall with the two *tehuantl* from his tent, Rothermel in tow behind him. The Melorian Keeper looked spent. His tangled head of hair was streaked with white, and his back was bowed like an old man's. He walked gingerly, as if each step pained him. Giving up his stone had sucked the life out of him.

"Rothermel!" Knox shouted. "Did he hurt you?"

The Keeper acknowledged Knox. His eyes looked vacant.

"Tut-tut. I did nothing of the sort," said Dankar. "I just made him an attractive offer—one I will make to you." He turned to face Evelyn. Then, he held out both hands. In one was the stone of Melor; in the other, a black stone of equal size and shape. The stone of Exor.

"They are beautiful, are they not? So perfectly formed. So similar, yet so different. Like brothers, forged at the same time." As he spoke, the stones began to glow from within. The darkness in the room retreated between the silvery-purple aura of the stone of Metria and the gold and amber light coming from the stones in Dankar's hands.

The Exorian troops were mesmerized. Dankar released them, saying, "Your work here is done; go find the others who came with these children. Bring them to me."

When the last warrior had exited, Dankar stopped Louis at the door and told him to stand guard. The *tehuantl* watched over Rothermel.

The large room suddenly felt very empty. Dankar took note of the hallway behind Evelyn, and flicked the hand that held the stone of Melor. Its walls pitched and bucked, and then collapsed, blocking their escape in that direction. The only way out now was through Louis.

"You have no right to use that stone," cried Knox. His face was red with anger. He looked like he might explode. "That is Rothermel's stone."

Dankar's eye twitched. One of the *tehuantl* snarled.

"Not anymore. And I would mind my manners, if I were you. The *tehuantl* are hungry." The glow from the stones in Dankar's hands intensified.

Evelyn was doing her best to maintain the grip on her stone, to fight off Dankar's pull on it, but the effort was taxing her. Sweat dripped from her brow and her hands shook.

Dankar took a step toward her.

"My, my. This *is* something—or should I say, *you* are something, my dear. You have the blood of an Other in those veins, if I am not mistaken. No ordinary human could handle, let alone ignite, a stone of power. But how, I wonder, did Rysta give it to you? For you did not have it before, I am certain."

Evelyn clenched her jaw, saying nothing.

"Very well. You do not have to tell me. But I should like very much to have your stone, girl-child. Would you give it to me?"

Evelyn shook her head.

Dankar took another step forward. The auras from the two stones in his extended hands began to mingle. He touched the stone of Melor to the stone of Exor and a cord of light spun between them, creating a humming sound. The cord expanded and began to creep across the room toward Evelyn. It stretched up her arms and across her shoulders, pulling her toward Dankar like a tractor beam. She resisted, crying out in pain.

"Give me the stone of Metria," commanded Dankar.

"Let her go!" shouted Chase. "She'll never give it to you!"

"We shall see about that." Dankar's eyes flicked to his, then Knox's. "I have found that attachments are very useful in this business. Ask Rothermel. He graciously surrendered his stone in exchange for his kin—and those hounds." Rothermel grimaced. "I had so wanted to set my *tehuantl* on them, but sacrifices must be made. Now—"

The cord of light wrapped itself around Evelyn. Her body began to shake. Her eyes rolled back in her head. The stench of burning skin filled the air.

"You must break the circuit, or it will fragment her!" shouted Rothermel, coming alive. The *tehuantl* snarled at him.

Chase responded by instinct. He launched himself into the air and plowed into Dankar.

Surprised by the force of the attack, Dankar tumbled to the ground and lost his grip on both of the stones. The stone of Melor rolled across the floor toward Knox. The cord of light dimmed.

"Get it, Knox!" shouted Chase.

Knox torpedoed himself toward the stone of Melor, but not before Louis had jumped in and wrestled Knox to the ground. The *tehuantl* sprang, tails swatting the air, teeth bared. Rothermel intercepted them, fighting them back with his bare hands. Chase wrapped his arms and legs around Dankar, trying to keep him immobilized.

Knox and Louis thrashed on the ground, each one trying to grab the stone—but Knox was quicker. He threw himself on top of it.

A bolt of green light exploded above them. The *tehuantl* screamed. Rothermel stood straight and tall, holding the stone of Metria in his hand. In the commotion, Evelyn had used the last of her strength to throw it across the room to him, and in the doing, gifted him its power. She was now slumped on the floor.

"DANKAR! Come fight me on *my* terms," Rothermel roared. The stone in his grasp radiated a great blue-green light, as if the hall had suddenly been plunged underwater.

Dankar rose to his feet, pulling Evelyn up with him, the obsidian knife pointed at her jugular vein.

"I don't think so!" he said, nodding at the knife. "Give me all the stones or this one dies."

"No more of this, Dankar. Enough bloodshed," Rothermel intoned. "I gave you one stone; I will not give you another."

Dankar's reply was to swipe the blade lightly across Evelyn's neck. A crimson line darkened her skin and sheet of blood began to spill.

Chase made an unintelligible sound.

Blood streamed from Evelyn's wound, spilling down her robe and seeping into the stone floor. She instinctively brought her hands up to her throat. Blood coursed through her fingers. She opened her mouth to scream but nothing came out.

Dankar watched her for a moment, then spoke to Rothermel. "Always, always, dear cousin, it comes down to this: the stones or the humans. A piece of rock or a life. Just give me the stone, and let's be done with it. You know you won't let her die. It's not in you." He held out his hand expectantly.

To his own astonishment, Chase began to cry. Great gulps of air and tears. He clutched his fists and screamed at Dankar.

"Why are you doing this to us? What have we ever done to you?"

"It's not about you. It's never been about you," Dankar sneered back.

Evelyn sagged against him. He let her fall to the ground.

Rothermel looked helplessly between Evelyn, Chase, and Knox. Reluctantly, as if it physically pained him, he relinquished the stone of Metria to Dankar.

"Take it," he said. "I give it to you."

"No!" yelled Knox.

"Thank you." Dankar snatched the stone from Rothermel's hand. "That is all I asked."

"Evelyn—" sobbed Chase. He crawled over to her and ripped off part of his shirt to try to staunch the blood.

"I will honor our agreement," Dankar pronounced, as if he had only decided to do so in that moment. "Besides, she is of interest to me."

He leaned over Evelyn's prone form.

Chase wanted nothing more than to take one of the stones and smash it into Dankar's face. Instead, he pressed the fabric harder against Evelyn's wound and willed her to stay alive.

"Help her," he said.

The stones in Dankar's hands began to glow, wrapping Evelyn and Chase in their combined light. In moments, she was able to sit up. Chase removed his blood-soaked piece of cloth. The wound was healing rapidly. Knox lifted her to her feet. She was very pale and weak, but she was alive.

Louis wasted no time. He shackled them together with Rothermel. The *tehuantl* flanked them.

"What made you think you could use the stone of Metria against Dankar?" Knox whispered to Evelyn. "It was exactly what Seaborne told you *not* to do."

"I don't know," she whispered back. "It just happened. One minute I was backing out of the hallway, and the next, I had the stone out."

"Shhh, children. What's done is done," said Rothermel. "The stones have a strong pull on one another. They are bound to one another and want to be together. I felt it myself. It is not your fault, Evelyn."

Dankar and Louis led the prisoners through the remains of the building, into the open air. The fog had withdrawn to the shore, revealing the remains of a watchtower on the ground, lying in pieces as big as trucks. Leaning against the heaps of rubble, flanked by Exorian warriors, were three people.

"Frankie!" cried Evelyn.

"Dad!" cried Knox, at the same time.

A woman, tall and pale, with colorless eyes and a black topknot of hair, stood to the side. Dust whirled in small eddies around her. She positioned herself directly in Dankar's path. The small eddies began to rise, growing into spinning columns of dust.

"Oh, man," breathed Chase. "I can't wait to see this."

# Chapter Twenty-Five

# BECKON

Grace, Teddy, and Bodi ran pell-mell across the courtyard with the broken fountain, not looking back. When they were safely in an adjoining alley, they stopped and waited for the others. After a while, when no one came, they went back to the courtyard, which was clear. Seaborne, Calla, and the Melorians had chased the Exorians to parts unknown. Grace tried the double bronze doors, but they still would not give, and the little side door she found led to a hallway that was caved in. Not knowing what else to do, they ducked down another alley and tried to stay out of sight.

They quickly ran into problems. Heaps of fallen stones and crushed buildings blocked their way, forcing them to turn back and find another route. It wasn't long before they were completely lost. They stopped to rest at the foot of an enormous pile of rubble.

"I'm tired," panted Teddy. Drifts of smoke obscured their surroundings.

"I'm hungry," said Bodi.

"Let's go in here," said Grace. She pointed to a nearby building. The doors and windows were blown out by the earthquake, but the structure was still standing. "Maybe I can find you something to eat."

Inside, the rooms were wrecked. At one time they had been well-furnished, with chairs and couches and tables, and fabric adorning the walls. Fire had consumed much of the furniture, and the rest was covered in dust.

"You two, stay here and rest," said Grace, pointing to the remnants of a low couch. "I'll see if there's any food." She went off to look for a kitchen.

"Now what do we do?" asked Bodi, looking around the destroyed room.

"I don't know," said Teddy. "My dad says that when you're lost, the best thing to do is to stay where you are. It helps other people find you."

"But what if it's bad people who want to find you?"

Teddy shrugged. "I guess we could stay here, but hide, too. Like hide-and-seek. We'll only come out if it's the good guys."

Bodi looked puzzled. "What's hide-and-seek?"

"It's a game. You play it with other kids. One person is the seeker, and everybody else hides, and the seeker tries to find them. And the way we play it, when you get found you go to jail. There's a jailer, and you can't get out of jail unless somebody who's hiding gives you a signal. We call it Beckon." Teddy put a hand up to his mouth and made a hooting sound, like an owl. "That's my beckon. When you hear it, you can escape from jail and you get to go hide again."

"Sounds hard."

"No, it's fun."

"I used to play games with my brother," said Bodi, matter-of-factly. She pulled a ripped sheet of fabric from the wall and wrapped herself in it.

Teddy said, "I'll play with you. But I need some rest first, okay?"

"Yes."

Grace returned with a loaf of bread and a couple of oranges. They sat together on the couch, eating without talking, exhausted.

Outside, an occasional shout or crash would bring Grace to her feet, but the combination of food and sitting was doing its work. Teddy was asleep in minutes. Grace's eyes blinked. She tried hard to stay awake, but she had not slept in more than two days. She covered them all with some large pieces of torn fabric, and soon, she, too, was asleep.

Bodi lay awake, listening to them breathe. She tried hard not to think about her own mother. All the mothers in the pit-houses had been put in the dungeon, along with their young babies. Older kids, like her, had been taken to the warrior barracks for training. If anyone resisted, they weren't given a second chance. They were hung on the rock spires and left for the vultures. Bodi swallowed hard, thinking of Emon. She watched dust motes spiral around in the smoky air, remembering the hut she used to live in. At night, the fire at the center sent sparks up into the air in just the same way. She used to watch them while her mother hummed to her.

Her eyes drifted over to Grace and Teddy. She wondered if Grace ever hummed; then, she put a hand to her mouth and hooted softly into it.

A hoot echoed back at her from outside the room.

She sat up abruptly. The sudden movement woke Grace.

Bodi hooted again.

Another hoot came back. It was coming from somewhere above them.

Bodi shook Teddy awake.

"Someone's here!" she whispered to him. "They gave me a beckon!"

"What?" said Teddy, sleepily.

"A beckon! Like you said." Bodi hooted again to show him, and again there was a response.

Teddy jumped to his feet, awake now. He pointed to the ceiling, and whispered, "Up there." He looked at his mother. "What do we do?"

Grace's brow furrowed. "I don't know. Let me think."

"Is it a good guy or a bad guy?" asked Bodi.

"I'll go up and look. You two stay here," said Grace.

Something crashed to the floor above them and broke into pieces. Then they heard a pounding, like a fist on the floor.

"It doesn't seem like a bad guy would make so much noise," said Bodi.

Grace looked at her. "You know what, Bodi? I think you're right. I think someone needs help."

They pulled off their hastily made covers and made their way to a set of smooth white stairs, coated in ash and dust. Teddy hooted again, and this time, the response was loud and quick, and came from a room near the top of the stairs.

"Hello?" Grace called up.

A woman's voice answered. "Help me."

They raced up the stairs and into the room. A jumble of furniture was lying at the center, but no person.

"Where are you?" cried Bodi.

"Here," said the voice. It came from under a pile of rubble where a wall had fallen down. "I can't move."

They found her halfway under a wardrobe that had fallen along with the wall.

"Teddy," Urza cried, when she saw him. "How did you get here?"

Teddy was speechless. He hardly recognized Urza under all of the blood and dust.

"I came with Seaborne and Knox and Chase and everyone else. This is my mother—and this is Bodi."

She nodded at them, and then, indicating the wardrobe, said, "I'm trapped; I can't move."

Grace, Teddy, and Bodi strained to lift it off her, but it was too heavy.

"Leave it," panted Urza, clearly in pain. "It's too dangerous for you to stay here. Exorians are everywhere." She pulled a piece of parchment from her robe and waved it at Teddy.

"You will find the entry to the underwater caverns marked on this map. Many of our people are in hiding there. You must get to them. Don't let the Exorians know where they are." She put her forehead to the floor and groaned in pain. "I sent anyone who could not fight into the caverns below the city. They could be trapped down there. They are the last of our kind. Do not let them perish there."

Teddy took the parchment.

"What about you?" he asked.

"Leave me," she said.

He and Bodi and Grace pushed again on the wardrobe, trying to dislodge it. It wouldn't budge.

Urza collapsed on her folded arms. "It's no use."

A soft little hoot came from the doorway.

"Who's there?" cried Bodi.

"Who do you think it is? And keep it down; the three of you are hooting like a pack of owls in here."

Seaborne stepped lightly over the debris in the room, coming toward them.

"Help me get this off her," said Grace, more than a little relieved to see another grown-up.

With Seaborne's help, they were able to lift the wardrobe high enough for Urza to drag herself out from under it with her elbows. When she was free, they let the wardrobe crash to the floor.

"Calla is waiting outside. We managed to round up a few more of our kind. We need to find Rothermel," said Seaborne. "Can you help us?"

He tried to lift Urza to her feet. Both of her legs were broken.

"I can't walk," she said, collapsing again. "I don't know where Dankar has taken the Keeper, but if you have a force, please go to the caverns. You will remember the way from your boyhood. Make sure my people escape."

Seaborne passed an eye over the dirty, frightened faces of Grace, Bodi, and Teddy.

"The city is overrun, Urza, and the earth has shifted. The caverns may have fallen in beneath us. Nothing is as it once was." He exhaled deeply. "The Fifth Stone has failed us. Ayda is spent. There is little hope for any of us now."

"What about Evelyn? Have you seen her?"

"That I have."

"Did she . . . did she mention the stone of Metria?"

"She did a lot more than mention it. She showed us the thing."

"Then she has it? Rysta gave it to her?" Urza looked relieved despite the pain. "All is not lost, then."

Outside the blown-out window, the air was still. A cold wind brought small white particles into the room. At first they all thought it was ash, but it began to collect in drifts along the edges of the wall.

"What is this?" cried Urza. "Has the fog been shattered and split? Has Dankar finally found a way to break it into pieces?"

Teddy walked to the window and put his tongue out. White bits landed on his tongue and dissolved.

"It's snowing," he said, amazed.

Seaborne joined him at the window. It was true. Outside, the fallen city was covered in a thin layer of white snow.

"Blimey," said Seaborne. "The world's gone upside down."

*Chapter Twenty-Six*

# THE VORTEX

"D̲AD!!"

Chase and Knox were shouting through the band of Exorians that had stationed themselves between them.

"How did you get here?" asked Knox. "*When* did you get here?"

"Mom's here, too. She's with Teddy!" Chase called out.

"Is that Evelyn?" cried Frankie, catching sight of her sister.

"Yes! She's hurt."

Frankie ran between the Exorians' legs, careless of their spears, straight to her sister.

"What's wrong with her?"

Evelyn lifted her head at the sound of her Frankie's voice; she was still very weak and unable to stand without leaning on Chase. She saw Frankie and raised her palm, fingers splayed.

"*Sa fè lontan*, little sister," she said, in their birth language.

"Too long," said Frankie.

She raised her fingertips to match Evelyn's.

"Are you all right?"

"I am now," said Evelyn, softly.

Louis yanked her back, harder than he intended, but the snow was an annoyance. It was stinging his skin, collecting in the cracks between his scales. It felt like tiny electric shocks.

Chase caught her before she could fall.

"Don't do that!" cried Frankie, defiant.

"That's Louis," said Knox. "He's a world-class jerk now."

Frankie's eyes shot up to Louis's, seeing the blue irises, so bold against the white of the snow that coated his warrior hide.

"Louis?" She could not believe it. "What did they do to you?"

"Do I know you?" asked Louis.

"Of course you do, dummy. You are *my* Louis."

She dove past her sister and jumped up, catching Louis around his neck and wrapping her legs around his middle. His right hand began to throb the moment she touched him. He felt a strange hollowing sensation and realized he was cold.

"I missed *you*, too!" said Frankie, oblivious to Louis's shock. "I came back to find you." She looked over her shoulder at Evelyn. "To find all of you. Chantarelle told me you'd be here! And you are."

She hugged Louis again. The sensation of her hands around his neck pierced the blankness in his mind and brought with it a memory: a night in the desert under a dark sky filled with stars. And then, the hole widened and more memories came: There was a house on a point. A sailboat. A little girl in a yellow T-shirt. Was this the same little girl?

"Louis, hug back!" Frankie demanded.

The snow continued to fall.

✛     ✛     ✛

Ratha had planted herself directly in front of Dankar.

"Brother," she said to Rothermel, bowing her head in greeting.

"Sister," he echoed.

"Nice of you to join our little reunion, cousin," Dankar sneered. "And with more humans, I see." He pointed at Jim. "They do make useful pets, don't they? As you can see, I have several of my own." He cocked his head at his prisoners. "And more on the way when we clear this fog."

Ratha ignored him.

"Let my brother go."

"Of course, of course," Dankar said, sounding reasonable. "It is a day of deal-making, and anything is possible for a price—say, one stone of Varuna?" He held out his hand. Snowflakes fell on it. He sighed and blew them off, saying in a huff, "Come on, Ratha. It's over now. I have *won*. I have the three other stones."

"You don't have hers yet, you loser!" Knox yelled out.

Dankar wheeled back and slapped him, hard, across the face.

"I told you to mind your manners!"

Jim Thompson broke through the line of Exorians and threw a punch at Dankar.

"Don't you ever touch my son again!" he shouted.

The blow glanced off Dankar's cheek.

"I see rudeness is a family trait," he said, touching his cheek. "No matter." He struck a hard blow across Jim's face.

Jim bent over double and staggered back, cupping his nose. Blood seeped up from a newly opened gash on his cheekbone.

"DAD!" both boys cried in unison.

"Go join your humans," said Dankar, shoving Jim behind him.

Jim stumbled. Knox caught him.

"Way to go, Dad," he said proudly.

Jim pinched his nose with his fingers, and tried to hug both his sons and Evelyn through their chains.

"Your mother and Teddy?"

"They're okay, Dad," Chase answered.

Jim choked back a sob.

"I thought I lost you all. I thought—"

He broke down.

Chase and Knox had never seen their father cry.

"Aww, Dad, we're here. We're all here now," said Knox.

Jim cleared his throat. "At some point, you will need to explain to me where *here* is, exactly."

Snow swirled harder around them. Ratha's voice rose, high and determined, arguing with Dankar. With it came an arctic wind whipping through the city, screaming through the alleys and waterways. Snow pelted them.

Louis put Frankie down. His skin was burning and itching under the snow. He clawed at it.

Evelyn watched him intently.

"I have an idea, Frankie. Take his other hand," she said reaching for Louis's right hand with her own. Frankie took his left, and Evelyn took her right, forming a chain. With the small well of energy that had been restored to her, she called upon her daylights. They rose, flickering and weak, but present. The amber network grew visible under her skin. It spun out until it encompassed both Louis and Frankie.

Frankie's daylights responded immediately, and together, they wove a web of energy that pulsed through them and into Louis.

Louis's brain shut down. He closed his eyes, no longer aware of the snow. He saw only a stream of images. All of the memories that had been kept at bay for so long by the fog of forgetting and the firewater came rushing to the forefront. He was pitched backwards through time, before the transformation at the arena, and his torment on the spire, and further still.

He remembered his journey with Frankie, and the day at the edge of the canyon in Exor. He recalled how he had risked everything to save Chase, Knox, Teddy, and Evelyn. How he had become the thing he was to save them. And still, his mind reached further yet, back to the house on the point, with humped ledges sloping off into the water. A sail flapping in the wind. His parents. His sister. Grace. He saw it all, and knew it for what it was.

*Home.*

He opened his eyes.

*Chapter Twenty-Seven*

# REVELATION

Dankar sprang into attack mode, grabbing at the stone that was in Ratha's hand, but she was quick.

The snowstorm kicked into a full gale, spinning sleet and hail.

In response, Dankar ignited the stones of Melor, Metria, and Exor, locking her in combat. A dizzying light grew up around them. The gale sparked and flamed. The earth trembled. The Exorians were paralyzed by the snow.

Ratha had kindled the stone of Varuna. Chase could feel it, and he, more than the others, could see through the blinding light that now encompassed the combatants. There were no blows between them; instead, it seemed that Dankar and Ratha were locked in an enormous test of wills. Ratha's colorless eyes had rolled back in her head. The stone of Varuna burned with an icy flame, blue and cold, as she wielded it against the other three. The energies of the stones of Melor, Metria, and Exor joined forces, and the humming cord of light that Chase had witnessed back in the hall began to buzz again. It flowed forward toward Ratha in a snaking tendril. The snow swirled more ferociously. The wind gusted, pushing against the coil of light. It was the strangest thing Chase had ever seen: a battle between air and light, both pressing against one another as if they had physical mass. The icy blue light of the stone of Varuna leapt forward.

"She's trying to pull the other stones toward her!" Chase yelled into the gale. For an instant, he thought she might do it. But then, the cord of light broke through the space between them and snaked its way around Ratha's body, wrapping itself over and over until she—and the stone of Varuna—were completely engulfed by it.

"It's pointless to resist!" Chase heard Dankar shout above the wind.

And still, she did. The gale blew harder. Snow whipped sideways.

"You may take it from me," cried Ratha, in an unearthly, high-pitched wail, "but I will never give it to you."

Chase could just make out her form, bent over the stone clutched to her chest.

He watched as the cord of light wrapped itself around the stone of Varuna, and pulled it from Ratha's grasp. The cord of light held it aloft, and then snaked backwards.

Dankar's triumphant cry rose above the gale.

"Follow me," Louis shouted, as the sound of Dankar's victory reached their ears. He put his head down and skirted the edges. Frankie followed.

Evelyn pulled at the chains still connecting her to Knox and Chase. She was feeling much better. Frankie's daylights had helped her as well as Louis.

"He's going to get us out of here!" she yelled, pointing at Louis's retreating back.

"Are you kidding me?" cried Knox, holding on to his father. "He can't be trusted!"

"He's good now! We fixed him!"

"Uh-huh—"

"He is! We have to go! Just trust me, okay?" she cried.

"Okay!" interrupted Chase. They set out together in Louis's and Frankie's direction, shielding their faces from the wind.

"Stick together and hold on to the walls!" Evelyn shouted. It was something she remembered from Haiti, after the earthquake, when it was pitch dark in the city. If you clung to the walls of buildings as you walked you wouldn't wander off and get lost.

"We'll never make it through this," called Chase.

The storm was thick. They struggled against it for some time. After a while, the wind and snow began to ease off. The storm was passing. They caught sight of Louis and Frankie ahead of them, and the steely glint of water at the end of the alley. They called to them.

When they had caught up, Louis took the opportunity to free Chase, Evelyn, and Knox from their chains.

"Glad you decided to fight for the good guys again," said Knox, rubbing his wrists.

"It doesn't matter anymore," said Louis.

"Why?" asked Knox.

Chase answered for him by pointing to the sky, where snow was barely visible now. A glare was shining through the overcast. Sunshine.

"Ratha lost. I saw it. Dankar took her stone."

"Did she give it to him?" asked Evelyn.

"I don't think so. He just took it."

"It's not over then—but it's still pretty bad."

As if to underscore her words, an explosion of dirt, snow, and wind erupted somewhere in the city behind them.

"What should we do?" she asked.

"We should run," said Louis.

So they did. They ran hard and fast until they hit the two poles that marked the entrance to the harbor of the city. Sun began to shoot through the dark storm clouds, hitting a cold and gray ocean. Out to sea lay the wall of fog, as thick and impenetrable as ever. It felt strangely comforting.

A hot burst of light raked the city, like the blast of a bomb. It shocked everyone into silence. Out of the alleyways, Seaborne, Calla, Grace, Teddy, Bodi, and a few Melorians came running with a band of ragtag Metrians, freed from the underwater caverns. They were chased by a horde of Exorians.

Jim saw Grace and Teddy first. He forgot about his injury, which had already begun to heal, and ran back toward them. He scooped up Teddy and grabbed onto Grace just as another burst of light threw everyone to the ground.

Dankar emerged from an alley, followed by his *tehuantl* and a much-diminished Rothermel and Ratha. In his arms, he cradled all four stones. He strolled past the crowd, toward the edge of the pier. A conqueror amid the conquered. The *tehuantl* slunk beside him, tails high.

When he reached the water, he turned. A sunbeam fell upon him and the stones. He lifted the stones over his head. The Exorians cheered. Everyone else groaned. Then, he motioned for Rothermel and Ratha to come forward.

Ratha's expression was inscrutable as always, but her eyes did not leave her stone. It had been wrested from her, but she had not gifted it to Dankar. He did not possess it, truly.

Dankar held up his hand, cradling the four stones in his other arm. He made a gesture of peace.

"Cousins," he crowed, "I cannot tell you how often I have dreamed of this day." He tilted his head toward the wall of fog out at sea. "Until now, we've been held back, fighting each other like caged beasts, kept prisoner on this island. But no more! There is an entirely other world out there, a weaker world; a world crying out to be taken in hand. The only thing that lies between it and me, is that"—he gestured out to the fog—"but no longer!"

He turned on Ratha.

"It is useless to deny me, cousin. I will be free of this island, with or without you. I have your stone; now help me to dispel this curse. If you do, perhaps I will give it back to you and we can go forward to our destinies as we were meant to, as kin."

"Our stones and the fog of forgetting were created by a power greater than you," said Ratha. "Far greater than any of us. You are a fool if you think you can control it."

Dankar's lips peeled back across his teeth.

"I am bored of this game. It is pointless to resist me. I *always* have the winning hand."

He cast his eyes over the crowd. They fell on Chase.

"Let's get this started, shall we? The sooner it is over, the better. Here it is: I will fragment one outlier for every minute you waste." He strode over and dragged Chase in front of Ratha. "And I will start with this one, as he is clearly a Varunan. I can tell by his eyes."

"Don't let him do this, Ratha," said Chase, in mindspeak. "He always uses us against your kind. He did it to both of your brothers, and to Rysta. Don't fall for it. I'm not worth it. None of us are."

Ratha's colorless eyes flashed purple but she said nothing.

"You said it yourself: Blood is an accident of nature. Choice is fate. I am choosing *you*, Ratha," said Chase, with mounting panic. "Please! Respect my choice. My fate. I don't care what he does to me!"

Still she said nothing.

Dankar frowned at her silence. "You think I am kidding?"

He touched all the stones together.

Chase felt a surge of energy hit him like a wall, and then he felt only pain. His thoughts began to recede, and he felt himself falling away from what was happening. Far off in the distance, he heard Knox and Evelyn and his father and mother shouting. He heard the cries of the Melorians and the Metrians. He heard Teddy and Bodi scream his name. He heard his mother's sobs. And then he heard Seaborne.

"Hang on, lad!"

*So this is what being fragmented feels like*, he thought to himself. It hurt, but not as much as he had imagined.

"Hold on, Chase!" he heard his mother cry, echoing Seaborne. But he didn't want to hold on. Maybe this *was* his fate. Maybe everything that had happened since they had first set foot on Ayda was leading up to this moment, right now. Ratha had showed him how time could just collapse, like the folds of a fan. Maybe this day was always going to be part of all the days that had passed, and everything that had happened was on purpose. Maybe everything that anybody does already has their death marked upon it—they just don't know it. And with sudden clarity, Chase understood that there was one last thing he could do that would truly matter.

So, just as Remiel had sacrificed himself for his mistakes long ago, Chase now offered up his vessel to help settle an ancient score between the Others. There was power in sacrifice. Dankar had been using their own love of life and each other against them. Now, Chase could turn the tables. He would choose to set his daylights free. He would not fight anymore.

He shut out all sound and went to the Varunan shelter in his mind. He lay on the straw pallet and looked up through the wind's eye.

And then he was flying, as he had done so often in his dreams, out over the endlessly blue ocean. Only this time, there was no orange life vest to catch his attention. There was only the sea, and the sky, and the horizon stretching vast and empty before him. He did not have to rescue anyone. He only had to keep flying.

# Chapter Twenty-Eight

# THE MARY LOUISE

Chase became aware of a rumbling noise that was filling his head. It was coming from the fog—an unnatural sound, as if thousands of large bees were swarming. He came to with all the people who loved him gathered around. His mother and father, his brothers, Evelyn and Frankie, and Seaborne were there. Calla. Bodi. Even Louis had come.

Ratha loomed over him, Rothermel's craggy face behind her.

She was saying his name.

Chase lay there, confused. One moment he was flying farther than he'd ever gone before, never to return, and the next, he was back here, on Ayda.

His parents helped him sit up.

Dankar glowered at him from a distance, distracted by the buzzing sound coming from across the sea.

"What happened? Is the stone his now?" Chase asked, not wanting to hear the answer. Ratha must have surrendered her powers. Dankar had won.

"No, Chase," said Ratha, reassuringly. "I would never."

"Then what happened?"

"You are a true dreamwalker now, Chase. But I think you should not dream that dream again for a very long time."

"Was it only a dream?"

"It was *the* dream. The most important one—the one that never ends."

"I don't understand," he murmured. "What brought me back?"

"I am not completely sure, but I have my suspicions," said Ratha, cocking her ear. "Listen."

The sound over the water grew louder; soon enough, its source was revealed.

"I don't believe it," said Jim Thompson, dumbfounded.

Pulling into the harbor and out of the fog was the unmistakable sight of Captain Nate's boat, the *Mary Louise*. It was headed straight toward them. A shudder of excitement went through the crowd. It was like the sight of an alien ship landing. Even Dankar was stunned.

"Captain Nate," Chase exhaled. If he had been brought back, all the way from the edge, by the arrival of the *Mary Louise*, it could only mean one thing. Captain Nate had brought them the Fifth Stone.

Dankar was pacing now, clearly unhappy at the disruption of his plans.

The boat swung gracefully into the harbor and pulled up along the jetty as if it were coming into port with the day's catch. Captain Nate silenced the engine, secured the bowline to the pier pole, and jumped out. Once the boat was safely tied up, he helped an old woman step out onto the pier.

"Who is this?" cried Dankar, his eyes on the old woman.

"Gran Fanny?" cried Evelyn.

No one made a sound as Mrs. Fanny Dellemere made her way toward them. Her white hair was looped impressively on her head and she still had her imposing height, but she looked impossibly old and frail—a strange sight on Ayda, where the daylights kept one's vessel strong. Around her, the air buzzed with electricity. Chase could feel the ends of his hair tingling. He tasted metal.

Captain Nate escorted her up the pier.

"Caspar," Dankar breathed, recognizing him. His hand went for the obsidian blade.

Fanny Dellemere's eyes lit first on Ratha and Rothermel, then Evelyn and Frankie, and then landed on Louis. In one glance, she took in his hand and his deep blue eyes. Her gaze traveled to the Thompsons and Chase, rising from the ground. And behind them the sorry state of the Melorians and the Metrians, and the altered vessels of the Exorians.

"So *this* is what you are up to these days, Dankar?" Mrs. Dellemere scolded, shaking her head. "Injuring and torturing innocent people and fragmenting children?"

She stopped directly in front of him, tsk-tsking.

"You've done quite enough, I think. Give me the stones and I'll set it right."

Her tone was so familiar and chastising that Chase almost burst out laughing.

"Who is this human?" Dankar cried, pointing at Mrs. Dellemere with the obsidian blade. He drew himself up, speaking loudly but not taking his eyes off of her. "And why does she think she may challenge me?"

"That is my grandmother," said Frankie, proudly.

Mrs. Dellemere smiled at her. Her gaze skipped to Louis's ruined face, then to Grace, and then to Chase. She cocked an eyebrow.

"Edward?" she asked.

Chase nodded.

"As in, Grace's brother?" Jim cut in, amazed at the news. "He's been here this whole time? Like that?"

"That's him," said Grace. "Well, sort of."

"Quite the shocker, isn't it, Dad?" said Knox.

"Poor boy." Mrs. Dellemere turned her eyes to Dankar. "All those poor men, and women! You've been playing at creation, I see."

"What do you have to say about it?" he snapped. He had stowed the four stones in his robe. Somehow, with the arrival of Mrs. Dellemere, Dankar himself seemed diminished.

"Quite a lot, actually. But I don't think you'd listen, so I will just show you."

As she uttered these words, the years fell from Mrs. Dellemere's face and frame. Her back straightened and she stood tall and beautiful, golden hair falling in ripples to her waist. Her face was gentle and kind, and filled with a radiant light. Anyone who saw her understood instantly how, once upon a time, a Watcher might have fallen in love with her and cursed the world.

"Mother," cried Rothermel and Ratha, in unison, bowing to her.

"My dearest children," she said, raising them up. "How I have missed you."

"Mrs. Dellemere is their mother?" whispered Knox.

"It looks that way," said Chase. "Which means she's not really Mrs. Dellemere. She's Rachel, Remiel's wife. The one he broke his vow for."

Knox swiveled his head between Captain Nate and Rachel as understanding dawned on his face. "And that means, *she's*—she's always been—"

Chase nodded. "The Keeper of the Fifth Stone."

"Holy—"

"—crap," Evelyn finished for him, amazed. "Gran Fanny. She's had it this whole time! Was Captain Nate living in Fells Harbor all these years just to watch over her?"

"And it, I guess," said Chase. "They're a team."

Captain Nate heard his name, and shushed them both with a look.

"There will be all the time in the world for explanation," Rachel was saying, noting the look on the outliers' faces, "but for now, I insist, Dankar, that you return the stones you took from my children and leave this place. Go back to Exor where you may live out the rest of your days. I require no further penitence."

Dankar bared his teeth at her.

"You hold no authority here."

His words were threatening, but beneath them lay a tone of confusion.

"And you do?" Her eyes danced. "That is where you are mistaken, nephew. You have *never* had any authority. None of us do. Not really. You've had the illusion that you were in control. There is only one source of real power in the world—the *atar*—and the Weaver grants us only shards of it."

She pulled a gray stone from her coat, similar to the hundreds of lucky stones that Chase and Knox had seen lining the shelves on the walls of Dellemere Cottage. The only striking characteristics were its perfect oval shape and the four concentric white lines encircling it.

"The Fifth Stone—at last," breathed Dankar, his eyes glued to it.

Rachel bent her fingers around it. It curved perfectly into her palm; as she did so, everyone in the crowd felt a calm, soothing sensation. Fear retreated.

"The power of the Fifth Stone has not been seen or felt in this world for more than five hundred years. Should I activate it now, you will never know peace again," she said to Dankar. "Your stones will become useless and your daylights will fragment. Do not follow this course, I beg you. Surrender your stones."

"No," he growled, like a spoiled child. "You surrender yours. I *have* won. I will be free of this forsaken island once and for all. I shall return to the lands of my birth and reclaim what is rightfully mine. You will not stand in my way. You owe me that much."

"Owe you?"

"My father and all of my uncles are dust because of you and your husband. Remiel should have died a traitor's death—but he didn't. He was rewarded—with *that*!" He pointed to her palm, where the Fifth Stone lay nestled like an egg. "Is it any wonder I would hate you and seek to end any remnants of your line? To take what should have been mine in the first place!"

Chase almost expected Dankar to stamp his foot. He looked so much like a ranting child compared to the majesty of Rachel.

She shook her head. "So much pain and suffering for this stone . . . so many ages spent hiding it, protecting it. And after it all, I wonder if you truly understand what you are asking for, Dankar." She uncurled her fingers from the stone. "This stone was forged by the Weaver and sent to Ayda as a gift to mankind—an apology for what befell the world after the Watchers broke their vow. It is the essence of a promise to never allow such an imbalance to occur again. For, you see, all of our kind—Watchers, Keepers, Others—have powers unfit for the world beyond the fog. We are capable of good, but the misery we have wrought instead is legion."

She pointed with her chin at the destruction of the city around her.

"Just look. This is but a taste of what occurs in the lands beyond the fog when the blood of the Others is awakened. The world was not made for us to rule like rabid dogs."

"They are my kin," Dankar argued. "They will rejoice upon my return." His eyes brushed past the outliers. "As for the humans, they will learn to serve me—or they will suffer. Their daylights are easy to control—as I will show you."

Rachel pressed her lips together, watching him in dismay.

He removed the four stones of Metria, Melor, Exor, and Varuna from the folds of his robe and held them together. A visible shudder went through all who were there—as strong and destructive as the earthquake had been to Metria, only on the inside. The group at the edge of the pier bent over double, their emotions and thoughts churning wildly.

"What's happening?" cried Knox, clutching at Chase.

Chase couldn't answer. He felt anxious and sick and happy and sad and confused all at once. Then he felt panic, and fear, and then, the telltale closing of his throat that indicated an asthma attack.

"Dad," he managed to choke out, but Jim Thompson was in no better shape. He had his hand to his heart and tears streamed from his eyes. Beside him, Knox was vibrating, his face as red as a beet. Grace held on to Teddy and Bodi, crying out.

Frankie bent over and retched.

Louis and the Exorian soldiers began to pull and tear at their scaled skin, as if it was suffocating them.

All around them, Aydans of every size and shape were in despair as the measure of their own daylights began to riot inside their vessels, uncontrolled and imbalanced.

Cries of despair filled the air.

Only Evelyn, Ratha, and Captain Nate remained calm, looking at Rachel: Ratha, because she was the Keeper of the stone of Varuna, whose powers she still contained; Evelyn, because she was called to the Fifth Stone; and Captain Nate, who had lived so long by its blessings.

Rachel looked sorrowfully at Dankar.

"I had hoped it would not come to this, but you have forced my hand. So be it."

She held up the Fifth Stone, and said, simply, "Rise."

The four white lines that circled the stone began to glow: one red, one purple, one blue, one white. They expanded from the stone in swoops of light that grabbed for the four stones that Dankar was holding. Once they touched, they set off a mushroom of flashing commingled colors that bloomed up and over the harbor, extending quickly beyond the *Mary Louise* and out, until the entire city and ocean lay under a dazzling tent of color.

And still it grew. The ocean around them mirrored the display in the sky, turning its waters purple and blue and white and red, as if an artist had spilled a paint box into the sea. Then, the lights massed together in the sky, cavorting and spiraling overhead and spinning tighter and tighter, drawing the wall of fog that surrounded the island into itself, and up, until the colors and the fog made a giant funnel, which poured itself down into the Fifth Stone. All was quiet.

The sun shone in a vast, blue sky. Out to sea, the horizon lay straight and unbroken as far as they could see. The fog had disappeared, and anyone within hundreds of miles felt only a pure and unbounded sense of joy.

"At last!" crowed Dankar, looking out at the clear horizon. "I am free!"

"Yes," intoned Rachel, sorrowfully. She raised her hand to his cheek. "Go now. Be free."

A look of panic crossed Dankar's face. His mouth opened to object, and a large winged moth flew out. And then another, and another. And then, like a petrified stone turns to dust, Dankar's vessel crumbled in front of them and broke into a thousand dun-colored moths. His gold circlet and the four stones fell to the ground; the *tehuantl* pelt that had draped his shoulders drifted after them.

The swarm of moths flew up and over the sea to the west, frantically seeking the heat of the sun.

Dankar, as he had been, was no more.

*Chapter Twenty-Nine*

# FIRST AID

The Fifth Stone had reclaimed the *atar* into itself, absorbing the four separate energies into its one. The four stones now lay inert and powerless. Ratha and Rothermel picked them up; but their vow and their allegiances had been fulfilled. They would never look fully like humans, these Keepers, but they resembled one another more now, brother and sister. In the exchange, Ratha had gained more substance, and seemed now to walk with her feet on the earth. Rothermel moved with more lightness and ease, as if a great weight had been lifted from his shoulders. Their reunion with their mother was brief and joyful. Captain Nate greeted Rothermel as an old friend. Ratha bowed her head in gratitude and said, "Well done, fisherman. You have brought my mother back from the dead."

Rachel held up the Fifth Stone and addressed the crowd before her.

"Our work here is just beginning," she said. "The Fifth Stone has returned to Ayda at last, but it alone cannot set things right. Its return is also perilous to Ayda, as now we are no longer hidden by the fog of forgetting. It is only a matter of time before one of the Others, or their kin, set out on the same quest that brought Dankar to our shores so long ago. We have a small window of time to gain our strength back, and we must do it as *one* tribe. One people. From this day out, you are all Aydans, no longer divided, and you will work together to restore our homes and lands. We shall see Ayda returned to her former beauty, for the Fifth Stone has returned."

As she spoke, her eyes scanned their faces, taking in the fear, injury, and torment they all had endured. She lingered longest over the Exorians, and then moved to acknowledge each of the outliers, honoring Chase, Knox, and Evelyn.

She raised the Fifth Stone and a beautiful light shone from it, as pearly and gentle as the first rays of sunrise on the ocean. It beamed out over all who stood before it, embracing them in its warm glow, and their hearts were eased and fortified. Memories of the battle softened, and the mourning for the dead began.

Rachel returned the stone to her pocket and linked arms with her children to walk among their people. She—and the Fifth Stone—were back where they belonged.

✣    ✣    ✣

In the days that followed, there was much to set right. All the remaining survivors were rescued from the underwater caverns. The bodies of the dead were buried, the rubble cleared, and the business of rebuilding the city began, aided with the grace of the Fifth Stone. But first, Rachel gathered all the Exorian soldiers in the city, Louis among them. They were crammed in the courtyard with the fountain, their bald heads and blood-red lips and scaled hides rendering them identical to one another. Rachel surveyed them, then spoke to Evelyn, who attended her with Frankie.

"You were not wrong in your thinking in how to reverse the transformation of the Exorians. It did not work because the stone of Metria did not have enough power to rebalance their daylights. What Dankar did was very dangerous. I am surprised so many lived—but those who feel the call of Exor have always been very strong."

"Like Ranu?" said Evelyn.

Rachel's face fell a moment at the mention of her eldest son, fragmented long ago during the first battle with Dankar.

"Yes, like Ranu, and"—she put a hand on Frankie's head—"like you, Frankie. Dankar tried to poison you—though more subtly."

"I don't remember firewater," said Frankie.

"Yes, but you were in Exor for some time. You did eat and drink. Dankar added small amounts of firewater to everything you ingested. A terrible experiment to do on a human child. But you are strong, my dear; you did not succumb. I knew you would not. As I said, Exorians are fierce."

"So, I'm definitely an Exorian?" asked Frankie.

"I think only you can answer that, my love," said Rachel. "Now help your old grandmother." She pointed to one of the shattered trumpet shells.

"You really aren't old anymore," said Frankie, running to pick it up.

Rachel filled it with water from the jet that had once fueled the fountain. Then she placed the Fifth Stone at the bottom. Its four lines began to flow, turning the water a rosy hue. She gave it to Frankie first.

"There you go; drink deeply, and all will be set right," she murmured.

When Frankie had drunk her fill, she and Evelyn went around and fed the water to all the Exorian soldiers. Rachel followed behind them, allowing the aura of the Fifth Stone to wash over the Exorians, bathing them in its light.

When they reached Louis, he took several big gulps. The shift he had first felt when Evelyn used her daylights to help him quickened. Now, it took hold. He grimaced, remembering how he had almost killed Knox; how he had treated Rothermel and the Melorians; and finally, how he had refused to help when Dankar had attacked Evelyn.

"I do not deserve to be saved," he whispered.

"Yes, you do, Louis. Yes, you do," said Frankie. "You saved me." She pushed the trumpet shell up to his face again.

"We are all darkness and light, Edward," said Rachel. "In equal proportion. Do not linger in the dark when there is so much for you to do."

She passed by him, letting the glow from her stone penetrate his skin. His right hand felt warm and alive. Blood pulsed from the fingertips up his arm and toward his heart. He could feel it laddering through his veins, running its course around his body. He felt his heartbeat slow and steady, and with each beat, the thick hide that had grown over his real skin began to fall away. Hair sprouted on his head and his old form emerged. He was himself again.

"There you are," said Frankie, proudly.

Around him, the effects of the cure were being felt by all the Exorians. Their scaled hides fell away to reveal individual features and faces. They returned to normal size, blinking and stretching in the light of the Fifth Stone as if awakening from a long and unhappy dream.

"Now, them," said Rachel, pointing to the *tehuantl* that had followed the Exorians into the courtyard.

⊹　　⊹　　⊹

In another part of the city, Chase was with Captain Nate.

"So the Fifth Stone was with Mrs. Dellemere this whole time—at the cottage?" They were going room to room, searching for any signs of life. "You knew, and you didn't tell me?"

"It was not my secret to tell," he replied. "The opposite, actually."

"Don't give me that!" cried Chase. "Why didn't you just bring her back? Her kids are here! I don't get why she had to take the Fifth Stone off the island in the first place."

"That is because you were not here at the time." Captain Nate gave him a weary smile. "You think you have lived through a tremendous battle, but that is because you have never lived in a time when the Others ruled. Such was the misery then that Remiel feared for the survival of the human race. He sent the Fifth Stone away with Rachel, and tasked me with her protection, as a guarantee that no matter what disaster the Others wrought, it could be healed. Ayda would survive.

"And those of us on the other side of the fog of forgetting lived in a relative time of progress—not knowing that our happiness was dependent on the balance that the Keepers on Ayda provided. Life got better for many people. But that is over now. The Fifth Stone has been awakened. The blood of the Others will rise again and try to dominate. It is only a matter of time. And they will eventually come here. There is no fog anymore to separate us; no safe place to hide. Imagine a hundred Dankars all vying for power, and you get the picture. This is why I did not leap to bring the stone back to you."

The sadness in his voice disturbed Chase.

"Then what's the point? Why did we do all this?"

"Because we did what was right for *this* time, in this moment. Dankar had to be stopped."

"But why us? Why were we involved? Just because we live near you?"

"That I cannot say. These forces—the *atar*—are mysterious, and come from a place that I don't even understand myself. The best way I can explain it is that all living things are joined by it, and thus are connected. For centuries, those who knew of the Fifth Stone wanted it revealed. Both Dankar and Ratha were intent on it; they sought it in all corners of the world as best they could, and, eventually, it came close to being discovered—"

"In Fells Harbor," Chase finished.

"Yes."

"A wise man once told me that intent is the greatest weapon of all," Chase said, thinking of Tinator.

"Indeed," said Captain Nate.

✣ ✣ ✣

Louis sought out Grace as soon as the antidote finished its work.

"Edward?" she asked, doing a double take. He looked human now, but he was a grown man. Not the boy she remembered.

"Grace," he answered, a little hesitantly. He, too, was having trouble reconciling his memory of the little girl in the yellow T-shirt, so vivid in his memory, with this grown woman in a Melorian poncho. He touched his fingertips to hers, and when their palms connected, a simultaneous flash of recognition swept through them.

"You're finally back!" she said, her throat tight. "I thought I would never see you again."

"I am, only I'm bigger. I—I—would have tried to contact you . . ." He broke off. There were no words.

"It's not your fault—"

"We have a lot of catching up to do," he said, sadly. "I'm so sorry for everything."

"It's not your fault, Ed," she repeated. "You were just a little boy. You got caught up in a terrible thing." She looped her hand through his elbow.

"We all did," he agreed. "Can we start over?"

"Of course. You're my big brother. Nothing will ever change the way I feel about you."

"There is one thing that needs to change."

"What's that?"

"Call me Louis," he said with a wry look.

*Chapter Thirty*

# ANACAONA

I t was a blessed time on Ayda—this time of reparation. Weeks passed in peace and activity, and life returned somewhat to normal. The presence of the Fifth Stone on Ayda encouraged the land to repair itself more quickly. The people were energetic and productive.

Metrians began to repair their city, and the Melorians stayed on to help. In return, the Metrians would repay the favor and assist them in rebuilding Melor. Many friendships grew between these tribes, and differences faded.

Captain Nate accompanied Bodi and the remaining Exorians north, retracing the path that Dankar had burned through forest. Once in Exor, they freed all the prisoners—including Bodi's mother—from the Palace dungeons. Husbands were reunited with wives, children, with their mothers. And the wounds that Dankar had inflicted on these people began to heal.

Chase, Knox, and Teddy set out on a tour of Ayda with their parents, showing them many of the places they had been, going as far north as the Broomwash and the low glacier field in Varuna. In their absence,

Evelyn and Frankie were inseparable, and passed many relaxing days together in Metria under Rachel's loving eye, tending to the injured, among them, Urza.

It was almost as if the world had not noticed the return of the Fifth Stone, and some began to say that the warnings Rachel had issued were unnecessary.

Until the day a ship was sighted steaming along the horizon. The sighting sent a flurry of anxiety through the city of Metria. Without the fog of forgetting to mask Ayda, voyagers would see the island, and tell stories of what they had seen along their ports of call. These stories would wind their way into the ears of the remaining Others and their kin, their daylights awoken once again. How long would it be before one—or a whole army of them—set out to find Ayda?

History would repeat itself, as Remiel had foreseen when he sent the Fifth Stone away.

A great cry went up in the city for Rachel to restore the fog. People grew afraid, and longed for the days when the Fifth Stone was banished, and the four were hidden in far corners of separate lands. Some even suggested that she bring back the four stones, and leave Ayda, taking the parent stone with her. Fear persisted, and a shadow loomed once again over the city and all those who resided there.

Rachel, Ratha, and Rothermel spent hours locked away in discussion. Evelyn and Frankie awaited the return of their friends. Nerves were frayed. An air of doom pervaded the city.

Finally, on the afternoon the Thompsons returned, Rachel announced that she would be taking a journey into Varuna with Evelyn. Chase, Ratha, and Rothermel would join her. It would be a long journey, on foot. Ratha's ability to transform into a bird had been stripped when her stone surrendered its essence. They would leave immediately.

✠    ✠    ✠

As the travelers walked north into Varuna, Rachel told them about the birth of the four stones, and how she and Remiel had scaled these snow-tipped peaks together, in the days when war lay thick on the lands below them. She spoke to them of their great love—for each other, and their children—and her grief when Remiel had passed away in the making of the four stones.

Along the way, they were met by several Varunans, who came out of their shelters dug deep inside the mountains, to welcome them, giving them fur robes and food. It was unclear whether any of them knew what had happened in the lower-lying lands. They were a gentle and small people, with light, purple eyes and quick steps.

Chase was surprised to see so many of them, and gratified by how warmly he was welcomed. He felt absurdly proud when they gave him his gift: a circle of leather that was strung with a web of clear string, woven from the tendons of a kind of mountain elk that had once been plentiful in Varuna. Beads and feathers adorned the leather.

"I had something like this in my window in Haiti. It lets all the good dreams in, and keeps the bad ones out," said Evelyn.

The Varunan who had presented it to him pointed at Chase's eyes, at the purple irises. Then he pointed back at his own. They were the same.

"Dreamwalker," he said.

They continued on, leaving the glacier that spilled across the plains and heading into the higher elevations. A flat light fell against the snow, playing tricks with the shadows.

Rachel came to a stop and held up her palm in greeting.

There, amid the gray shadows, stood Calyphor and Deruda, like creatures out of another time. They fluffed their wings and raised their palms in greeting.

"This is where we leave you," Rachel announced, turning to Chase.

She signaled to Ratha and Rothermel, who were clearly in on the plan.

"My daughter longs to show her brother the marvels of her home, and you, Chase, will accompany them. Evelyn and I have other business."

Calyphor and Deruda stepped forward.

"Wait," cried Chase, as Calyphor took hold of Rachel and Deruda grabbed on to Evelyn. "You're coming back, right?"

"She will not be gone long," said Rachel. "Do not worry."

Evelyn turned back to grin at him, sending his heart into overdrive. "I've always wanted to do this!"

"Good-bye, Mother," said Ratha, softly.

Rachel and Evelyn swooped up into the sky.

Chase stood below, next to Rothermel, waving both his arms.

They watched until the figures had flown out of sight.

✢　　✢　　✢

Rachel and Evelyn were deposited on a vast peak that looked as if a meteor had hit the top. A huge gouge had been taken from the tip, and the bones of the mountain were visible. Spindrift glittered in the cold air.

"I have often wondered if you knew why I came to Haiti so often, my dear?" said Rachel. Her tone had deepened, and to Evelyn it was as if she were speaking to her Gran Fanny again.

"You knew my mother when she was a girl. After she died, you felt responsible for us. That's what my father told me."

"That is true. I do feel responsible for you, as I did for your mother, and her mother, and your entire maternal line back for hundreds of years."

Evelyn chewed her lip, listening.

Rachel moved into the crater, pulling out the Fifth Stone from her robes, and then, the four other stones. She put them to one side and brushed away the snow. Then, she carefully picked up each of the four smaller stones and laid them out in opposing directions: the white one to the north; the amber one to the south; the blue one to the east; and the red to the west. She cradled the Fifth Stone in her palm.

"You remember when Dankar spoke of his kin? Well, Evelyn, you and your sister are his kin. You and Frankie are descended from a Watcher. But in you, the Other blood is very strong. It is called to the Fifth Stone—and this is a potent combination. It can be the most glorious of occurrences, or the most lethal, depending on how it is manifested upon the world. You possess a great gift, and you will go on to do many important things if you choose to follow the human part of your heart, and not the Watcher."

She looked down at the arrangement of stones.

"You and your sister are descended from a great princess, an Other of the Old World. Her name, when I met her, was Anacaona, and she was a brave and generous person. There were some noble Others in those days, very few, but she was one. She and her husband ruled over the lands of your birth. For a thousand years, her people lived peacefully, enjoying its fruits and riches, largely undiscovered by the outside world. Does this sound familiar?"

Evelyn nodded, thinking of Ayda.

"But as we know, whatever happens on Ayda is reflected in the other world, and as Dankar strove to find the Fifth Stone, so the Others who reigned at that time grew hungry for more power. Not all, mind you, but many. Their desire for more wealth and land led to a migration into the Americas, and with it, strangers to the shores of Haiti. And not just any strangers, but power-hungry *conquistadores* who wished to lord over all they encountered.

"At first, your ancestor Anacaona and her husband welcomed the newcomers, but soon the situation turned deadly. Anacaona's husband was taken by the invaders and sent to Spain. He died in a shipwreck. The other noble people in her village were invited to a feast to honor them, but once they were inside, the doors were chained and the building was set on fire. Anacaona herself was imprisoned and told she could live out her days as a Spanish slave, or die. She chose death, but not before sending her only son into hiding. It is from him, Anacaona's son, that your line continues."

"How do you know this?" said Evelyn, aghast.

"Because when I left Ayda with the Fifth Stone, my boat floundered in the Sargasso Sea. We were rescued by a captain on a Spanish caravel bound for Haiti. Caspar—or Captain Nate, as you call him—was with me, sworn to protect me and the stone in my possession.

"We hid on Haiti, under the protection of Anacaona's son and then his heir, and so on, for a very long time. They were the family I grew to love after the loss of my own. Years passed and Ayda slipped into legend. Haiti, on the other hand, saw more than its fair share of misfortune. I longed to use the stone to aid in its struggles, but I knew I could not. It was difficult, but the stone had to remain hidden, so that Ayda would remain hidden.

"We moved many times, to many lands, with secrecy as our only goal. Chantarelle was helpful; he scouted potential hiding places. Eventually, we found Fells Harbor, and the stone has been safe there—up until now.

But even after all this time, though my heart resides in Ayda with my children, my soul lies in Haiti, with your kin."

"*That's* why you came to get us after the earthquake. That's why you adopted us," said Evelyn, understanding.

"Yes, my dear. I promised your father that I would protect you, always."

"But what about Frankie? What about when we were lost in the fog? You must have known then! Why didn't you help us? Frankie could have died!"

"It was very hard for me to see Frankie suffer, Evelyn, but I have spent an age, half a millennium, upon this Earth, and have seen much suffering. And though it pained me deeply to have misfortune fall on those I love, I have never let go of the larger suffering that would occur if I used the Fifth Stone. If I have gained any wisdom in my long life, it is that most decisions are between what is best for oneself and what is best for others. Sometimes, if one is very lucky, they are the same. In most cases, they are not. It is a paradox. Our salvation is also our doom."

Her tone grew pointed.

"And that is why we are here. For today, my sweet girl, you are now faced with a decision. You have witnessed the earliest signs of what will befall Ayda because I have rekindled the Fifth Stone."

She bent down and placed the Fifth Stone at the center of the four surrounding stones. As she did, a closed circuit of light began to hum around the stones and into the center.

"You know now that Ayda is no longer a sanctuary. Now that the Fifth Stone is activated, the blood of the Others will eventually lead them here. There is but one way to stop it: Ayda must once again be hidden, and I think you can guess how."

Evelyn stared transfixed at the circle of light. It flickered and spun between the stones, electric and alive, but contained. Balanced. As she watched it, she felt her own daylights awaken and rise to the surface. She also could feel Rachel's, and knew instantly what she had planned.

"You are going to restore the four stones, and send the Fifth away again!"

"Not me," said Rachel. "*Us*. I spent much of my power on Dankar, and I am not strong enough alone. I need your help, but first you must make a decision."

"What kind of decision?"

"A life-changing one. You must decide if you will take possession of the Fifth Stone. If you do, you will have to leave Ayda forever to protect it."

"And if I don't?"

"We will stay here and face whatever sails into our future, and the uncertain outcome."

"So my choice is to leave forever, or stay forever? Staying doesn't sound so bad."

"Not now, but the other world will be tempting. Ask Captain Nate. It is difficult to live in between, one half longing to be in one place, the other, longing to be in another. Life is long on Ayda. I can see how you might be satisfied for the foreseeable future, but let me ask you: What happens in a hundred years? Two hundred years? Can you swear that neither you nor your friends would be tempted? And during that whole time, as your curiosity builds, the Others and their descendants will be searching for you—and Ayda. It is inevitable."

"What about the fog?"

"The fog will return only if you take the Fifth Stone from these shores. You may use the stone to take you and whomever chooses to join you through the fog. Once you are on the other side, it will close behind you. The stone will sleep."

"Why me? What about you and Captain Nate? Can't you just take it back?"

"No, Evelyn. Our lives have traced their course. We can no longer protect the stone. You know this. You and your friends paid the price for our weakness. I am only human, blessed with long life because of my husband and the Fifth Stone. If you take the stone, the Captain and I will fade, but that is not a sorrow. We have found peace again after a very long journey."

"What about Frankie, and Chase, and the other Thompsons?"

"The ancient law applies: Any person who comes to our shores is free to leave with you should they choose to. Once they pass back through the fog, however, Ayda will become like a dream at the edge of memory. All on Ayda are free to make their own choice. You must not make them come with you if they do not want to, even your sister. I want to be clear: I am not making you do this; I am only asking you."

"What about Chantarelle's tunnels?"

"Without Chantarelle's permission, no one will find their way through them. And he will not give his permission unless the Keeper of the Fifth Stone asks him to do so."

Evelyn gulped. She didn't want any of this—the Fifth Stone, the decision. It was too big a responsibility.

But then she thought about all the people she had come to love on this island, and its beauty before Dankar's war. She thought of Tinator and Mara. Of Seaborne and Calla, and the children they would have. She thought about Urza, and remembered Hesam. And then her mind recalled the small, quirky Varunans in the mountains, and the way the light fell through the trees onto the springtime glen in Melor. She saw the desert of Exor and its red rocks and canyons, and then the swift-flowing Hestredes as it approached the towers and blue-domed houses of Metria. She imagined it overrun and ruined, again and again, as more

Others came to her shores, seeking the Fifth Stone. Hadn't she seen her own country in upheaval, and witnessed the wages of endless struggle?

The only answer was for her to take the Fifth Stone from here and protect its secrets with her life—as Rachel had done herself, for five hundred years.

"I'll do it. I will take the Fifth Stone away."

"And so it is done," said Rachel.

Rachel's daylights welled forth and expanded over the stones to join with Evelyn's. The stones between them added their glow, and a vast corona of light crowned the mountain peak, as if another daybreak was at hand.

✠    ✠    ✠

Evelyn came down from the mountain alone, carrying with her the four restored stones of Metria, Melor, Varuna, and Exor, and the Fifth. It had taken all of Rachel's daylights to revitalize the four stones, as she—and Ratha and Rothermel—had known it would. Her vessel had fragmented, and her daylights had returned to the source.

The four stones would be put to use, to rebuild Ayda to its former state, and then Evelyn herself would leave the island with the Fifth Stone, never to return. Unbeknownst to her, a deep bank of fog was already amassing out to sea. Soon it would move in and surround Ayda in secrecy once more.

Calyphor and Deruda were waiting for her at the lip of the glacier. They flew with her to Ratha's terrace. Chase had been told what might happen, but until the minute he saw her, he had no idea what she would decide.

"You did it," he exclaimed upon seeing her exhausted face. The transfer had taken a lot out of her, too.

"It is done," she said, with a new gravity in her voice.

"I've been thinking about it, Evelyn, and I'm going back with you. Like Caspar did with Rachel. It's too much for one person. I'll help you keep it safe."

His offer cracked something open deep inside of her, and the cold thing that had lived within her for so many years evaporated. She smiled gratefully at him.

"You know you'll have to follow me around for hundreds of years. You'll turn out cranky and mean like Captain Nate. You'd better take some time to think about it."

"Don't need it." He held up his palm, fingers splayed. "I swear on my daylights to protect you and the Fifth Stone as long as I live."

Evelyn pressed her open palm to his, then leaned in and kissed him on the lips.

# Chapter Thirty-One

# FAREWELLS

Thick fog returned to shroud the island of Ayda, and any ship that attempted to pass through was left floundering for days. The island was safe. The four stones were balanced. And all of its peoples, without the unnatural strife and division caused by Dankar, began to thrive.

Rothermel took back possession of the stone of Melor. He used it to undo the dam that Dankar had created, restoring the flow of the Hestredes to the sea. Then, he turned his attention to the great forest of Melor. Soon, tree shoots were springing up through the ashes and the springtime glen was renewed. In the evenings, his deep laugh could be heard rumbling along the Vossbeck as he did his work, often with a howler monkey on his shoulder. *Tehuantl* were still seen with frequency in Melor, but were no longer feared.

Evelyn gave Urza the stone of Metria, and helped her learn how to use it. Once Urza's daylights grew accustomed to the power, she used it to rebuild the city. In time, high towers rose again above the fog, and red-sailed boats could be seen traveling up and down the Hestredes, trading goods and transport with Varunans who now came openly to the shores of the Voss.

In Exor, there was no obvious choice as to who should inherit the stone, so it was decided that its powers would be shared by all the people. Dankar had sired so many children in his time that the Exorians were, as a whole, powerful enough to mind their stone without a Keeper. And they did so with pleasure. The desert bloomed with swathes of oases, and the new river was flush with waters from the mountains. It fed new crops and welcomed many animals that had never traveled so far west. The wadi became ripe with life, and the ten stone heads of the Watchers looked over a greening valley. The katari, the gifting trees, were covered in long tendrils of pink and yellow flowers—something that had not occurred since Ranu's death.

Ratha brought her stone back to Varuna, though her psychic powers were now more tempered by open exchange with the other stones. She spent much of her time with Rothermel in Melor, helping him to reseed the forest with spring winds. His influence offset some of her more unnerving qualities, and she could often be seen walking the lowlands of Varuna, and visiting with her people. It was rumored that she even smiled now and then, and wore her hair flowing freely to her fingertips. To Chase's great relief, it seemed that she had even given up prowling his dreams and interrupting his thoughts with mindspeak.

As promised, Hesam's remains were retrieved from her shallow grave, and she was given a traditional Metrian burial at sea. As the funeral dory floated out into the fog, Seaborne used the crossbow to set it alight with a burning bolt. The remains of Hesam disappeared into the mist like a flame, lighting the way to another world.

☩    ☩    ☩

After many moonrises, it was time for Evelyn and Chase to leave, and a greater choice had to be made by the people who loved them: Stay on Ayda, or go with them.

It was an easy decision for Frankie, and for Louis, too, who longed to see Summerledge and the world he had once known. Jim and Grace chose to go back, as did Teddy. And so, it was only Knox who could not decide. He did not want to leave Ayda, and yet he did not want to remain behind when his family left. He argued alternately between them staying and Seaborne and Calla going back with them.

"My home is here, lad," Seaborne said. "My daylights are happiest here. Besides, can you imagine what they'd do with the likes of me in your lands?"

He scrunched up his eyebrows, and waved a hand across his crazy getup.

"True," said Knox. "They'd probably have you arrested, even if you didn't have a sword and a machete."

"It won't be so bad to go back," said Seaborne, halfheartedly. "They are your family. You will doubt yourself for staying. Trust me."

"You are my family, too," said Knox.

Seaborne was touched. He spoke gently to Knox. "Trust your instincts, lad. If you go back and your heart is not in it, the daylights will drive you mad. Consult with them. Let them lead you."

And so Knox found his way to the clearing outside the remains of Seaborne's cabin. He sat on the little footbridge, recalling all the small moments he had passed there and the skills he had learned. He thought about Summerledge, too, and school, and his brothers, and his tree fort. He thought about his mother and his father. He fell so deeply into remembering that the sudden appearance of Axl and Tar in the clearing startled him. The two hounds sat quietly on either side of him on the bridge, and together, they looked out over the trees, limbs budding with new growth.

A presence behind him made itself known, like a tree branch rustling. Knox looked over his shoulder. At the other end of the footbridge, looking as if he had sprung up directly from the dirt and rocks and trees nearby, was Chantarelle. The little man crossed the bridge, using his gnarled walking stick to lead him. It thumped against the wood with each step.

"How now, Melorian," he said, raising his wrinkled palm, fingers splayed. His brown, weathered lips pulled back to show his yellow teeth. "I see you are troubled."

Knox sighed deeply. "I am. I don't know what to do."

The hounds moved off the footbridge to make room for Chantarelle, who stood eye-level with Knox, and uncomfortably close. The little man's earth-colored eyes bore into his.

"You are worried about your family," said Chantarelle.

Knox shrugged. "No matter what I choose, I'll be unhappy. I feel like I should go back, because it's where I come from. And my mom and dad, and my brothers—they need me. But Ayda feels more like home now. I'm happier here. I fit in. Seaborne and Calla and Rothermel are my family, too."

"I understand. Your bonds are strong with your blood, especially with your mother. She is a Melorian, like you, and would feel your absence most profoundly. You do not want that. But perhaps you suffer needlessly. Sometimes an absence that seems like forever does not turn out to be so. For example, her brother has been returned to her."

Knox gave him a strange look.

"So, if I stay here, I could go back someday, if I wanted to? You'd take me?"

"I might; but that is not my decision."

"It's Evelyn's."

"Yes, though it would not be made lightly. I would not count on it."

"Then why are you telling me this? It's not helping."

"I tell you this so that you do not forecast grief with this decision. The longer one stays at a crossroads, the harder it is to move forward. There is no telling now which road is best, as every path has its hazards. You cannot predict them. You must simply get up and walk. Whatever direction you take, there will be sorrow, it is true—but also, joy. One can only hope that they come in equal measure. Perhaps you will not make the best decision for everyone, but you will make the right one for yourself."

"But which one is right for me?" groaned Knox. He threw himself back against the footbridge.

"I do know that not many Melorians are left in Ayda. There is much yet to rebuild, and a tribe to replenish. It will take time, and Rothermel will not live forever. Even Keepers must pass eventually. They are half-human, after all. He will need to give his stone to someone."

Knox closed his eyes and briefly imagined himself as the Keeper of the stone of Melor. Then, he thought about his parents, growing old without him. How much he loved them.

"Arrgggh!" he gurgled. "This is making me crazy."

Chantarelle took pity on him. He put down his walking stick.

"You must listen to your daylights, child. Trust them. The future will take care of itself." He lifted Knox's face in his hands, moving his own face closer.

"Here. I will help you."

Knox could smell his breath, warm and sweet like fresh dirt being turned in the sunshine. Knox's daylights rose with Chantarelle's touch.

He became aware of the earth rotating beneath his feet, and the roots of the trees that held it in place, and the pulse of the stream that ran beneath the footbridge. He felt the beating hearts of the hounds, thumping in time with his own. He saw the sky reflected darkly in Chantarelle's irises. He saw the meridians of energy that connect all living things, no matter how distant or near, and knew that he was not only in the forest, but *of* it—no longer just a boy, but part of an inexorable whole, undivided and eternal. A sense of contentment unlike any he had ever known flowed through him. He would be okay.

Chantarelle dropped his hands.

Knox stood and walked with the hounds back to Metria.

He had made his decision.

✣    ✣    ✣

And so the day dawned when the *Mary Louise* was pulled up in front of the two poles that marked the entrance to the city of Metria. A great farewell party was planned. Aydans from all four corners traveled to the city to feast and say their good-byes to the five strangers who had changed the course of their destinies. Captain Nate had given them his boat, since he was staying on Ayda. He brought Bodi and her mother back to the city to say a final farewell.

Chase gave Bodi his dreamcatcher to take back to Exor.

"Keep it safe for me, okay, Bodi?" he said. "Maybe Evelyn will let me come back for it someday."

"Swear?" she said.

He spit in his palm and shook her hand. "Spit-swear," he said, hugging her one last time.

The Thompsons, Evelyn, Frankie, and Louis made their way to the *Mary Louise* through a formation of fully armed Metrians, and a host of Melorians including Urza and Letham, and Ahna and Adhoran, who had managed to survive. They walked down the tide-stained stairs to where Seaborne and Calla were waiting.

Seaborne couldn't speak. He was too choked up. He just kept pounding them all on their backs, wiping his eyes and saying "Blimey."

Calla came forward holding a handful of leather strings, each strung with a pearly, gray stone. One by one, she fastened them around their necks, though she did not give one to Evelyn or Chase.

"What's this?" asked Jim, holding the stone on his necklace up to the sun.

"It's a moonstone," said Calla, "collected from the shores of the Voss. Evelyn helped me make them. They will ward off the effects of the fog, so you will not forget us."

"Why don't I get one?" asked Chase.

"You don't need one. You and Evelyn are pledged to the Fifth Stone. You need not worry about the fog."

Evelyn touched the Fifth Stone to the moonstones on each of their necklaces. They began to glow with an inner radiance, like opals.

"Now we all carry a piece of the Fifth Stone with us. Our memories of Ayda will not be forgotten," she said.

"I know it sounds strange after all that I've done, but I am happy for that," said Louis, looking down at his necklace. "I'm tired of having my memory wiped."

He took Frankie by the hand.

As the outliers made their way down to the pier, Knox lagged behind with Seaborne and Calla.

His mom noticed and stopped, her heart sinking.

"Knox?"

"I'm not going, Mom. I'm staying here. I won't be happy back there."

His father was caught up short.

"Knox. We aren't leaving you here forever. You are still a child."

Chase caught his brother's eye and understood.

"He's not though, Dad. Not here," said Chase. "His daylights have spoken. On Ayda it means he's grown; he can make his own choices. You can't make him go back. It'll make him go crazy."

His mother began to sob, reaching for Knox.

"You are my child. No parent should have to leave their child behind. We still have so many years to be together. Must I always live with the loss of someone I love?"

Evelyn intervened.

"I'm sorry to say it, but yes. That is the weight that humans must carry. We must all live with loss, because no one lives forever."

"But he is my baby," Grace wept.

Knox went to her. "I'm sorry, Mom, but I can't go back. I'm not meant for that life anymore. Calla and Seaborne will look after me."

"Then I will stay with you," she argued. "I cannot bear to be without you."

"Is that what you truly want?" asked Evelyn.

Grace looked at Knox, and then at Jim and Teddy and Chase. And then at Louis.

"I don't know what I want." The pain in her voice was awful to hear.

"Yes, you do, Mom," said Knox, hugging her. "You want to go home. And I want to stay here, because this has become my home. I'll be all right. Tell her, Chase."

Chase started to argue on Knox's behalf, but his father stopped him. He put a hand on Knox's shoulder.

"I understand, Knox. It's your choice. You do what you need to do," he said. "I love you, and I am very proud of you."

Knox's face crumpled. He threw himself into his dad's embrace.

Grace turned to Calla and Seaborne, tears falling from her cheeks.

"You will take good care of him?"

"As if he were my very own," said Seaborne, solemnly. "He shall never want for anything."

Grace drew Knox to her.

"Chantarelle told me that you are a Melorian—that means, you know, we're the same," he whispered in her ear.

She hugged him tighter. He hugged her back.

"Yeah, that's right, Mom. In me, you go on."

✛    ✛    ✛

It was a diminished and more sorrowful group that made their way to the boat. Ratha, Rothermel, and Captain Nate stood by the *Mary Louise*. Rothermel bowed to them. Ratha instructed Chase and Evelyn one last time: They could use the Fifth Stone to get the boat safely through the fog, but once they were on the other side, the stone must be shut down and hidden where no one would find it. Under no circumstances could they *ever* use it on the other side of the fog.

"I understand," said Evelyn.

"See that she does," Ratha said, challenging Chase with one of her formidable stares.

"I will; I know you'll be watching," he joked.

"That I will," she said. "Go now, Varunan, and do not fear. When you are most alone, I will be with you."

"That's a cheery prospect," said the Captain, smiling. He pulled Chase aside.

"There's a good spot on my dock to keep an eye on the watchwater. And mind the fog. Things have shifted, no doubt, since the Fifth Stone was used. Be prepared. The Others are out there. You and Evelyn must always use caution."

"I will," said Chase. His eyes drifted to the Keepers. "Look out for them, and Knox—and Bodi?"

"It will be my privilege." He placed a hand on Chase's shoulder. "As it has been to fight alongside you. You are a brave man, Chase. Don't let anyone tell you otherwise."

☨   ☨   ☨

Evelyn and Chase lingered a moment longer with Knox before getting on the boat, not wanting to go. They had been through so much together. It was hard to believe it was all coming to an end.

"I guess I'll be seeing you in my dreams," said Knox, chucking his brother softly on the arm.

"Count on it, little brother," said Chase, grinning.

Evelyn touched the glowing moonstone on Knox's necklace.

"Chantarelle knows how to reach me if you need to get us a message." Knox caught her eye.

"We do not say good-bye," he said.

She embraced him.

"No, we don't. May your daylights protect you, Melorian, until we see each other again. In this world, or another." Then she and Chase boarded the boat.

Grace took the wheel. Louis and Frankie settled themselves. The engine roared to life. Captain Nate cast off their line and Jim stowed it. From the stairs, Seaborne, Calla, and Knox, the hoods of their Melorian ponchos raised, lifted their palms, fingers splayed, in a final salute. The crowd assembled behind them did the same. Axl and Tar howled. Beside them, a *tehuantl* roared.

Teddy yelled back at Knox, "IF YOU SEE BOB, TELL HIM I SAY HI!"

Beneath his hood, Knox grinned.

"YOU BET, TEDDERS. TAKE CARE OF MY TREE FORT!"

Teddy gave him a thumbs-up.

Evelyn went to the bow and took out the Fifth Stone. A rosy glow emanated from it. All around it the fog receded, creating a hole of clear air. Grace tipped the wheel and pointed the boat through the hole.

Chase stood alone at the stern, looking back at the shore toward his brother, and all the people who had loved and helped him on Ayda. He watched without blinking until the fog closed around them and he could see them no more.

# GUIDE TO THE
# FIVE STONES TRILOGY

## FELLS HARBOR

**Chase Thompson,** almost fourteen, eldest of the Thompson brothers.

**Knox Thompson,** twelve, middle brother.

**Teddy (Edward) Thompson,** six, youngest brother.

**Grace Thompson** (neé Baker), mother of the Thompson boys and wife of Jim Thompson; inherited Summerledge in her twenties.

**Jim Thompson,** father of Thompson boys, husband of Grace; chief of medical research lab with a focus on immunology.

**Edward Baker,** only brother of Grace Thompson, lost at sea for almost forty years.

**Fanny Dellemere,** the Thompsons' nearest neighbor, owner of Dellemere Cottage, and adoptive grandmother to Evelyn and Frankie.

**Captain Nate,** old sea captain who lives down the road from Summerledge and Dellemere Cottage.

**Evelyn Boudreaux,** thirteen, adopted granddaughter of Fanny Dellemere, born in Haiti to her Haitian mother, who died in childbirth, and her French-Canadian father, who was killed in the great earthquake.

**Frances (Frankie) Boudreaux,** nine, Evelyn's younger sister, born in Haiti (their mother died giving birth to her); also adopted by Fanny Dellemere.

# AYDA AND THE MYTHS

## The Watchers

Ten immortal brothers sent to Earth by the great Weaver at the very beginning of time to teach humans how to control the daylights so that life could thrive on Earth. Of these ten, **Remiel** is the first to break a promise that has vast repercussions on the other nine, marrying a human woman named **Rachel.** They have four half-human, half-Watcher children who become the Keepers of the four stones on Ayda: Ranu, Ratha, Rothermel, and Rysta. In due course, all the Watchers follow his lead, and the world is never the same.

## The Others

Half-human, half-immortal children of the forbidden union between Watcher and human. They live unnaturally long and powerful lives, and throughout history, most—but not all—have used this power to enslave their human kin and hoard the Earth's riches. Legends of their deeds are the source of folktales and fairy stories in all countries. After Remiel's sacrifice, they were weakened. Their daylights grew rigid and unyielding, many turned on one another, and they became easier to kill. Several of those that survived are the fathers and mothers of great dynasties. Traces of their Watcher blood still flow, albeit diluted, in many human veins.

## The Daylights

*Daylights* is the common term for the divided *atar*—the energy that flows between and around all living things and binds them together. According to legend, the undivided *atar*, which is the force of all creation, was too strong to be contained in a human or animal vessel. To harness the *atar* so that life could thrive, the Weaver split it into four essential energies. They are seen in the physical world as the elements, and in the metaphysical world, as humors or temperament, and are known on Ayda as the daylights. One's daylights define where one is most at home, and to which tribe one belongs. A person on Ayda is considered fully grown when his or her daylights have spoken, regardless of chronological age, since time passes differently on Ayda.

## The Melorians

**Rothermel:** Keeper of the stone and lands of Melor. He influences those bound to their Earth daylights, and cares for green and growing things. His realm is the forest of Melor, and of all the Keepers, he is closest to human. He has grown battle-worn and afraid during his watch.

**Seaborne:** An outlier who washed onto the shores of Ayda while serving as a cabin boy during the Napoleonic Wars.

**Axl** and **Tar:** The great hounds of Melor, descended from a line of ancient Aydan animal tribes. They are bound to the Fifth Stone.

**Tinator:** Rothermel's captain, a Melorian of noble birth; husband of Mara, father of Calla, and a skilled soldier and teacher.

**Mara:** Tinator's wife, a healer and provider. She is kind and beautiful, though damaged from a former fight with the Exorians, who tried to abduct her.

**Calla:** Daughter of Tinator and Mara, and a soldier in her own right. Strong-minded, skilled with weapons, and devoted to her family, she becomes a friend to the children.

**Duon, Duor,** and **Sarn:** Melorian guardsmen.

**Duelle:** son of Duon.

**Adhoran:** A Melorian warrior.

**Ahna:** Adhoran's wife.

## The Metrians

**Rysta:** Keeper of the stone and lands of Metria and protector of all those bound by their water daylights. She rules the waterlands of Metria and influences all waterborne creatures. In humans, she impacts memories, empathy, wisdom, and comfort. She holds the archive of much of Ayda's history, and seems consumed by a secret grief.

**Hesam:** Captain of a Metrian ship.

**Urza:** Rysta's most trusted attendant; a Metrian descended from a long line of Aydans.

**Letham:** Captain of the Tower Guard.

**The Hestredes turtles:** An ancient breed of large amphibious creatures related to prehistoric sea turtles. They are bound to the Fifth Stone, and as such are able to travel up the Hestredes to nest on the sandy beaches of the warm bay outside the caverns, though they live primarily in the brackish waters outside the city of Metria, where the Hestredes empties into the Atlantic.

## The Exorians

**Dankar:** Cousin to Ratha, Rysta, and Rothermel, and usurper of the stone of Exor after his murder of Ranu in the first battle of Ayda. He, like his cousins, is half-Watcher, half-human, but born from a different union. He cares little for his (or anyone else's) humanity, and longs only for power, revenge, and the Fifth Stone. He will sacrifice anything—and anyone—to procure it. The stone of Exor under

Dankar has bound those who are dominated by their fire daylights into his service.

**Bodi:** A daughter of the pit-houses, possibly of Dankar, which gives her Watcher blood.

**Emon:** Bodi's older brother, a scribe. He was taken from his mother and sister at the beginning of his adolescence, as are all males in Exor.

**Scribes:** Servant class of males taken from their mothers before adulthood to wait on Dankar. When they begin puberty, they are tested, and if found strong enough are sent to become warriors. Every boy is tested, and how they perform dictates their fate: scribe or warrior.

**Exorian army:** Fierce and hideous warriors who undergo a transformation through ceremonial firewater that scorches their memories and armors them in a scabbed, scarred hide. They fight with flaming, poisoned spears and broad shields. They are sworn to Dankar and his mission to bring down the protective wall of fog that hides Ayda from the rest of the world.

**Louis:** An outlier who came through the fog and is under the protection of Dankar. He is the first human to successfully transform into an Exorian warrior—an important test for Dankar's ultimate plan. However, his right hand and eyes resisted transformation. He is known as the "blue-eyed warrior."

**The *tehuantl:*** An ancient race of jet-black jaguars whose daylights have been perverted by Dankar to hunt humans, though they may not harm fellow Exorians.

## The Varunans

**Ratha:** Keeper of the stone and lands of Varuna and protector of those bound by air daylights, she influences the wind, space, and all creatures that fly. A solitary and unearthly Keeper, she is wise and all-seeing, and can mind-read. Of her siblings, she most resembles a Watcher.

**Calyphor and Deruda:** Two of the very few remaining ancients who have lived on Ayda since the time before the Keepers. They are bound to Varuna.

# ACKNOWLEDGMENTS

No work of this size or scope could have been accomplished without the support of legions of people, especially my growing tribe of Aydan fans. My most heartfelt thanks to the readers, friends, colleagues, bookstore owners, and teachers who have invited me and my ragtag bunch of heroes into their hearts (and classrooms). I do not exaggerate when I say I could not have done it without you.

Thank you to Dean Lunt at Islandport Press, and to my warrior-editor, Melissa Kim, for seeing this long project through and never losing faith—and to Jen, Shannon, Holly, Michelle, Teresa, Anna, and Taylor, for all of their hard work behind the scenes. A big shout-out to Tyler Bouchard and Stephanie Tade, who were early readers, editors, and huge fans of this work, and especially to Melissa Hayes, who works her own magic. Heartfelt appreciation to Elena Stokes and the team at Wunderkind, for going the distance. To Alex Ryan, for her beautiful rendering of detail of the map in Book One. And to Ernie D'Elia, who used his pens and his imagination to bring the characters in these books to life with his wonderful cover illustrations.

ACKNOWLEDGMENTS

To Brooke McIlvaine and Nick Howard, my sister and brother by choice, for always giving me a beckon. To John C. McCain, for his unwavering support and his knowledge regarding all things metaphysical. To Eddie and Patty Howells, for keeping me fed and sane. To Kate Christensen and Brendan Fitzgerald, for being willing to stay up and talk writing until daybreak. To Peter Nichols, for a last-minute Hail Mary of the nautical variety. To my circle of girlfriends (you know who you are) for listening to me go on all these years.

Of course, none of this would have been written without the works of J. R. R. Tolkien, C. S. Lewis, Frank Baum, Ursula K. Le Guin, Enid Blyton, Philip Pullman, or Frank Herbert. There are no words good enough to follow theirs. I found the work of Ross Heaven, a shaman trained in Haiti, to be especially illuminating.

Above all, a huge debt of gratitude to my family, especially Tom Morgan, who has kept me safe and cared for since I was a girl, and to my boys, Graham and Wyeth. Thank you for being so brave and adventurous and inspiring this tale. I am grateful we are here, together, in this world.

May your daylights shine.